# Seas of Antrana

## Book Two of the Erskan Trilogy

First Edition

Published by The Nazca Plains Corporation
Las Vegas, Nevada
2007

ISBN: 978-1-934625-01-9

Published by

The Nazca Plains Corporation ®
4640 Paradise Rd, Suite 141
Las Vegas NV 89109-8000

PUBLISHER'S NOTE
*Seas of Antrana* is a work of fiction created wholly by *K. McVey's* imagination. All characters are fictional and any resemblance to any persons living or deceased is purely by accident. No portion of this book reflects any real person or events.

Editor, Karen Martin
Cover Art, Michael Manning (www.thespidergarden.net)
Illustrations, Atrao
Art Director, Blake Stephens

# Acknowledgements

For LGO: classic FemDom, modern-day Warrior;
always facing fears and forever living her dreams.

# Seas of Antrana

## Book Two of the Erskan Trilogy

First Edition

K. McVey

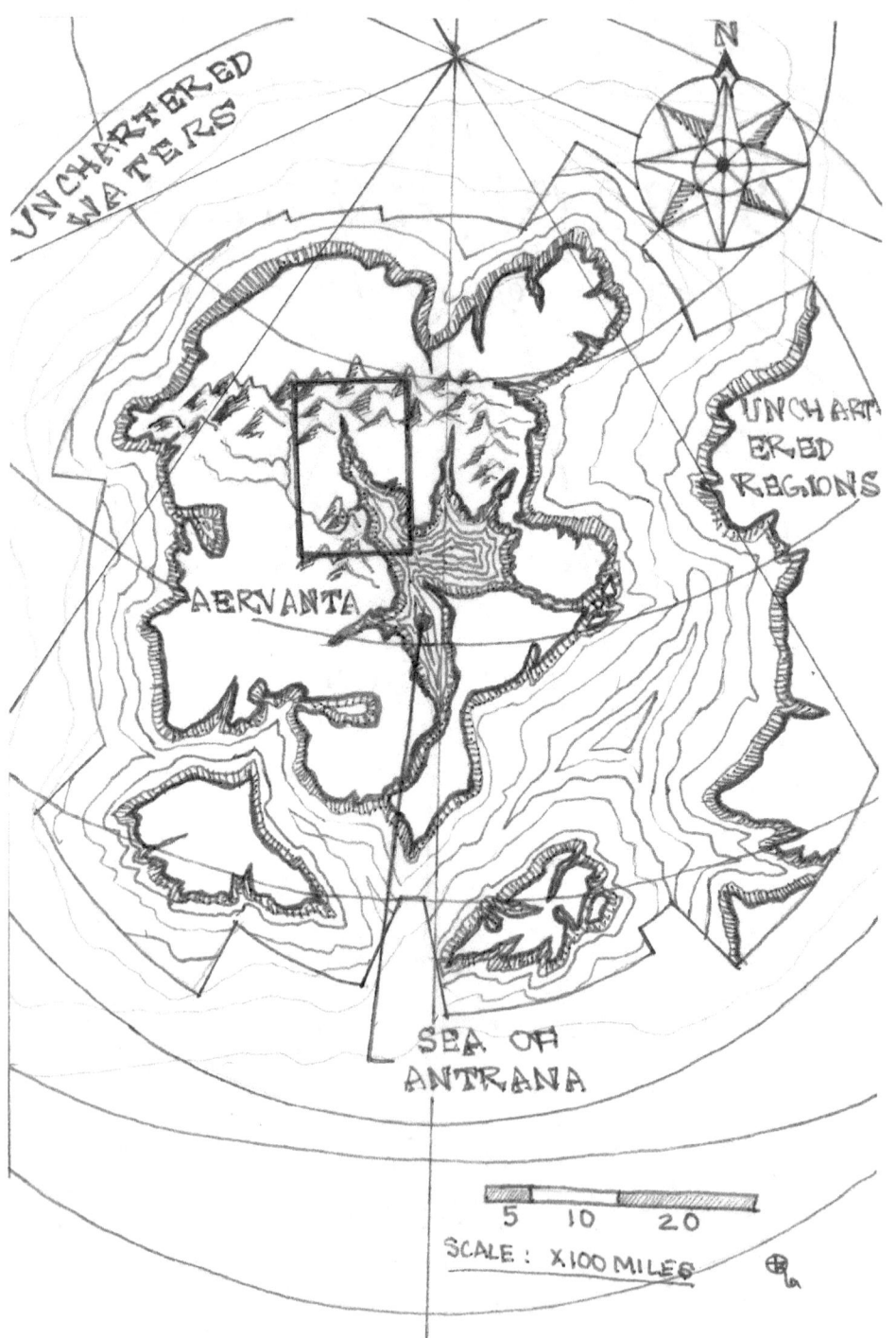

# Contents

# Introduction

We have not always owned our men. Our world changed two thousand years ago when the great coastal city of Erska was demolished following the collision of the dual moons of Netra and Heron. Netra disappeared, leaving only her eleven small orphans in orbit around Aervanta, third planet from Solana, our bright and warming star.

Erska was known throughout the world as a prosperous center of commerce, athenaeum of knowledge, and sanctum of art. A sparkling metropolis of six million people, half the population was killed by the onslaught of towering white waves from the sea. The survivors, bruised and aimless, retreated inland where they suffered through unimaginable centuries of famine and drought.

Morata Kretahla took control of the desperate and hopeless calamity facing the people. She created an enduring warrior culture that led to the establishment of a new city, Antrana, and together the survivors fought to sustain life when there was no hope.

Civilization struggled to advance. The proportion of males to females dropped to a debilitating level. Morata instituted the only plausible remedy to keep the species from extinction: males had to be protected at all costs. Ownership of males became the law of the land.

Prosperity returned two hundred years later. Food became plentiful. Animals again roamed the grassy plains and dense forests. Antrana grew and eventually rivaled that of Erska.

But the male population remained stagnant. Wars were fought over just a handful of men. Over time, the Erskan warrior became the most powerful and feared woman in the world.

A precarious stability endured for centuries.

Danger once again came to us from across the mysterious and fearful sea when Antrana was attacked by the Treaslok people, nine months ago. The Treaslok were aided by ruthless criminals from Earth. These invaders would have been successful if it were not for Alexi

Malind, Earth Police Ranger, tracking the trail of greed, blood, and sorrow.

But we knew the Treaslok, licking their wounds now, would assail our defenses again. Stunned by their defeat, they would return with renewed vengeance. Soon.

As an Erskan warrior it was my duty to protect our people, destroy the Treaslok, and, finally, kill the Earth criminal known as Louis Corrigan.

As a direct descendent of Torino Morata Kretahla I would ensure that there would be no sacrifice too great.

No distance too far to travel.

No sea too far to cross.

No mountain too high to climb.

My name is Vercella Tural.

This is how our world changed again.

# Chapter One
# Third Art of War

Alexi lay at my feet. His body was curled, head resting on the blanket that covered my bare feet and his collared, naked body. Drifting into and out of sleep, my frey appeared relaxed and content.

My feelings were opposite of his.

There was something not right in the order of things.

"Netra!" I cussed as the lead tip broke again. I pressed my lips close to it and puffed until the tip fell off the edge of my desk.

"Mistress Tural?" Alexi asked, lifting his head. He blinked his eyes and then rubbed them with his left hand.

"I cannot write the *eta*," I growled. I resisted the urge to grab the sheet of paper and crush it into an insignificant ball.

Paper was too expensive to waste; instead I placed the lead-filled writing stick onto my desk.

Alexi slowly got to his knees and then looked at my attempt to use the new writing instrument.

"It looks good," he said, after a pause that led me to question his sincerity.

"The paper is good. But I cannot write this letter." I jabbed the lead-filled writing stick at the deformed *eta*. "Look. It is not graceful, there are no curves in the letters, and ..."

I lifted the writing stick. My knuckles were white. I made a loud breath. Then I added, "And the tip keeps breaking on the lead-filled writing stick."

"'Pencil,'" he corrected.

"Mistress," he added after a moment in a not-so-subtle attempt to appease me.

He failed. I glared at him for a moment until he shrunk away an inch or two.

On the right side of my desk, abandoned, was the cloton hair brush and skrow ink bottle that Hirlana, my mother, gave to me when I was a child. The glass bottle had been passed down among the women of our family for almost one thousand years. I reached across the table and ran my fingertips on the smooth, cool glass.

My goal this year was to gain competence in writing Erskan with the pencil so that I could better translate my writings to English.

"May I?" Alexi inquired. He took the pencil from my hand and then carved a tip into the cylindrical wood with a sharpening knife. Then he wrote the first six of the thirty-five letter Erskan alphabet. "Like that."

It was effortless for him. The letters, though cleanly written, were lifeless and of single thickness.

Alexi offered the pencil to me.

Instead, my right hand lay flat on the paper a few long seconds – before my fingers crunched it into a small ball. "Netra," I cussed again, half under my breath.

Alexi untied a ribbon from around a cloth bag. He carefully removed one of the ten remaining sheets of paper. He placed it gently before me and then sat the pencil beside it.

The pencil rolled to the side of my desk. The sound, though soft, only soured my thoughts.

The clock on the wall showed that it was early afternoon.

I stood, almost kicking the chair out from under me. "Let us go outside. I require fresh air."

Alexi pulled on my boots, laced them, and then kissed each. He wrapped a heavy leather coat around me which he buckled snugly about my waist. I shook my head *no* when he pointed at my sword. We would stay within the palace grounds.

I reached inside my coat and adjusted my leather pants as I waited for him to get dressed in a similar heavy coat and thick soled boots.

Guards acknowledged me as I passed them in the stone-lined corridor of the palace.

With a near-silent sigh, I watched Alexi pull open the heavy wood door.

Frigid air attacked my face. Winter had come to Antrana, and she was not friendly.

The formerly green and lush grass parade grounds were now a brown, frozen field of horse hoof pockmarks and wagon wheel ruts. A light dusting of snow covered some areas, especially those in the shade running along the inner palace wall. In my field of view, dozens of small streams of smoke rose from camp and house fires.

A giracha of warriors marched from the gate entrance, along the gravel path. They looked like new recruits, young, bright, and shivering. A giracha was composed of nine warriors. Nine giracha made a harfala of eighty-one warriors, plus field support staff. It was the basic fighting unit of the modern age.

We were mid-way through winter. It was nine months since we repelled the Treaslok from our land. Plans were being made to deal with the threat of our most hated enemy. I was frequently questioned about my previous mission to northern Treaslok territory.

It was rumored that our defensive strategy was to be revealed soon.

Across the sky, at about a ten-degree angle, Hera's orphans glowed.

My frey looked as cold as I felt.

"Would you like a bowl of hot wadu soup?" I asked.

"Yes, Mistress."

He followed my steps according to protocol. I glanced over my right shoulder and smiled.

Alexi was only my second personal frey. My criteria for a frey was, perhaps, too restrictive. Most warriors of my seniority would have owned four frey.

As an Erskan female, I did not lack for male sexual conquest. However, my elusive search for a unique male was finally satisfied when this powerful, intelligent, and strangely aggressive creature came to Antrana. I faced greater challenges by owning him, but with –

"The Erskans have avoided the sea for two thousand years?" Alexi interrupted my thoughts.

"Yes."

"Why?" he asked. "I know the history. But it is surprising that your people have not made an attempt."

"We do not need the sea. Everything we need is here on the land."

My frey frowned.

I feared the repeat question.

"Never?"

"Some go to the sea," I admitted.

"I do not mean to make you uncomfortable, Mistress," he told me.

I was suddenly aware that my teeth bit onto my lips. I forced a smile for my frey to see. "Is there nothing that frightens you, frey?"

He nodded. "Heights. High places. I do not like being on... *ladders*, eh, boshimi."

"You? You have come to us from highest of all places."

Alexi shrugged his shoulders and turned the right corner of his mouth, which usually meant he was struggling to express his feelings. "Yes, Mistress."

I probably held my eyes on him for many seconds. It was surprising to learn this.

Best of all, I could use it against him some day for entertainment purposes. Meaning, of course, for my own *sadistic* purposes.

"Ah, I will offer you assistance in the future should you require my help," I offered, quite selfishly.

A gust of frigid air stung my face and forced my eyes to water. I wiped away the tears with a leather-gloved hand.

Alexi faced the frozen city. "We need to cross the sea to take the battle to the Treaslok."

I shivered and crossed my arms before me as windblown snow pelted us from above. Hera's orphans faded from view behind dark, ugly storm clouds that rolled in from the east.

I tried to convince myself that the cold weather made me shudder. But I knew otherwise.

"Yes," I finally replied. "We must cross the sea."

I led us beyond the front courtyard and through a shorter route, nearest the school.

We stepped around the southeast palace walls and fell upon a pitched battle.

My right hand stayed my frey as I waited for an opportunity to intervene in the sword play. Alexi's chest pressed against my glove for only a moment.

I counted five females, two groups, with one versus one, and two versus one.

Heavy winter clothing hid their features, if not their height.

The shortest female was holding her own against two combatants. They tried to get on opposite sides of their single opponent; yet she would circle in her position in an effort to have them interfere with one another. It was a good tactic, but only effective until they detected what was happening.

The plogos, tightly grasped in their gloved hands, crashed loudly with the sound echoing off the stone palace walls.

Alexi's face tensed as the shorter female raised her plogo high to deflect a blow, exposing her body to attack. However she effortlessly glided over the snow and struck outward offensively. Her sword arm was quick and accurate, graceful and powerful.

Then the shorter female changed her strategy: she slashed her plogo wildly, and pushed hard into the closest opponent. This further prevented the two from organizing an offense.

I smiled at her skill. She would be a worthy opponent.

Finally, the shorter female caught one of the two combatants in the arm. The defeated fighter exclaimed a scream of horror and fell down into the snow, clutching her arm. Writhing, she rolled through the snow.

"Thank you, Volsa!" the other teammate said to her short opponent. "Now I take all the glory for myself!"

Her shorter adversary, Volsa, charged at the source of the taunt.

Farther from me, the two other females continued fighting. Their plogos clashed in the air, brushed the snow at their boots, and collided dangerously close to their bodies. Puffs of air turned into clouds around their heads as they became winded.

They resorted to making verbal insults as they fought, with both trying to out-do the other's volume.

Closer to me, the sword fight was nearing an end as the taller female made several careless strikes.

Volsa slashed low, then crossed high, then maneuvered to her right. I realized that she was toying with her enemy, enticing her to swing outward in wider and wider defensive moves.

I recognized the strategy and chuckled.

My frey, though adept at many forms of combat, knew not enough to recognize the true situation unfolding before us.

Finally, after trying to deflect a feigned knee-level strike, the taller female was unable to pull her plogo in close enough to defend a solitary horizontal, direct impact to her abdomen. It was a perfect and clean strike.

"You are dead," I declared loudly. I was about twenty feet distant from them.

The taller, older girl reeled on her heels to act out her death. Instead, she turned toward me and dropped her wood plogo, obviously surprised, recognizing my presence for the first time.

Volsa quickly turned toward me, plogo firmly in her hand, which she brought to an initial defensive posture.

The other two girls heard me speak and both, by mutual consent, stopped fighting.

They looked completely winded. One put her hands on her knees, bent slightly over and wheezed.

"Who are you?" I asked the two closest girls. I walked toward them. I guessed their ages to be about twelve.

"Tymia," the oldest said, as she reached to retrieve her plogo from the snow.

"Volsa," the shorter girl replied.

"You are the daughter of Korina Jurina Emla," I asked for confirmation of Volsa.

"Yes...?" Volsa trailed off.

"I am Tural," I told them.

I stood before Tymia and put my boot on her plogo, preventing her from lifting it from the snow. "Why did you drop your weapon?"

"You startled me," she said. She released the hilt of the plogo and backed a step away from me.

"And you are dead now," Volsa said. Her voice was even and non-confrontational; but her eyes projected conquest.

I nodded. "Very well, that is one excuse I can accept."

The two other girls shuffled to us. One of them looked at Alexi. He remained standing by the entranceway. "Is that the Earth frey?"

The answer was obvious since Alexi was the tallest and largest man in the country.

I nodded. "Alexi, here," I ordered. My finger pointed to the snow-covered ground behind me.

My frey joined us and stood slightly to my left.

"This is Tymia, Volsa, and..." I said, and then pointed to the first "dead" warrior.

"Ila," the "dead" warrior replied.

"Solalee."

"Myna."

"This is my frey, Alexi."

Alexi stepped forward.

He took their left hand, kissed each glove, and addressed them as "Lady Tymia" and so on.

I reached down and handed the plogo to Tymia.

She nodded and took it from my hand before brushing off snow.

"Your school break should be over now, yes?" I suggested to them.

Tymia replied, "Thank you, Tural. Mathematics class. Bah! Mathematics."

Ila brushed white flakes off her coat before heading toward the door with her school comrades. She stole another look at Alexi.

"Volsa, I will speak with you now," I said.

Volsa stopped in her tracks and turned to face me.

The other four girls looked after us from the doorway for a moment before heading inside.

Volsa returned to me without nervousness. She slid the plogo into a ring on her belt with a smooth action that was achieved only with substantial practice.

"Your mother is teaching you the Third Art of sword fighting?" I tried to hide the skepticism from my voice. Emla was an accomplished archer, not a swordswoman.

"No, Netratoh Tural. Nelia Tega is my teacher."

"Ah, yes. I recognize the style – the way you hold your weapon."

Volsa blinked. "Tega was your teacher?"

"In a manner of speaking. On your way to class," I ordered, giving her a salute.

Volsa snapped as crisp a salute as any of my officers would make before she turned and rushed into the palace doorway. The faces of her schoolmates peeked from the inside of the door.

"Mistress," Alexi said, "you have mentioned Tega before."

My former student, Tega, was now an instructor. How many times did I kill her during six years of War University?

"Yes, I have," I replied.

Volsa was a quick study; she had identified the siglets of my rank.

"Where were we headed?" I asked, knowing the answer.

I would hear if he was placing my interests before his.

"To get hot wadu for my Mistress and her frey."

My right hand pushed into his coat, grabbed his collar, and drew his head toward mine. I kissed him, pressing my teeth hard against his lips.

"Correct," I replied. I aimed again for the warmth of the senior officers' canteen.

\* \* \* \* \*

For an hour, all was peaceful. The sensation on my feet had lulled me into a half-sleep and allowed me a time to hide the anxiety I often experienced in the void between consciousness and oblivion.

The nightmare returned: The Treaslok constructed new ships.

Blacksmiths manufactured hundreds of deadly swords a day.

Warriors charged across the field, slashing and hacking their way into hay-filled bags dressed in Erskan uniforms.

Limbs flew from the bodies.

Heads rolled onto the black, charred ground.

Strands of blood-soaked straw flew into the air and showered down on those that had been torn and wounded.

The bags were ripped. Lifeless.

One of those bags looked like me.

The Treaslok were coming for me.

My eyelids flickered.

I balanced on the edge of sleep and fear. My frey was supposed to be licking my toes and --

A knock at the door jarred me.

My chest rose as I gasped for air.

Netra! Twice this week the nightmare had invaded my sleep.

I blinked and felt my legs contract.

Alexi released his hands from my ankles and he sat up straight. "Mistress?"

I tried to reassure him. "I am well, thank you."

Or was I trying to reassure myself? It was only a bad dream.

Alexi looked at the door.

"Yes, frey," I commanded, half-pointing to the door.

Alexi stood and then walked to the door, pulling it open.

With his back turned to me, I clenched both of my hands to remove the spiky tingling that chilled my fingers.

Cinzia, one of my sister's most-decorated jurinas, or "generals" as Alexi knew in his native English, stood in the doorway. She was dressed in her palace uniform. Alexi immediately stood to the side to allow entrance.

Cinzia strode in, followed by her frey, Mermak. He paced exactly three feet behind her and one foot to her left. A privilege of the rank of Jurina was the allowance of a personal, full-time frey from the highest of the frey caste.

Mermak had been Cinzia's property for several years. Her choice of such a young male was little surprise to those of us that knew her.

Cinzia approached and stood beside me on the left. She flashed a pleasant smile, which in most cases would quicken my heart rate.

Jurina Cinzia was of average Erskan height, but she was solidly more muscular than most of us, with dark brown hair pulled into a tight tail with leather bindings. Tattooed eyebrows arched above her eyes. She talked with her arms folded across her, in a manner that was comfortable, but not confrontational or indifferent. She displayed painted gray fingernails. Her heavy winter leather skirt and leather long-sleeved top did little to conceal her curvaceous shape. My eyes were drawn to her full breasts and cleavage, rather than to the several scars she sported on her arms, right hand, and shoulders.

Her left bicep had one particularly lengthy scar that reflected a near loss of her arm. I had been in that particular battle and remember well how she self-tied two strips of leather around her upper arm and continued fighting.

I was stretched out on a chaise, my winter skirt pulled to my right side, my feet resting on a small pillow. Alexi shifted his position and kneeled to my right, looking down.

Military protocol was not in effect while in my own quarters. Still, I politely saluted her.

"You look comfortable, Tural."

The truth was that my heart was still racing.

I patted Alexi on his head, "I might keep this one."

Cinzia laughed. She knew well my intentions about Alexi.

"We will begin moving the Tamagra through the city tomorrow morning. Will you be attending?"

Moving the alien space wagon from the desert was a difficult task. Twenty miles of sloping terrain, two-hundred fifty miles of desert, and then eighteen miles of city roads were the least of concerns. Our engineers and foundry constructed special metal wheels and axles to carry the massive weight of the Tamagra. Winter's arrival allowed us to utilize the smooth and ice-coated passage through the dormant yiminee desert. Still, a crew of four-hundred women and twenty men labored three months to move the Tamagra into the outskirts of Antrana, our capitol city.

After early supervision, Alexi told us that there was nothing anyone could do to harm it and he left the matter to Cinzia and Kendra, the chief engineer.

"Frey, would you like to see the Tamagra tomorrow?"

"Yes, Mistress, I would, please."

"We shall attend," I replied to Cinzia. "What time?"

"At first light of day. It should be *interesting*," she smiled, using the English word.

Alexi looked up at Cinzia and flashed a momentary smile before returning his gaze at somewhat-floor-level.

"Will you be retiring for the evening now?" Cinzia inquired.

Did Cinzia have something in mind?

"That was my plan." I wanted to probe other possibilities with her: "I would consider other ideas."

I resisted an impulse to reach between my legs. With my frey licking my feet, and the presence of Cinzia and her breasts near me, my face became warm.

"I am weary of eating in the officer's cantina," Cinzia said. "We have been working hard for months. I will dine tonight in the city and would enjoy your company."

I sat straight, brushing my legs off the chair. That was an excellent idea!

"Frey, have you eaten in the city?" I asked.

Alexi shook his head.

"Have you eaten at any dining place?" I pressed.

"I have had no time with civilians," Alexi replied.

"None?" Cinzia asked, surprised.

"None, Mistresses," Alexi replied again. He almost gave me a "Did you not listen to me the first time?" glance. I would have to do something to stop that from happening again. It was slightly disrespectful and would have been detected by Cinzia.

"We will remedy that situation this evening," I told Alexi. I had intentions of first resolving the lack of civilian interaction and second of reprimanding him for his behavior. He was smart, but I wasn't sure he recognized the duality of my answer.

"It would be my pleasure to dine with you," I said, standing to face Cinzia. She was almost close enough that I could touch her. The faint scent of pionas petals drifted from her hair to my nose. The perfume was nearly intoxicating.

We locked eyes for a moment. I could see my reflection sparkle in her blue eyes. She smiled and then nodded.

"Shall we depart from the East palace gate in one hour?" Cinzia asked.

I wanted to tell her, "We can forgo dining and go straight to your bed."

But, instead, my reluctant reply came out as, "Yes, one hour."

Her rank was superior to mine and such a bold request to sleep with her was considered improper and slightly rude. Though I had heard it said that Cinzia could be enticed to bed with crude remarks, it seemed best to wait for the proper opportunity.

"Mermak," Cinzia stated as she walked toward the door. It was neither an order, nor a request. In typical Erskan fashion it was merely spoken so that the frey would make action to satisfy his owner. It was certain that Cinzia expected anticipatory service at all times; however we knew that the males were not capable of reading minds.

With the spoken affirmation, Mermak dashed to the door and held it open for his Mistress to pass.

After they left, I turned toward Alexi and licked my lips. The evening held great promise. A hint of Cinzia's perfume floated in the air behind her. It was the same floral petal that Hula used.

It had been several months since I had seen Hula, my closest lover of many years. She was coordinating western mining operations to supply us with a steady stream of ore for Alexi's re-inventions.

Hula's soft skin, the smile that melted my eyes, and –

Dinner.

I wasted no time getting prepared and directed Alexi to obtain my clothes.

"Mistress," my frey asked. "Are there special rules of behavior for me to follow in the civilian population?"

"Yes, there are. I will explain those after you dress me."

Alexi laced my boots and I stood, pressing down on the heels. The boots glistened as a result of his shining and leather care.

I was tall, for Erskans, but had the typical narrow waist, long lean body, ample breasts, dark hair, and light complexion. My frey said that Erskans were, as a people, smaller in size than Earth humans.

Tonight I was dressed in my finest: medium gray long-sleeve leather shirt hanging out, skin-tight but thick, dark gray leather pants, heavy black leather boots, and wide two-inch black leather belt with a silver buckle. It was a rare occasion for me; I adorned my ears with pendant earrings that matched my bracelets and necklace, all made with platinum from our mines. I crossed my arms before me and flexed my forearms; I could look quite fierce for a thirty-year-old warrior.

Rarity was the fashion for the evening so I applied a small amount of perfume oil, the scent of the asonga flower, at my wrists. Then I breathed on my fingernails to ensure the gray color had fully dried.

The final piece was hidden from view; an Earth StacGun was concealed in my right calf-high, front-lace boot.

"I love that sound, Mistress," Alexi said, standing slightly behind me, to the left.

"What sound, frey?"

"The low growl you make."

I grinned. "Get dressed with the clothes I set for you."

He turned away, typically naked in my room except for his metal collar, and went to the front room. His clothes were draped over his cage. I watched him for a moment as he pulled on a matching gray, heavy leather skirt and winter shirt, with low ankle boots.

Muscles flexed on his shoulders as he leaned and grabbed his winter skirt.

There was that sound again, coming from deep in my body, as I examined him.

My frey was six-foot, two-inches tall, about two-hundred ten pounds. He was the most muscular male I had ever seen. He had wavy, short-cut, light brown hair that became darker during the winter. Alexi looked over at me for a moment, watching my inspection of him. Those dark obsidian eyes were beautiful. His skin was darker than an Erskan complexion. Earth men had higher cheekbones and their heads were blockier than my people. We converted the years and found that he was one year older than I. Earth time periods and measurements were not so unlike Erskan conventions. For example, an English "foot" was approximately twice the length of an Erskan "vi."

"Protocol," I told my frey as he held the door, two coats folded over his left arm.

We walked along the hallways toward the East palace gate. "Frey will not eat at the table as the women, except at a small stool placed beside my chair. When you enter the dining room, you must not talk until spoken to. You must look down at the floor at all times, unless spoken to and given permission to look up. I will present you with food and will tell you when you may eat. Never finish your meal before I have done so."

I continued, "You may not engage in any conversation with anyone unless it is a woman that is talking to you. Limit your questions. Cinzia is my superior. Her frey, Mermak, is therefore first ahead of you. Perform well. She will be watching you. Do you have questions?"

Alexi flinched as I reached around him and lightly slapped the back of his head. "That was for the manner in which you replied to my question about interaction with civilians."

"Yes, Mistress. I apologize."

Quick to change the direction he asked, "Who will be serving the food? Do I serve the food to you?"

"No. You will be near my side at all times. This is much similar to our military rules, except that you are more closely restricted from social behavior. This is women's time for enjoyment. Frey are there as an afterthought. If, perhaps, the women desire involvement from frey it will be at a different place and time. Not at evening meal."

I stopped walking and looked at him. "In contrast to this afternoon, your greeting to the girls this morning was well done. Thank you."

"Yes, Mistress." The corner of his mouth betrayed a slight grin.

"Do you know why I appreciate your proper etiquette?"

"Because if your frey looks good, then you look good," he replied.

"Correct." I continued walking.

"Mermak is Third caste?" Alexi asked.

"Yes. First caste is reserved for the frey of the Torino. She may have any number of permanent frey, but at the moment I believe she has four. Second caste is for the Korina and then Imaya Jurinas, where the Korina may have three frey, and the Imaya may have two trey. Third caste is the Jurina and she may have one permanent frey." I knew what his next question would be.

"How much longer may I be your frey?" he asked.

"You are on a military assignment. This is a special circumstance. Still, you will be required to complete many more of your etiquette and training classes in order to justify the Fourth caste you have been granted. Despite the unusual circumstances, there are still those that have expressed concerns about your caste designation. It is mandatory that you achieve your caste designation in the proper manner."

Just as it was mandatory that I achieve my own military rank by demonstration of competency and performance.

"Yes, Mistress," he said.

Much of his time was consumed by the persistent and impatient engineering staff. It was time to intervene on his behalf so that he could focus on learning his responsibilities as a frey.

"But, Mistress," he asked, hesitancy in his voice, "how much longer?"

Alexi buttoned my coat; then he wrapped the belt around my waist and tied it.

"As long as I want to own you," I told him.

Alexi faced me and blurted, "Mermak said he has had six different owners."

"Mermak is twenty years old," I explained. "Of course he has had several owners over that time. You are not in the same situation. Now, stop worrying about this."

Alexi shrugged before pulling on his coat. He opened the door.

The cold evening blast of air bit at my nose and ears. "Ah! It is cold."

Cinzia and Mermak stood outside. Cinzia hopped on one foot and then the other. She disliked winter more than I.

"Netra!" Cinzia shouted. "By my heart, it has never been this cold!"

"Alexi has our glass factory making *thermometers*. It tells us how cold it is."

"Frey, what do I need with something to tell me it is cold? I know that now!" She scowled at him.

"I believe it is so that we may share the misery of the weather," I explained, quick to answer, in case Alexi tried to reply.

"Oy, oy, oy," Cinzia laughed.

She pulled her coat tighter around her waist and then faced toward the inner wall gate. "Shall we dine?"

I nodded and walked to her left side. Mermak fell in behind Cinzia while my frey followed in my steps, precisely as instructed.

It took us about ten minutes to walk beyond the castle grounds and enter the city streets. It was dark, despite oil lamps strung overhead at every intersection. For such a cold night there were many people walking about. We observed several people heading to evening meal at the various cafes that lined the main street.

Cinzia paused, abruptly breaking the rhythmic sound of our four pairs of boots on the road side walkway. She pressed her hands onto the glass window of a weapons shop. "That is a fine sword," she said, pointing at a standard-length draguire.

I resisted the temptation to tell her that, in another few years, swords would be a battlefield relic. We were in the early stages of developing our own gunpowder. Then we could build a gun, called a musket. In a few years all Erskan warriors would be equipped with these first generation weapons.

Cinzia looked at my frey and added, "Or, it *was* a fine sword. I must tell you, frey, that there are those that are not happy about casting their weapons aside to adorn their mantle or, worse, to rust in the rubbish pile."

"But," she looked at me, "change is here and we must make it to our advantage."

Alexi nodded, but did not speak. Complaints about the advancement of technology were not new. He was the oftentimes target of criticism, despite my attempt to deflect the verbal attacks.

"Would you enjoy dining at Shula?" Cinzia asked. She had a tendency to jump from topic to topic. In private, Alexi called her an "A D D Personality."

I remained suspicious of the true description when he further claimed it was a title of honor for those that were aggressive performers.

Mermak grinned. He was pleased at the cafe suggestion.

"It has been several years," I replied. They had a tasty greintol. Trimmed with steamed riti and renza sauce. It was almost on my lips. "Yes!"

We walked another ten blocks until the four of us arrived at the red stone building that housed Shula on the ground floor. The other three floors were illuminated by oil lamps as the residents moved about above.

The frigid air added to my enthusiasm to get inside. Proper protocol called for the frey to open the door, but if they delayed for one moment, I would rip it off the hinges.

Thankfully, Mermak quickly opened the door until Cinzia and I passed; Alexi held the door for himself and entered last. I would need to later acknowledge his proper use of protocol. He was performing well.

Shula was warm and cozy. Dark oiled woods paneled the walls and ceiling. Numerous oil lamps brightened the dozen tables which were neatly lined in four rows of three, each table suitable for seating of six persons – any combination of women or frey. There were two fireplaces, on either end of the lengthy hall, logs blazing.

The aroma of traditional spices brought a smile to my lips. A hint of deldo, familiar from my childhood, reached my nose.

"Jurina Cinzia!" the owner said, approaching from a table where she was writing an order. Both women embraced. "It has been too long!"

"Blia," Cinzia said, "It is good to see you."

"You have brought a friend."

"Blia, this is Netratoh Tural."

"Netratoh," Blia said, reaching to hug me.

Blia was much older than I, short for an Erskan woman, with a few streaks of gray accenting her closely-cropped cloton-black hair. Her smile was warm and inviting.

I held her for a moment, smiling my best, and told her to call me "Tural."

"I have seen you before," Blia said.

"Almost three years ago," I admitted. "That was my last visit here."

"Is my cooking so awful that a brave warrior, such as you, is afraid to enter?" Blia laughed.

"No. The life of a military officer is to blame," I replied.

"And a busy one, yes," Blia said.

Mermak removed Cinzia's coat while Alexi took mine. They placed all four coats on the coat pegs and then returned to our side. I observed that Alexi was keeping his head down.

Nine of the twelve tables were already serving, with typically two or three women per table. There were only two other frey in Shula. Both were quiet as the women talked and laughed.

I followed the sound of cooking utensils and glanced past the chest-high kitchen door to see a frey carrying a metal skillet.

"Is this table good?" Blia pointed.

"Yes, it is good," Cinzia replied, sitting in a single chair. Blia pulled a chair for me. After we were seated, Blia removed two other chairs and replaced them with low stools. Mermak sat on Cinzia's side of the table. Taking his lead, Alexi sat to my left on a stool.

"You are our war hero," Blia said, pointing to a wall nearest the cooking area.

Among several painted portraits and assorted parchments was a framed portrait of me, standing on the Luchian battlefield, the vanquished Treaslok scattered about my feet.

"Is it too warm here?" Cinzia laughed. "Your face is red."

"No, it is not," I asserted.

Still, it was a good painting. I contemplated asking her where she had purchased the art.

I did not recall ever wearing my hair in that style, however. And my right arm appeared shorter than the left arm.

Rita leaned over to my ear and whispered, "Is this the frey that is making all the new conveniences?"

I nodded.

"It is allowed to thank him?" she whispered.

"I will convey the message at a later time," I replied.

"I do not mean to be disrespectful," Blia again whispered.

"It is an appropriate question. Thank you for conferring with me," I smiled, trying to reassure Blia.

Blia stood up again, "Now, what can I make for my war heroes?"

"Greintol," I said, abruptly, ready to move away from the prior topic.

"A good choice," Cinzia said. "You must try it with the riti."

"And for Jurina Cinzia?" Blia asked.

"The same. With renza."

"Renza sauce?" Blia looked at me.

"Of course, please," I answered.

"Nerlu?" Blia asked.

"For us both, yes?" Cinzia looked at me.

"Yes." A little bit of nerlu might get me closer to bedding Cinzia. I had almost said that out loud!

"Two glasses of nerlu. Please excuse me," Blia said, stepping away.

"Is that why you have not gone out into the city?" Cinzia asked, looking directly into my eyes.

Hiding my discomfort was now impossible. I had been exposed. "Yes. There were many war 'heroes' on that day. My frey killed more Treaslok than any of us. Socially, a frey cannot be a war hero. But the public knows. Do you know what Blia asked of me?"

"Tell me."

"She wanted to know how to thank him."

Cinzia laughed. She crossed her arms and leaned forward. "This is not a secret anymore. By my heart! I am moving an alien space wagon through the center of Antrana tomorrow! We have electric lights in the palace court. The gunpowder factory will be operational by the summer. Our doctors have words to describe sicknesses and use English words such as *infection* and *hygiene*. I received my first fifteen sheets of paper yesterday. And a lead-filled writing stick. My daughter... my daughter does not want to learn the bow; she told me last month that she wants to fly in a space wagon and go to the stars! They make drawings of the Tamagra in her school. The roads do not need repair as often because of the new paving and heating of bricks. Our cattle are living longer and producing better leather because we feed them differently and have new ways of agriculture. We grew so much food in the fall harvest that we ran out of storage in the granaries."

Cinzia abruptly stopped. "I was going on, yes?"

"It was enjoyable," I replied. "The future is bright for little Beshiana. That is what we want for our daughters, yes?"

Cinzia nodded. "Yes."

"Do you know who I met this morning?"

"Tell me."

"Volsa Emla," I said.

"Oh! She is about eleven years old?"

"I believe so. Close to that age, yes. Her plogo is almost as long as she is tall! She took down two of her classmates during a break in mathematics studies. I watched nearly the entire fight."

"I recall that Volsa is small for her age, yes?" Cinzia cocked her head a bit, "And she beat two of them?"

"Third Art skills," I explained.

Cinzia leaned closer, "At that age?"

"She is good."

"I could cut her mother down with a butter knife," Cinzia said in a hushed voice. She lifted said knife from the table and waved it in front of her face.

"Korina Emla is not teaching her daughter," I told her.

"No? Besides you, who else can teach Third Art?"

"Tega."

"Hmm. Tega has been very aggressive since her sister was killed in *that* battle," Cinzia jerked her chin toward my portrait on the wall. "She appears to be teaching this to the very youngest."

"I have my doubts about the wisdom of this," I told her. "Not to criticize a Korina, though," I quickly added. Recalling a KoVerian parable, I had just backed into a sandstorm without a scarf.

Cinzia grinned. "Do not worry. Your concerns are valid. I will look into it, discreetly."

Cinzia took her left hand and ran fingernails down the neck of her frey. Then she looked over the table to Alexi, who was silently listening. "Frey Alexi, are you being rewarded for your help to the Erskans?"

Alexi moved his head slightly up, but not to make eye contact. "Yes, Mistress Cinzia. My reward is being the personal property of Netratoh Tural."

Cinzia laughed. "Now, what is the real answer? And, look at me."

Alexi glanced at me for permission.

I frowned. "Do not delay; it is disobedient. Answer the Jurina now."

"Yes, Mistress Cinzia. I live in the best place in the Erskan Empire. I have nice quarters and food. I am allowed to create new things to help the people of my new home. And I am rewarded by being the property of Mistress Tural."

"Does your Mistress use you for her sexual pleasure?"

"Yes, often."

"And how do you feel about that?"

We paused as Blia delivered the drinks: two tall glasses of nerlu and two small empty glasses. A full pitcher of nerlu and a carafe of water were also set down on the table.

Cinzia and I raised our glasses: "Shia-talso," we said in unison.

We drank deeply.

"Oh, that is good," Cinzia said. She smiled and rolled her shoulders.

I returned the smile. "Continue, my frey."

I could see Alexi struggle for a moment with the answer. "Sometimes it is hard. And it hurts badly. Other times it does not."

Cinzia reached over to Mermak's ear. Her fingernails ran under his ear and he responded with a grimace. "The Erskan way is that for every time a male experiences the pleasure of sex, he must also experience pain to remind him of his place at the feet of women."

"Yes, Mistress Cinzia. I have come to accept that."

"Good. We do not experience pain, do we?" Cinzia affirmed with a lick of her lips.

"Only pleasure," I smiled. "Much pleasure."

Cinzia leaned in closer to the table. She took my left hand in hers. "Perhaps," she stroked the top of my hand once, "we will see how much pleasure."

My feet tingled. I was wet. I rubbed my thighs together.

"Perhaps, we should not have ordered a meal," I offered, thinking we could cancel.

"Hmm. The strength from a meal is important. A nice walk in the cold to the Palace will make my chambers feel even warmer."

"Good," I smiled. *Her* chambers. Her statement trampled any doubts I entertained about the evening's direction.

I suppressed the inner growl…for the moment.

I poured a glass of water and handed it to Alexi.

"Thank you, Mistress," he said.

Our food arrived. Over bites of food Cinzia and I talked about old battles and, at times, discussed the social ramifications of the technology changes.

The greintol was superb and the nerlu was fresh and spicy – it also made me slightly intoxicated. I resisted pouring a third glass.

"Frey, did you enjoy the greintol?" I asked.

Alexi held his bowl on his lap and rested his hands on his knees. He looked up at me and smiled, "Yes, Mistress, it is good." From my height I could barely observe the two missing teeth on his bottom right side, the result of his crash in the KoVer Desert.

Cinzia looked across the table to me. "Tural, I have a busy morning and then a truly dreary state function to attend. How do you feel?"

"We should not have told so many old war stories," I laughed. "I mean to say, old *lies*."

"Tomorrow we will have our meal earlier in the evening," she suggested.

Mermak and Alexi retrieved coats and dressed us for the outside. I was barely able to pay Blia for the meal; Cinzia did not want me to pay; nor did Blia.

It was a brisk walk through the mostly deserted streets to the palace.

We arrived at the hallway door to Cinzia's chambers and she ordered the frey to kneel and wait for us. Alexi and Mermak pressed their knees to the stone floors.

Cinzia shut the door behind me and I followed to her bedroom.

In thirty seconds our coats and clothes were haphazardly cast on the floor.

Her warm, wet mouth was inviting to mine as we embraced. Both of her hands wrapped around my waist and then on either side of my buttocks and she pulled us closer, pressing our warm flesh against one another.

A shiver climbed my spine and we pressed harder. Her breasts rubbed against mine as my nipples became hard and my breath hot. Our mouths melted for a moment longer before I stole a deep breath. I pushed my head under her hair and kissed her left ear, then ran my tongue inside while breathing softly.

Cinzia's hands continued to massage and probe. I spread my ankles slightly and moved my hands to her side, stroking her body. I closed my eyes and a growl escaped from my body.

"There," she gasped, "is that sound."

She pulled her ear away and melted into my mouth again, our hot breath heaving as we exchanged air.

I pushed my hand between us and found Cinzia's inner thigh. She was as hot and wet as I.

I gently brushed her, teasingly; she tensed at first and then let out her own sensual moan, succumbing to my massage.

Her bed was only six feet from us, but it appeared so distant that my legs would not make the journey.

Cinzia moved toward the bed; together our feet shuffled until reaching the edge. She crawled onto the bed, on hands and knees. I stroked her back until she rolled over, feet away from me, her head hanging off the edge of the bed slightly. She reached out and pulled my hips toward her.

Still standing, I shuddered and moaned loudly as her tongue flickered out to me, gentle at first, and then pressing. My legs twitched. With eyes closed, waves of pleasure rose up from my clit, as she licked... one lick ... after ...another. Cinzia was so, so hot.

My hands explored for her and found her breasts. I pressed on her nipples and listened to her moan.

Cinzia's moist lips brushed the middle of my right thigh. She ran her teeth against my skin.

My leg tingled.

Then she bit into my flesh, easy at first, and then harder.

I growled.

Cinzia released her bite. Then she dived into my left thigh and bit, hard.

My hands grasped her breasts as Cinzia continued to bite.

She let go and then pressed her tongue into my undulating mound.

I clenched her breasts harder, my nails digging into her skin.

She moaned and increased the frenzy of her tongue's sweet torture.

The waves built up, crashing again and again on me until I let out a loud growl, my ankles jerking towards the other. My hands shook. "Oh, oh," I barely whispered as the nika came.

Cinzia let out a soft sound of happiness.

I released my grasp on her breasts; lovely red fingerprints bruised her skin.

Then I crawled onto the bed, and quickly straddled her until I could bury my face in her wet heat. My lips and tongue drank heavily of her wonderful taste. Cinzia moaned and thrust her hips higher against my lips. Her hands pulled my hips down onto her as she continued to lick. We moaned, our bodies heaving.

Cinzia bit into my thigh. Then she bit again.

I growled. My tongue strained to please her.

Cinzia pressed her head deep into the bed, "Tural, oh......oh. Almost....al – " she shuddered and came. "Tural, ah, yes, yes."

We embraced for an unknown time.

I stroked her flank with my hands, running the length of her body with the tips of my fingers.

Eventually I rolled off of her and pulled soft, scented sheets over us both.

She relaxed. But to catch her off-guard, I grabbed onto the back of Cinzia's hair and brought her mouth to mine.

Cinzia bit hard onto my lips as our tongues playfully licked and kissed one another. Blood was on my mouth.

"Plans for tomorrow night?" she asked, her voice high pitched and dreamy.

My hand continued holding her hair. "With you, I hope."

Cinzia arched her back and sighed. She rubbed a finger on my lips. "I insist."

"Mmm," I purred.

"Tural?" she asked. "Does your frey continue to worry about being with you?"

All the time.

"Yes." I licked her finger.

"Do you want to keep him?"

"Yes, of course."

Cinzia reached around my back and pressed a hand against my buttock. "Then brand him, right *here*." Her finger stabbed me to emphasize the location.

"I hadn't thought of doing that so soon," I told her. "Besides, only a jurina may own and brand a frey."

"Everyone else has thought about taking him."

"What's stopping them from challenging me?"

Cinzia chuckled. She moved in closer to my face and bit my lip.

I grabbed her hand and squeezed her wrists.

This frequently happened after rough sex: my 'aftercare' transformed into sex again.

But, she released her bite and licked her lips. "A healthy respect for your skill, that is what. I may challenge you if you wait too long."

Referring to Mermak, I said, "You may have only one branded frey."

Besides, she wouldn't stand a chance on the field in competition with me.

"You believe I'm going to be a basic jurina forever?" Stronger than I, Cinzia twisted her wrists from my grasp.

"I have no doubt that you will own many branded frey," I replied, complimenting her.

"Mermak was insolent, too, at times, before taking my mark," Cinzia said. She rolled on top of my body and pinned my wrists to the bed, at my shoulders. "And after you rog him following the ceremony, I want to be next to get that big earth penis inside me."

"You don't have to wait," I said. "You can rog him anytime. Now, if you want."

Cinzia pressed her lips to my ear and whispered, "It is not only Alexi that appears insecure. The branding will help you as well."

"There will be a long queue after the ceremony," I laughed softly.

"Call our frey," Cinzia said.

"Mermak, Alexi! Inside!" I shouted.

I heard the door open and close.

"Sleep in there," Cinzia told them.

Cinzia released my wrists and moved to my side.

Reluctantly, my hand gradually released her hair.

We were asleep within minutes.

# Chapter Two
## The Ryinka lo Troynya

I cocked my head to the left, left ear touching my shoulder. The Tamagra was on its side, wrapped in a metal and wood frame. A thick steel base ran the length of the space wagon. A combination of wheels and skis protruded from the bottom of the base. Safety chains at the top of the frame were secured to outriggers.

"Two-hundred women, fifty horses," Cinzia replied to my question.

"No problems?" Alexi asked. He was buried in a heavy winter coat and scarf.

Cinzia laughed. Kendra walked up at that time, with a frey in tow.

"There has been no significant problem. None we cannot address," Kendra said. Her coat was stained with black, glossy grease. "We knocked down one pole while making a curve. Two of the horses slipped and are now at the stables. And," she said, sheepishly, "we broke a wall of the House Poyta. Not too *shabby*, after all."

"You are using many English phrases," I told her. "'House Poyta?' Jurina Cinzia will hear about that."

Cinzia frowned. Poyta was a supplier of military weapons.

Kendra nodded. "That is because we meet with Alexi almost every day." She looked at my frey, "And because he talks a great deal, especially for a frey."

For two hours a day, every day, Alexi and Kendra sit in a meeting with Kendra's team of thirty-seven engineers, both military and civilian. Using the writing paper pressed in the fledgling mills, Alexi drew pictures to capture as many things as possible that he can recall from his Earth civilization. Though at the present time we are unable to manufacture most of the items, we maintained a chronology of dependencies of each phase of inventions.

For example, we know how to produce a semi-automatic pistol. In fact, we have several of Alexi's guns. Our expertise has been in metalworking, thus producing the weapon itself is not too distant; but we are having difficulty in making reliable gunpowder.

Kendra's engineers recently produced the first hand-polished steel ball bearings, which are used in the axles for transporting the Tamagra. *Making* the ball bearings was not difficult; we had never *thought* about using such an invention.

"Yes, Mistress?" Alexi asked.

"What, frey?"

"You are smiling," he looked at me.

"Yes. It is a good day," I told him.

Sunlight was about to break through the gaps in the two-, three-, and four-story buildings on the main road. Despite this early time, there were more than a thousand onlookers. Most lined the sidewalks, while some peered down from the windows of their homes and stores.

A giracha of warriors passed by us; they were here to increase protection for the Tamagra. Cinzia returned the salute of the giracha lead as they dispersed ahead of the working teams.

There were many verbal commands from the team moving the Tamagra. The onlookers were pointing and talking about what was happening. Children ran alongside the walkways.

A junior officer arrived on foot, wading through the crowds. "Netratoh," she said, saluting me. And then she recognized the others and saluted Jurina Cinzia and Kendra. "The Torino and the Jurina Prima Council requires your attendance."

"Let us go," I said, pointing to the junior officer to lead.

Cinzia followed. "I shall walk with you."

Alexi and Mermak pursued us as we moved briskly through the crowds until the streets were more open.

"Do you know what this is about?" I asked Cinzia. My suspicions were strong.

"I am not saying 'Yes' and I am not saying "No," Cinzia grinned.

A gust of frigid wind swept through the streets and chilled my face. Puffs of warm air blew from my mouth.

Finally we entered the palace grounds and crossed the parade field to the Grand Entrance.

Dozens of life-sized, marble statues decorated the grounds of the palace. The Grand Entrance, however, was unique in that it included statues of males.

A tall, powerful warrior, the first Torino, was posed in the middle of the courtyard, her rock-hard eyes peering at nine kneeling frey, encircling her. The white marble dress of the warrior included thigh-high laced boots, small thong, and long-sleeved open-cleavage top. An actual steel sword was held in her gloved right hand, leveled evenly before her.

The statues of the frey were in a darker marble. Each male was naked except for an actual steel collar and chain that lay to the side. And each one was on his knees, wrists crossed at the back. Finally, each male statue displayed an erection.

The meaning of the display was not only to show female dominance, but to reinforce the importance of fertility.

The junior officer led us inside and then directly to the Torino's Council of Jurina's, the meeting place of her top twenty-four jurinas.

"No frey," one of the Palace Guards said as we approached the door. "This is women's matter only."

"Enter that door," I told Alexi. "Follow Mermak. The frey of the Council will be there. Remember, your position is at the end of the line. You may talk freely in there."

I stepped inside. Two palace guards barred the doors behind me.

The Torino sat at her throne in the far back center of the room, the ancient stone wall, a remnant of Erska, shadowing her. It was the original stone wall of the first palace of Antrana, and seat to the first of our ancestors of the modern era.

Unknown to all but three other persons in the room was that the Torino, our leader for twenty years, was my older sister by fifteen years. It was our mother's order that I would make my way to the ascension of command and to the throne by right of my own accomplishments and not only of bloodline. Though it would always be an option to claim the throne outright if necessary, it was best that my achievements could stand upon their own weight. There were other women in the House Kretahla, but I was the next in the line of succession.

The Torino was dressed in a winter weight black leather military uniform of long-sleeve blouse and heavy pleated skirt. The four silver siglet rings of her position were on her blouse collar, which matched four small silver rings hung in a row on a small strand from her ears. One ear was pierced; the other earring was clipped-on because her lower ear had been cut away in battle. A wide black leather belt was wrapped around her waist, adorned by a three-inch wide silver buckle with the etched image of an attacking cayilita. It was an ornate symbol of our most powerful bird.

My sister was an expressive woman, prone to accenting her point with her hands. She and I were of the same height and similar build. But her hair was cut short, sheared roughly at the ends, and had changed from black to a gray color several years ago. Her voice was deep and slightly raspy, but rarely loud. I admired how her presence always commanded the attention of those about her.

To her left and right were curved tables, encircling one-half of the room, in greater circles away from the throne. The first row of tables seated three jurinas on each side – these were the top six jurinas. They were each wearing the same winter uniform as the Torino; these korina jurinas had three silver siglets on their uniforms.

The second row of tables seated the imaya jurinas, with two rings. Four of these warriors sat on each side.

The third and final row of tables seated the jurinas, with one ring. Cinzia walked to my right and took a seat. There were seats for five jurinas on each side; however, there was one empty seat on the far left back row.

If all seats were occupied there would have been twenty-four jurinas and the Torino present in the chambers.

"Netratoh Tural," the Torino said.

I saluted in a most crisp manner, "Yes, my Torino. How may I be of service?"

Cinzia was on the inner aisle. Her expression moved from one of consternation to one of…what?

"The Jurina Prima Council has come to me with grave concerns. These concerns may have a bad effect on our people and the military."

"Yes, Torino?" I asked. Thoughts ran through my head at great speed. Had I forgotten an important task? Had there been an accident? No, I was certain that all was going according to plan.

"Since the Treaslok invasion we have begun to prepare for the time when they may yet again soil our land," the Torino said, standing. "We do not know what the Earth dictator has been doing for the last half of a year. He could be attempting to build another force to attack us. He could be making reinventions as we have done. In any matter, we can expect that soon the Treaslok will attack us."

The Torino stepped off the dais of the throne. As she was apt to do, she waved her hand expressively around the room. "We will *not* allow another attack," she exclaimed, pounding her right fist into her left open palm.

"The Council has decided that we take the fight *to* the Treaslok and we will conquer *them.*"

I found myself blinking. The… the scale of such an effort. I thought we would attack merely to inflict harm upon them and to do damage. This was unexpected.

"Your frey has said many times 'The best defense is a good offense.' We will adopt that strategy. His people's history has proven time and again that waiting for an attack will result in defeat."

The Torino swept the Council with her eyes and then looked at me. "We shall prepare new defenses and equally shall make for an attack. At the end of this year we will subjugate the Treaslok."

I nodded.

"The Council has a great task ahead of them. Our people, all of our people, have a great effort before us. It was your foresight to recognize the value of infiltrating the Treaslok three years ago to learn their language and ways. It was your foresight to value the knowledge of the Earth frey. You proved your valor and bravery in tactical planning. You proved your perseverance and competency in combat, time and time again."

The compliments warmed my face.

"Netratoh Vercella Tural, you are ordered by the Torino, and further ordered by the Council of the Jurinas, that you be promoted to the rank of Jurina."

In my thoughts I believed a commendation would be forthcoming. But I did not anticipate a promotion!

Cinzia beamed a knowing smile.

"Thank you, Torino. Thank you, Council," I said, catching myself after a moment's hesitation.

"Approach," the Torino ordered.

I marched to her and saluted again. She returned my salute. A palace guard came up and handed the Torino two silver siglet circles. The Torino reached past my coat and found my collar. She removed the Netratoh bars and replaced them with the silver rings, one on either side.

I saluted again.

"As I said, we have a great task ahead of us…you may take your seat." With her hand the Torino indicated the empty seat on the left.

I nodded and moved to take my place. Pleasant smiles greeted me. It was a good feeling.

Yes, it had been a great day.

"Sonda, please begin," the Torino said, taking her seat at the throne.

Korina Jurina Sonda stood from her seat on the aisle left, first row. She was my sister's most trusted and long-term comrada. At age forty-five, Sonda had earned several prominent scars in combat. A few were concealed within her dress uniform, a few were exposed. It was well-known that Sonda had taken an arrow to the shoulder during a battle six years ago to prevent my sister from being hit. She consistently won sword fight competitions. But she and I had yet to face one another.

I could take her.

There were few Erskan warriors that were without battle scars. One thing about us was that you were either good or dead; it was rare to find a half-capable warrior above the rank of Kuretno, and unheard of for a Jurina to possess minimal fighting skills.

Sonda pointed to the ceiling. One of the palace guards lowered an expansive map, created in the traditional ink-on-cloth manner.

"We will have two primary efforts under way. Jurina Yannta will be in charge of the land attack. Jurina Iona will be in charge of the water attack.

"For the attack," Sonda moved to the map on the right side, pulling out a wood pointing stick. She pointed to Renest, our small city on the eastern coast. "Renest has been repopulated and will be the base from which we launch our attack. We have positioned two harfala as temporary protection; we shall move another harfala into the city next week. The city walls are complete and are fully armed with archers. One of the two small power units from the Tamagra is now connected to the light source for Renest and it has field lighting for a two-thousand foot radius around the defenses.

"Belenda has also been reinforced with two harfala. The height of the walls have been increased five feet and the second of the two small Tamagra power units is in place providing light and power – we will need this for construction thirty hours a day.

"The twenty foot wide road between Renest and Belenda has been paved in stone and provides smooth passage. Two new armored escort wagons are nearly complete and armed with a rotating turret for the archers. Eight additional wagons are being constructed.

"Iona, please continue," Sonda said, stepping aside.

Jurina Iona stood, carrying a few sheets of paper in her hand. "The decision to build a navy has been made, obviously. We would not begin these preparations without having a way to advance upon the enemy," she smiled. "Unless our newest Jurina would like to swim to the Treaslok?"

There was a ripple of laughter.

No one liked being in the water.

I hated the thought. Riding in a boat made of wood. On water that stretched for hundreds of miles.

I would rather be made of straw and face down an armed Treaslok.

At least in my dreams there was solid ground at my feet.

Iona continued, "We believe that the Treaslok have already had surveillance of Renest. Most likely this is by using their sea ships. That is why we have concentrated on making the appearance that we are merely working on the city's defenses. We believe that building a growing base could signal that we were preparing for attack. Instead, we want them to believe we are on a defensive posture.

"We will start the effort of ship building in Belenda in two weeks. We will, of course, need frey Alexi to stop all civilian efforts and begin to direct the supply of materiel, further design, and construction of ships. I am confident that he has enough knowledge and information for us to make our first ships.

"We will create three types of ships. The first ship will be used for carrying our warriors across the sea. This is called a *troop ship* and we will build twenty of these ships. Each troop ship will carry two-hundred warriors. This will carry about 4,000 warriors per cycle, with arms and supplies. We will make five round trips, eventually bringing 20,000 warriors to Treaslok. Each troop ship will have a crew of ten warriors. Based on our intelligence, we believe the distance to be approximately two-hundred and fifty miles. It takes approximately twenty-five hours for a round trip, and thus four days to transport all invasion forces, accounting for loading and unloading times. We will attempt to produce more troop ships as time permits.

"To provide escort, the second ship is called a *sloop-of-war*. This is a fighting ship. A crew of twenty-five will be operating crew and three will be weaponry crew. It will have two masts for sails and have a body made for speed and turning. Each ship will be armed with the most powerful of the Earth firearms. We will build three of these ships for escort across the sea.

"The third ship is the *caravel*. It is a smaller, very fast ship that will be used for patrols around Renest and Belenda. It will have a crew of fifteen, and will be armed with the remainder of the Earth weapons. We will have three of these and there will always be at least one of them on patrol at a given moment. They are to intercept any spy ships that the Treaslok may send to us. They are small in size so that they will not give the impression to Treaslok, should they escape, that we are preparing the other two types of ships. Caravel ships will have two masts for sails. They are suitable for use close-in to the shore.

"The caravel ships will be created first and then deployed in the bay. The sloop-of-wars and troop ships will be created next and stored in Belenda until we are ready for the attack. We will have trials of each of the three ships early in the mornings and will train as many crews on the sea as we can. We know that our level of shipbuilding skill is deficient and that our knowledge of sea combat is null. We will persevere and shall spend months practicing. We will begin recruiting the navy in one week. "Emla, would you like to address the defenses?"

Korina Jurina Emla stood beside Iona. Emla looked at me for only a moment. Did Volsa talk to her? Or did Cinzia say something?

"The caravels," Emla said, "will provide protection of the new crews and ships while they are in Erskan waters. We are aware of a defensive device called a "mine" that would be excellent for defense of our coasts; however our inability to find the correct ingredients for gunpowder has slowed this. In the meantime, armed radio patrols will monitor the coast line until we have the ability to place explosive mines in the water. I am seeking other suggestions for defense beyond the traditional methods."

Yannta continued: "Our warrior army is now at thirty-thousand. We will add another twenty-thousand to that number. Included in this first attack force will be called *Marines*. This is a word from Earth."

Several of the jurinas attempted to pronounce the foreign word.

The number "fifty-thousand" was also mentioned. This was a tremendous number of warriors.

"We will train another five-thousand warriors for home defense, bringing our forces to fifty-five thousand."

Sonda took over: "This is a bold plan. We have never attempted this...an *invasion*, or *ryinka lo troynya*, on this scale. The operations eight years ago at Hikevo, and, to a lesser scale, KoVer, can be viewed as training missions for the invasion of Treaslok.

"To ensure our victory, first we will need to double our current forces. This will require growing our training facilities and uniforms and supplies and weapons. And, perhaps the most difficult, will be to acquire the women we need for the fight. The civilian population continues to have high morale and support for all of our past campaigns; however, for us to conscript so many at one time may be a burden on all houses. The mandatory age for conscription will be expanded from ages nineteen to twenty-two upwards to include twenty-four years of age. We take the war to Treaslok's land to ensure that we are safe for the long future. Leaving one's home for a year is a small price to pay for the security we will feel for decades.

"We will," Sonda continued, "also have an unprecedented materiel and supply need. In the past, this has been left to the leaders of the attack and defense; now Imaya Jurina Alsada will take command of these responsibilities. Imaya Jurina Ryokoa will be in command of weapon and armor production.

"Korina Jurina Imonsa will retain command of all training. This is especially important because we will now include language training. We must know the language of the enemy. All warriors must become fluent in the Treaslok language. Also, senior officers will be trained in the basics of the rather complicated English language. This will allow us to communicate in a secret manner amongst ourselves.

"Korina Jurina Keka will retain command of administrative operations. Korina Jurina Hedida will retain command of internal Security and Intelligence."

They distributed hand-drawn sheets of paper that identified the areas of responsibilities.

The Torino spoke, sweeping her hand, "All command assignments for Jurina officers remain the same, though your chain of command will change as the navy is deployed. With one exception in that Jurina Tural will now have responsibility for a new position taken from the Earth language. It will be called *Skunk Works*."

The room was full of puzzled faces, including my own.

The Torino walked over to the large map and tapped it on the presumed coastline of Treaslok. "If we are to protect our people, we must attack and defeat the Treaslok. To do so with the least harm to our warriors requires that we must employ every new weapon we can create. The key to our last victory was the introduction of superior communications and weapons. Indeed, I believe the Erskan Empire may have fallen had it not been for the willingness of the Earth frey, Alexi, to use his weapons and equipment. How many of you have asked yourselves, when no one was nearby to hear you, about what may have happened to us if the Treaslok had attacked unabated? We would all be in chains or dead.

"In the past few months Kendra and her teams have been working to provide our civilization with advances, both civilian and military. We need to finish the civilian improvement projects we have begun, but then we must concentrate on developing and deploying new military capabilities.

"I have had several private meetings with frey Alexi and he has an uncompromised willingness to assist us. We will borrow from his people's history and experience. This is for two reasons: first, because he knows well the Earth technology that is two-hundred years ahead of us. Second, because the trenama Corrigan is undoubtedly making similar efforts in his alliance with the Treaslok.

"The knowledge of Earth military technology is to have a special factory where new weapons are created and tested. This is named after a *skunk*, an Earth animal that is somewhat like an eeneta. However, when you come close to a skunk, it will spray a foul odor onto anyone nearby. Because of this, skunks are pushed as far away from everyone. Thus they are secret. Our Skunk Works will be commanded by Jurina Tural and she will report directly to Sonda. Kendra will report up to Tural. All civilian engineers will finish their projects and begin working on the preparation for the invasion."

With my promotion came new duties. This was a pleasant surprise. Before I could think about it in detail, the Torino swept her hand across the Council.

"What is the time line?" the Torino asked aloud. "All civilian engineering projects must move to military objectives by the end of eight weeks." She lifted a sheet of paper from her throne and read, "Design and building of the navy must be completed in six months; one month after the snow melts. Land-based training for the navy begins in eight weeks, and then moves to the sea when the first caravel is ready, which is in four months. Marines will begin training one month later. We will attack three months after the navy is complete."

There was a quiet over the room.

"Yes," Sonda said, "we will invade Treaslok in nine months with an untested navy."

"It is nothing that the Treaslok, or Corrigan, can expect us to do," the Torino added.

She was correct. I estimated our attack would be in a year's time, or perhaps longer, twenty months from now.

"The precise invasion date," the Torino told us, "will be determined at a later time. Until then, Sonda will pass down command dates and assignments. Kendra's use of the Earth planning techniques will be taught to all officers over the next two weeks. Without using this tool, we will not be able to accomplish our timeline.

"Questions you may have about the invasion can be directed up your chain of command. The Council will meet every week at this time. I leave it to the Korina's for your next orders." The Torino walked to her throne. She turned on her heels and straightened herself.

"Shia-talso," the Torino said, wishing all of us good fortune.

"Shia-talso," all of the room's occupants replied, standing.

The Torino strode past us to the doors which were opened by palace guards.

It was apparent that the majority of the jurinas in the Council were aware of most or a substantial part of the invasion plan. But it seemed that the scale, and the time line, of the invasion was quite a surprise. The jurinas had grouped into small clusters, talking.

Sonda walked over to me at the same time that Cinzia approached.

"Congratulations, Tural," Sonda said, nodding her head.

"It is an honor," I replied.

"It is overdue," Sonda told me. "How much time will it take for you to brief your frey on the invasion plan? He knows several pieces of the plan by answering previous questions from the Torino."

"I would need about a half-hour," I said. "I must translate words to English for him to understand."

"Good. Bring him with you to the War Room after the noon meal. Bring Kendra and her two senior engineers, eh, Uimisla and – "

"Nerua," I added.

"Yes. And, Jurina, for the time being, your frey is not allowed outside of the palace walls unless he has at least one of the Elite palace guards with him."

This was obviously not because of an escape risk, but because of the need to protect his safety.

The Elite palace guards were carrying my frey's StacGuns.

"That should not be an issue," I said. "My frey trained all of them to use firearms."

Sonda smiled. "It is a shame that your frey is not a female."

I smiled. "Then I would have no one to feel the kiss of my whip."

Sonda laughed. "You are dismissed until after the meal."

I left the room with Cinzia immediately behind me.

Alexi and Mermak were on their knees inside the second hall. Both stood as we exited and turned the corner. I walked about ten feet and then spun to face Cinzia.

"You knew!" I accused. My finger stabbed the air in her direction.

"By my heart, yes. Of course. I knew about your promotion two weeks ago."

Cinzia looked over her shoulder, checking the hallway. Alexi and Mermak had stopped, about six feet away from us. "Did you really believe I would have been sleeping with a *junior* officer?"

Cinzia smiled and then walked on, with Mermak on her heels. "I believe you have some explanations for your frey, Jurina Tural?" she said loudly to me.

Alexi blinked. "Jurina?" His eyes darted to the shiny new siglets on my uniform.

"To my quarters," I grinned. I reached my fingers into the welded loop on his collar and tugged. "You are going to hear about an amazing morning."

"What happened?"

I walked beyond him, my hand guiding him to follow.

# Chapter Three
# Skunk Works

"What can we do to prevent another attack?" Cinzia asked aloud.

We were meeting in my Skunk Works offices, in a rear area of the palace. Several of the jurinas and top officers sat around the table. Alexi was the only male sitting near the table, just to my right and back about an inch. The room had several other frey nearby, each of which was the trusted and branded personal property of the jurinas.

"We will have adequate defenses in the cities," Yannta said.

"What if we could keep them from getting that close?" my frey wondered.

"It will be many months' time until we have ships on the sea," an officer noted.

Alexi looked at me and asked, "Is there a fast way for us to reach the sea from here by using a *river*?"

"What was that?" I asked.

"What was *what*?" Alexi replied.

"The last word you used," I told him.

"River?"

"Yes. What is a *rivers*?" Yannta interceded, typically impatient.

"You have a river near KoVer," Alexi said. "Water running by the cliffs...."

I nodded. "Yes, that is a rivers then. The word is 'yelnoc.' There are no others."

"There is only one yelnoc? Where does it start? Where does it end?" Alexi inquired further.

"It ends in the ground...in the rock," someone told him. "A mile before KoVer. It goes down and we cannot follow."

"Where does it begin?" Alexi asked. His question was addressed to all in the room.

I did not know the answer.

A few of us looked at one another.

"How far has someone searched for the start of the KoVer River?" Alexi asked.

"Fena went ten days along the rivers, yes?" Jurina Shalana asked.

"No," Resvana countered, "Fena only went five days. She said she was searching for Glata's body. Do you remember Glata?"

I remembered stories about Glata, lost when I was a child. She was from the House Halina, a relative of --

Alexi looked around the room, his face twisted, before stopping to look at me. "No one knows where the KoVer Yelnoc starts?"

"We have not explored to the west," I said. "The sand makes travel difficult beyond several days because it becomes softer. Our horses sink."

"Has anyone tried to go *on* the Yelnoc by boat?" he asked.

"Why would we do that?" Resvana scoffed.

Alexi came over to me and sat down, his shoulders dropped.

We knew the lands of the Aervanta continent to the north, east, and south. But we did not know much about our western territories. I could sense that Alexi was… disappointed. At times before, though rarely, he seemed unhappy that we were not as advanced as his people were.

This seemed to be one of those times. Usually, it was not easy for others to know what he was thinking; but he appeared tired and was not shielding his feelings.

I decided to re-start the conversation at-hand and keep the room from feeling self-aware at our own failings. "We need ideas on protecting Renest and Belenda while we build our navy."

"What does the coastline look like?" Alexi asked, turning his attention to me.

Cinzia had been there recently. Alexi followed my gaze when I looked at her.

She went to the chalk board. "The coast by Renest is rocky. There are many great rocks protruding from the water. There are only two or three locations that anyone could land upon the shore. But it was much farther south where we found evidence that the Treaslok landed. They crossed west to KoVer. Radio patrols monitor that point now."

The chalk clicked on the board as Cinzia sketched a rough picture with water and boulders. "Our patrols can fire down upon approaching boats because of this elevation change, of about thirty feet."

She sketched a side-view of another coast. "Belenda is better for us, which is why we chose it as the location to build the navy. We can construct the boats in the city and then roll them to the water. It is a long, sloping drop in elevation for two miles to the coast. There is no rock for five-mile wide area on the coast, but there is a desert."

"How wide is the – eh, desert?" Alexi asked.

"It is several hundred feet from the grass and fields to the water."

"Interesting," he said. He made a notation in his papers. He walked to the chalkboard and wrote an English word, 'b – e – a – c – h.'

He turned toward us, "I have not heard anyone talk about *tides*."

"I do not know that word," I admitted.

"When the moons, the larger of Netra's orphans, move around this planet, they create an invisible pull onto the seas."

The room was deathly quiet.

I never felt that the orphans were pulling me toward the sky.

"Please explain," Kendra asked softly.

"Let me try this," Alexi said. "I am holding this chalk in my hand. What will happen when I let it go?"

"It will drop to the floor," Kendra answered.

"Yes, it will. We all know that it will. It always drops to the floor, yes?" He let go and it dropped. "Why does it drop?"

"Because it is heavy," Kendra replied.

"Yes, it is. It drops because it is being pulled by your planet to the middle of the planet. This is called *gravity*."

"We have a word for that, *emi-shon*," an engineer said.

"You cannot see emi-shon," Alexi said. "But you know it to be there, yes?"

Alexi drew a circle with several small circles around it. "This is the Aervantan planet. Around it are Netra's orphans. They are small moons. They are larger on one side. All of them are moving around the planet. They all have their own emi-shon."

Kendra nodded and said, "The larger the moon orphan, the stronger the emi-shon."

"Yes. As the larger moon orphan moves around the planet, it draws the water of the sea toward it. Not enough to make it move like the chalk falls to the floor, but there is enough water in the sea to make it move up in large amounts. This rising and falling of the water at the coast line is called a 'tide.'"

Another engineer raised her hand. "Belenda has tides. The depth of the water changes four feet in a thirty-hour day."

"Lina, you have observed this?" Cinzia asked, surprised.

"Yes, Jurina. Many years ago. I was experimenting with skrow to learn if they could live with the salt water."

"What is that, *skrow*?" Alexi asked.

"A water animal we cut open to make our writing ink," I said.

"Does it have legs or is it a –" he stopped. "Does it swim in the water?"

Cinzia drew a half-circle on top, then a squashed circle with the tentacles of a skrow.

"Looks like a *jellyfish*," Alexi nodded. "They live in the sea?"

"For only a few months," Lina replied. "We cultivate them."

Alexi looked confused.

"We *grow* them," I explained, sensing his lack of vocabulary.

"Do they bite?" he asked.

Lina rolled her eyes, "Worse! They are very painful." She exposed her right calf.

Several jagged scars ran five inches along her skin. "This is from merely one of the legs that touched me."

Alexi put his hands out, about four inches distant. "How big are skrow?"

"No," I said, expanding my hands three feet, "this."

"The legs, or tentacles, are four feet?"

"Oh, no," Cinzia told him. "The legs are twenty feet or more."

"How many of these do you... grow?"

"We farm several thousand skrow," I replied. "The ink is used for writing and for dying our leather and other fabrics."

Alexi smiled. He tapped the chalk against the board twice.

"What are you thinking?" Cinzia asked.

Alexi drew three crossed sticks on the Belenda desert.

"We can make traps. We will put them into the sand, on the beach, at low tide, when we can go out and push them deep. Then we tie them together. We put metal points on the top. When the tide is low, the Treaslok boats will have great difficulty landing to the shore. When the tide is high, the Treaslok boats will be damaged."

"Five miles of coastline," Kendra said. "How many spike traps will be needed?"

"Three of these per every thirty feet."

"That is five-hundred," Kendra counted in her head.

"Done," Cinzia replied. "Now, what are you thinking about the skrow?"

"Whether the Treaslok exit their boats at low tide to walk up the beach, or if their ship is sinking, they will get into the water." Alexi grinned again, "Is it possible to seed the coastline with skrow?"

I bit my lip and nodded. Then I smiled at Lina and asked her, "Yes?"

Lina's hands ran through her hair as she thought about the idea. "I do not know how long they will live in the sea. Since we got the first skrow from the sea we can expect they will be fine."

"Take a couple of skrow to Belenda and find the answer," Cinzia told her.

"Understood," Lina replied. She received Kendra's nod as an affirmation.

"I would like to see a skrow, please," Alexi asked.

Lina glanced at one of the clocks in the room. "Now is not a good time. Two hours from now would be better."

"We will be there," I told her.

Cinzia surveyed the room. "I invite any other discussions." There were no comments. "Good. Tomorrow, same time. Dismissed."

I saluted Cinzia before she walked out.

There remained only Alexi and a few of Kendra's staff. They busied themselves with plans to make spike traps.

"Tell me, frey, what you think of our preparations?"

Alexi nodded. "I am impressed, Mistress. The target of nine months did not seem likely to me. Now, I believe it."

"This is only one day of preparation!" I laughed. "How could you possibly make such a statement? I only wanted your thoughts of today's topics."

"Organized now means organized later," he said, probably quoting an Earth phrase, as he was often apt to do.

He appeared to speak but changed his mind.

"What else?" I demanded.

"Now my Mistress has something to do," he admitted. He stepped back a couple of steps and added, "and maybe she will have a sense of humor again."

"Here!" I ordered, pointing to the ground directly in front of me.

Alexi moved close and then suddenly dropped to his knees to kiss my boots.

His tactic was to avoid being slapped.

The fingers of my left hand latched around his collar and pulled him up. Then I cupped his cheeks with my hands and delivered a very light slap. "Just because it is true, does not mean you can think it."

"Yes, Mistress." His voice was serious, but he smiled.

It was almost time for the noon meal.

I could eat.

Or I could rog my frey.

Eat.

Sex.

Hmm.

Sex wins.

"Kendra, I will return in an hour," I told the engineer.

She nodded, barely looking away from a pile of scrolls and a few sheets of paper.

Without a word I pulled on Alexi's collar and led him to the doorway.

Alexi reached out for the door latch.

The door swung in.

"Mistress Hula!" Alexi exclaimed. His voice sounded almost that of a little girl. Then he caught himself and tried again, "It is good to see you, Mistress Hula."

Hula made a sharp salute to me. "Have you been taking care of my frey?" Then she smiled and added, "Jurina."

I returned the salute. "*Your* frey? Perhaps I need to send you to Renest to encourage you to show proper respect."

"Netra! Not that! Do you think there is snow and ice here in the capitol?" she laughed. "You should see what it is like on the coast. It is gray. An ice-rain falls during the day; snow at night. *Eagh!*"

Hula patted the head of my frey as she walked by him. "Alexi would love it there."

I hugged her.

"Does this mean you are not sending me to Renest?" she returned the hug.

"No. Something much worse."

"Oy, oy, oy," Hula laughed.

I continued to hold her body close to mine.

"You can let go now," she said, somewhat uncomfortably.

She attempted to pull apart.

"I received special orders this afternoon. You and I are going on a mission," I told her. I maintained my grasp around her cold leather coat.

"Where?" she asked, shaking her head. It seemed she knew the answer.

"Treaslok."

"Could I return to Renest?"

I released my grasp on my lover. "There is a war coming and we will take first blood."

"What is this place?" Hula asked.

"This is our Skunk Works. It is where we will build new weapons. I can only show you some of the battle plans to invade Treaslok."

"When?" She looked around the large room, with several tables covered with large sheets of paper and pictures. Maps hung on the walls.

"Door!" Kendra said, again keeping her head down in design work.

Alexi closed the door.

"In nine months."

"What?" Hula turned on her heels. "That is madness."

"Yes, it is. That will help us have a surprise advantage over the Treaslok."

Hula looked at a few of the maps. She turned to me again, "How, exactly, are we to begin the attack?"

She looked at my frey, "Have you been teaching everyone to swim in the sea?"

I laughed. "We are building a number of boats…ships that will transport our warriors across the sea. Before we are ready for the invasion we must accomplish two tasks. First is to create sand spikes." I pulled a diagram of the steel-tipped wood spikes to the table before her. "Second, we will scout their coast line and find their seaport. We need to learn the current state of their navy."

Hula pushed the picture of the sand spikes away. "When do we go to Belenda?"

"In five weeks," I told her.

"Who is in charge of the operation?"

I paused.

"You?" she asked.

"I am not sure, but it is likely," I admitted, not too confident.

Behind Hula, Alexi's arms twitched. The wait was causing him more agony than my three-foot whip.

"Alexi, wait," I commanded.

He sat on his heels.

"Yes, yes," Hula nodded. She turned around to face him and snapped her fingers. "Come here, frey."

Alexi launched to his feet and wrapped his large arms around her, engulfing Hula's body.

I often forgot the difference in our size; Alexi was several inches taller than I and he was considerably larger and heavier.

"He is so warm," she said. Hula pressed the right side of her face into his chest and looked at me.

"I did not know you were recalled to the palace," I admitted.

"I was not. Not yet, anyhow, until I got here. I am here to participate in Otra's Glow Ceremony tomorrow. But Yannta intercepted me and said I was assigned to work with you. No, she said, to report *to* you, but I did not know that meant you had a new rank."

Hula had a tendency to talk until interrupted.

"What is a Glow Ceremony?" Alexi asked.

"Otra is pregnant," I explained. "This is, understandably, a special occasion and celebration."

"Do you remember Otra?" Hula asked Alexi.

"No, Mistress."

"Oy, oy, oy," Hula laughed. "Otra did not like you. She thought spending time with you was a waste of effort."

Alexi's face scrunched. Then he nodded, "Oh… Yes… The 'Choker of KoVer.'"

"She would have got rid of you if it were not for someone's intervention," Hula told him. Then she released her grip on Alexi and looked at me. "I do not know how you found the authority to change the regular system in your favor."

"Yes," I admitted, avoiding a portion of her comment. My sister had intervened.

Hula also failed to mention that she, initially, did not want to teach Alexi our language – until she actually met him. Then she would not even consider a regular payment for her lessons, and eventually taught him at no cost.

"You need to take what I know about Treaslok language and deliver training to our warriors," I informed her.

"Understood," she nodded. "Why am I still holding this?"

Hula handed her rucksack to Alexi. "How many warriors?"

It was my turn to laugh. "No. You do not understand. To our warriors. *All* of our warriors."

Hula's eyes popped. "Twenty thousand?"

Kendra and Uimisla approached. "Fifty-five," Kendra said.

"What?" Hula looked at them. "What kind of game are you playing with me?"

"Fifty-five thousand," I said. "And... English for the top three-hundred command staff."

"Netra!" Hula glared at me. "Where am I going to find help with English?"

Uimisla waved her hand.

"Oo hauf mi dikshun iree?" Alexi asked Uimisla, in English.

She held a paper book in the air.

"Uimisla and I will help you, Mistress," Alexi replied.

Hula frowned.

"Frey," I addressed Alexi, "deliver Hula's belongings to my room and then meet us in the officers' cantina."

"Yes, Mistress."

I moved to the door and waited for Alexi to open it to the cold air outside. "Let us talk over hot soup. I have much to tell you."

"How will you and I get to Treaslok?" Hula asked.

"You will not be happy with the answer," I told her.

"Seems like the day for that, oy, oy, oy," Hula answered.

It was great to have my lover in the city.

We stepped into the dreary cold weather. But I looked at Hula and felt a warm feeling surround me.

# Chapter Four
## Mistress of Freydom

I pulled on Alexi's collar with my right hand and forced my frey to his knees.

He knelt and pressed his lips to my right boot. Then he gently kissed my left boot. He moved to lift his head, but I pushed the back of his head down hard, holding his lips against the leather. He made a muffled sound in surprise; I continued to press.

His back tensed; I could see those powerful Earth muscles ripple and flex around his shoulders.

My frey remained the largest person anyone had ever seen; he was two hands taller than the largest female; he was three hands taller than any male. I always felt the satisfying feeling of power over any male; but Alexi was unique beyond all on my world.

Ah, to find a way to go to his planet, capture their males, and return with gifts to my sisters...

I eased my grasp on his hair and he came upward some distance before kneeling.

Silent.

Obedient.

Mine.

The fire in the cabin roared, with the dranta wood crackling on the iron frame. The fireplace was on a raised circular dais in the middle of the large cabin. The cabin was suitable for holding 20 troops. Four cages were in each corner for frey. But this week the cabin would not be attended by troops.

"Bring me something to eat from our pack," I told Alexi.

"Yes, Mistress," he replied.

I sat deep into the plush mattress of alta feathers and stretched my legs out before me. I rolled to my left side and looked toward the heavy wood door. Wind whistled as it escaped into the corners of the door frame. Snow pelted the wood-shuttered windows. Two more months of this, I thought. Two more months of cold and snow and ice.

"You knew your mother, yes?" I asked Alexi.

He was cutting open a wera fruit for me, exactly as instructed; in quarters, sliced on the edges. These he placed on the hammered-metal plate.

"Yes, she lived until I was twenty-five years old... uh, twenty-five Earth years old."

I did the conversion in my head.

"That is a young age for people of Earth, yes? You have said that most people live until one hundred and twenty years."

"She was murdered. Run down by a person in a space wagon on Io, a moon of Jupiter. It's...never mind."

"I am sorry," I said. "Both for your loss. And for not having anyone of your kind to talk to."

"It was almost six years ago," he said, looking past me. I could sense that he pushed away painful memories.

"It was then that you became a trenama hunter?" I wondered.

"No, Mistress. I had been a Ranger for two years by that time. My family has a long history of being *police* officers, eh, trenama hunters."

"I understand," I nodded. "Our males are removed from their mothers after the first twelve weeks."

"And their fathers?" Alexi asked, bringing the plate to me and offering it as he bowed.

"They never know the father. I never knew my father. Children are placed into separate lives immediately, depending on their House. Mine is House Kretahla, and my sister and I share the same mother. She was Torino for thirty-nine years. Because the bloodline is part of the Torinoship, it is important that the descendents mate with as many males as possible. My sister, however, has been unable to conceive."

"And you?" Alexi inquired. He was almost hesitant in his question.

"You must not worry about asking these questions. You may freely ask of what you do not know."

He nodded.

"I am also unable to conceive. We have relatives within the House Kretahla, but no other direct descendents at this time. The problem of not bearing children affects others."

Alexi held one of the slices to my mouth.

"You have heard about the medical reasons that caused our female-male ratio to be so different, yes?"

"Yes, Mistress."

"You were told that it was thirty-to-one." I took a bite of the sweet fruit. "You must not repeat this to anyone: the ratio is changing."

My frey nodded..

I took a breath. "It is getting worse," I told him. "It is approximately forty-to-one."

"Over how much time?" he wondered.

"The last twenty years it is sliding."

"That will cause more problems," Alexi noted.

"Yes. Scarcity. More wars over the males. But if this continues… how long could our race survive? Could we live with a fifty-to-one ratio?"

"The Erskans are extremely aggressive, sexually, in comparison to Earth women," Alexi said. "It's understandable why there would be more fighting."

"We take what we need to survive," I said. "We have minor conflicts with other nations to the north, and with the Treaslok in the east, for many centuries. You are aware that we cannot travel west across the desert. We have the same problem south. East is the sea, and our… irrational fear. Just north of the others is an almost-impassable mountain range. We are locked in."

Alexi was silent for a moment. "You traveled the mountain route to reach the Treaslok."

"Yes. It took us two months to make the journey. It took me three months to return."

"You said 'us' and then you said just 'you,'" he noted.

"It was a successful mission in that someone returned with intelligence. But I lost seventeen warriors."

Alexi's eyes widened. He looked into mine and his lips mouthed an open "O."

"Yes. It was almost a complete disaster."

"What happened?"

The memories flooded my heart. I bit my lip for a moment.

"On the outbound journey, while on the mountains, one giracha fell into an ice hole. The line pulled all nine of them off the edge of the cliff."

The frantic cries for help from my sisters echoed in my head.

"Mistress?" Alexi asked.

I blinked.

How many seconds had gone by while I looked into nothing?

"The rest of us went on. Two weeks later we came down from the mountains into a great forest. We were attacked by animals on our first night. I used a rope to climb a tree. No one else had time to get off the ground."

"What animal?"

"We have no word for it. They are narrow sticks of flesh that move on the ground. They have a head and large teeth. They bite into the skin and deliver a poison that paralyzes."

"I think I know what those are," Alexi said. "What happened after they attacked you?"

"The screaming stopped. I fired twenty arrows and made twenty kills. But then I sat in the tree and watched the vile animals devour my sisters. Then, at first light, there was nothing left but their equipment and torn uniforms."

"I am sorry for your loss," Alexi said, his voice soft.

He reached out to touch my knee.

"My location saved me. I could have been the first woman to be bitten. Instead... Life and death... there is no understanding for all that happens to us."

I looked over his shoulder and then, with great resolve, forced my eyes to focus on him.

"I continued the mission. Spent two weeks and interrogated four Treaslok, executed them, and returned home. I traveled the forest only during the day. The most valuable piece of information I found were children's educational scrolls."

"Five months of travel for only two weeks of being there," Alexi noted.

"Yes. That was not the original mission. The eighteen of us had specific objectives. I did the best I could for the situation."

"That must have been hard."

"It still is," I admitted. "But we fight on."

"Yes, Mistress. We do."

I wanted to change the topic.

Alexi felt my intentions and returned to our previous topic. "Who knows about the change in the male to female ratio?"

"Only a handful of our leaders know this. But people in the population are beginning to notice that the price of males is increasing. We have a good understanding of what you call *economics*. Inflation, brought on by the cost of males, is unsettling our economy for the first time in several hundred years."

"I have limited medical equipment that survived the crash," Alexi said.

We had already tried his medical devices. We found no answers.

"No more talk of problems tonight," I decided. "No more talk of wars. No more talk."

"Yes, Mistress."

I parted my skirt and exposed the length of my legs. "Here. Service me for a moment, and then you will rest."

Alexi moved up and placed his head between my legs.

I grabbed onto his hair, roughly at first and then, somewhat more softly than before.

My toes tingled and I let go of his hair as his tongue moved as he had been trained.

Days ago I had him please me in this manner for two hours; reaching nika at least a dozen times. I gasped for air as he pushed his tongue into me.

I grabbed his hair again and pushed him back.

"In the bed with me," I ordered.

He had a surprised look on his face. Was he concerned that he had displeased me?

I grabbed onto his collar and pulled him the rest of the way up, placing him on the bed in front of me. We sunk into the deep cushions and among the two dozen pillows scattered about. "On your side," I told him.

My frey lay on his right side.

"We will rest." I pulled a sheet on top of us and cradled his naked body against mine.

Our attack plans were drawn.

Warriors were being recalled to the palace.

I knew that moments like these would be rare until after the battle. My arms involuntarily tightened around his body.

First would be a reconnaissance mission to Treaslok shores.

Beyond the great risk in making the journey, we faced perils of concealing our presence among the population.

If successful, we would return later with a large invasion force, followed by dangerous inner-city combat.

Alexi made a soft snoring sound.

It was clear he was concerned about being my frey.

My thoughts teetered from one side to the other; was it reckless to brand him as my own property if I was exposing myself to the high possibility of death? Or would it, at the least, provide comfort to him for the present?

I ran my fingers in his hair.

He pressed his body into mine.

Branding him would require that I identify my heir to ownership.

Hula.

No question about that.

He would belong to her in the event of my death.

Maybe that is what concerned me the most.

He was not the typical frey.

Yes. The proper woman must own him.

It was time to petition the Torino for the Rite of Ownership.

And then...

I slid my hand down to his buttock and pressed softly against him.

Yes. *There*. Just to the right of the spine, and low.

* * * * *

Alexi twitched.

He tried to be brave. Still, his shoulders betrayed his fear. He shuddered again.

"Are you cold, frey?" I asked.

"No, Mistress," he whispered. "Uh. Maybe I am a little cold."

I pressed my back against his and wrapped my arms around his sides for a moment. Then I ran my hands against his body, pressing slowly from under his arms and running down until his hips. His skin was not cool. The unknown frightened him.

Alexi was in the center of the room, naked except for his original steel collar, locked around his throat so many months ago, and four steel cuffs. His arms were outstretched to the left and right. Chains from the corners of the ceiling eye bolts kept his limbs angled at about thirty degrees.

His legs were pulled shoulder-width apart, chained to the floor.

As a necessary precaution, soft strips of leather were wrapped inside the steel cuffs to protect his skin from being cut.

The large room held more than fifty of my friends, plus a number of frey. The women sat in chairs that encircled Alexi and I. Frey kneeled beside their owners.

The room was darkened, with only half of the usual oil lamps burning.

I wore my favorite dress uniform: Leather thigh-high laced boots connected with a gold ring to my leather thong, leather double-buckled cleavage-revealing strap top, with leather shoulder-length gloves. All of the leather was a dark, almost-black, purple. Gold siglets of my rank were on my bicep bands. My sword was cross-buckled at my back.

Everyone silently watched as I comforted my frey.

"What are you thinking, my slave?" I whispered in his right ear and used the English word 'slave' to reassure him.

"I... I'm proud, Mistress. But I am afraid."

"The worst of it will be over soon. Then, the best for us."

He nodded. Sweat beaded on his neck. Rivulets of moisture dropped along his spine.

As he had done a dozen times in the last ten minutes, Alexi looked over to the far right of the room. Placed there was a burning steel cauldron. It cast flickering shadows on the stone from its red-hot coals.

He shuddered again.

Hula sat cross-legged near Cinzia. Both smiled. Hula made a slight, comforting nod.

All eyes were drawn to the Mistress of Freydom, or chief frey hunter, as she entered the silent room. Her boots clicked on the stone until she approached us in the center of the room.

She wore the traditional uniform of the frey hunter, black leather thigh-high boots with metal spikes at the outside of the heels, black leather short skirt with side slits, cross-over black leather buckled bra, and shoulder-length black leather gloves. A nine-foot triple-braded whip, pair of leather locking cuffs, and a length of silver chain hung from the wide belt slung low on her inviting hips.

A couple of centuries ago there still existed numerous teams of frey hunters that tracked and captured roaming males in the wild. It was a rare occurrence that an uncollared male would be found today.

Required traits of the frey hunter was to be uncompromisingly attractive, overwhelmingly seductive, and cruelly expedient.

The Mistress of Freydom approached me and caused my heart to skip a beat. She definitely met the first of those two traits.

I glanced again at Hula and saw her lusting after the frey hunter as well.

I stepped a couple of feet distant from Alexi and faced the Mistress of Freydom. She nodded and I returned the greeting in the ancient style: my right hand made a closed fist to which my left reached around it.

"Tural, you are ready to partake in the ceremony?" she asked, her voice smooth yet commanding. It was easy to understand how a male would be intoxicated by her voice.

Virtually all Erskan women of experience possess an aura of command that was capable of enticing males. The Mistress of Freydom drew those powerful women under her alluring spell.

"I am ready," I smiled, trying not to sound too eager – for Alexi's benefit, of course.

She turned and slowly rotated to address my friends. "Jurina Tural's petition of the Torino was approved this morning. Jurina Tural now comes to the Freydom Court to claim ownership of the frey, Alexi, as her right of gender and her privilege of rank. This evening we shall make her ownership of the frey clear to him and for all."

Her assistant walked in. Clad in a simple black cloak, she was likely a younger woman of similar beauty. She presented a key to the frey hunter.

I moved to Alexi's front side and stood before him.

He was making a valiant effort to stand without shaking. Usually when he was bound in this manner his penis was erect and he would gyrate his hips; however, in this situation he was shrunken and motionless.

"Relax," I whispered.

He half-nodded.

The Mistress of Freydom moved behind him and reached onto both sides of his plain metal collar. She took the key from her assistant and removed the padlock. She removed the collar by opening it on its hinges and pulled it to his left side, giving both to the assistant.

I unsnapped the new collar from my belt and held it high in the air for a few seconds before bringing it to Alexi's lips.

"Kiss it," I ordered.

He kissed the glistening steel collar.

It was the finest collar I could find, easily worth three month's standard payroll. My name was hand-chiseled into the thick, one-inch wide band. The seal of the House Kretahla, representing the airborne cayilita, was chiseled into the other side.

I lowered the collar and placed it around his neck.

The Mistress of Freydom took her padlock and locked it into the collar.

"You are mine," I said, loud enough that my friends could hear. "With, or without, the collar."

"Yes, Mistress," he whispered.

"Speak up," I told him.

"Yes, Mistress!"

I took in a deep breath.

Mine.

The Mistress of Freydom flashed her teeth.

I nodded to her.

She stepped to her right, her assistant beside her.

Alexi's lips trembled. I pressed my body against my frey and held him tightly.

He buried the left side of his face against mine, pressing his cheek downward. I could feel him about to speak.

"Shh," I reassured, stretching out the sound.

The frey hunter moved behind Alexi. She held a white-tipped branding iron in her thickly-gloved right hand.

Alexi could sense her presence. His body shook.

"Frey," she said, taking her left, free hand and touching the small of his back, "this will be quick. A proper branding only requires one second. You will make a bad mark if you move your body."

Stern in her appearance to him thus far, her voice changed to soothe him. She ran her fingers through his hair on his head. "You will remain still, yes?"

"Yes, Mistress," he said, his voice barely above a whisper.

"It is good to scream," she told him. "But do not move."

I looked, for the hundredth time, at the chains to be sure they were taught. Then I wrapped my arms around his waist to further hold him steady.

She pressed the brand into his right buttock.

"Ah!" he screamed. HIs body tensed. The chain links clinked and the anchor bolts strained against the stone walls.

Tears poured from his eyes and ran down onto my shoulder.

"Done," she said, after only a second or two.

"Ah!" he continued, his air running out.

The Mistress of Freydom handed the branding iron to the assistant in exchange for a medicated cloth. She placed it on Alexi's skin.

Tears continued to stream down his face. His breathing was labored; but he stopped screaming.

I held him for almost a half-minute while he fought the tears and attempted to straighten his body. Though the chains secured him at four points, he had managed to slide an inch through the wrist cuffs.

"Well done, Jurina Tural," the frey hunter said. I knew the compliment was actually directed to Alexi, but protocol prescribed a different approach.

"Women of Antrana," she addressed the room. "I present you with Jurina Vercella Tural and her owned property, frey Alexi."

My friends clapped nine times.

"Thank you," I told her.

She tilted her head and blew a slight kiss to me.

Damn her!

Then she left the room, hips swaying the entire distance to the doorway, assistant in tow.

Hula and Cinzia came to their feet and approached Alexi and I. Others stood and held conversations.

I released my grasp on Alexi.

Hula knelt to release the ankle cuffs. She looked at his right buttock. "May I see?"

"Yes," I said.

"Let me look," Cinzia said.

I reached around him and lifted the cloth.

Other women changed their positions to look at the brand.

There were several "oohs" and "ahhs" from my assembled friends. The bright red skin was burned into the half-circle that represented the frey, topped by the *kora* letter representing the House Kretahla.

"Beautiful," Hula said. "Let us cover it so it does not become ill."

I placed the cloth again onto him.

"Mistress Hula," Alexi asked, "it looks good?"

"Frey, it is beautiful. You should be proud to wear such a brand."

"I am," he replied. "I am."

I unlocked his wrists.

As expected, he practically collapsed to the floor. Cinzia and a friend of mine from War University were prepared and they caught him.

Alexi looked up into my eyes. "I am."

"I also," I said, kissing his forehead.

His eyelids fluttered.

"How do you feel?" I asked. I allowed him several seconds to reply.

He moved his right hand backwards to touch his buttock. Instead, Cinzia intercepted his wrist.

"You must not touch it," Cinzia told him.

Alexi was quiet for a half-minute. Then, "Mistress?"

"Yes, frey?"

"That really hurt," he said in a matter-of-fact tone.

I glared at him.

Cinzia ran her fingers through her hair and then shook her head.

"He is fine," Hula said. She stood and wiped her hands.

"Brieneia," I ordered and stood to my feet.

Alexi made slow and deliberate movements to get on his hands and knees. Cinzia reached down to his right shoulder and gently prodded him forward.

He kissed my right boot and then left.

"Hand that to me, please," I pointed to the wall.

Hula pulled a four-foot leather leash off a pin.

I clicked the lead around my frey's collar. I walked in front of him.

"Crawl," I tugged.

Alexi followed me on his hands and knees for a few feet. I stopped and turned to face the women.

Cinzia and Hula remained standing. Cinzia had her arms crossed in front of her; Hula clasped her hands. They appeared unsure as to move or not.

"Yes, please, come with me," I grinned.

Cinzia nodded. Hula grinned.

I tugged on the leash again.

Alexi struggled to keep up with me as I led the four of us down two flights of stone stairs. He shuffled his hands and knees quickly to keep the collar from pulling too tight around his neck.

We reached the breeding dungeon. This dungeon was strictly for the use of palace staff and their frey. It was not for the incarceration of trenama or military prisoners – we had several of those elsewhere.

I pulled the metal-plated wood door open and looked inside the well-lit dungeon. It was approximately three-thousand square feet in size with twenty frey stations. To the right, on a long, sturdy wood table was a male on his back. An Erskan warrior straddled his hips. Wide leather strips on her skirt enveloped the naked male. Her hands pressed down against his chest and she arched her back.

She smiled down at him. Her face was flushed.

A silver steel collar encircled his throat. He was naked save for steel ankle and wrists cuffs that stretched his body on the table. He lay motionless.

Then she moved forward and covered his body with hers and wrapped her arms behind his back.

"We missed something good," Hula told me.

"We have not missed anything, yet," Cinzia replied.

"Here," I told Alexi.

He followed me toward the rear corner.

I looked at the wheel that dominated this area of the dungeon.

Heavy black leather slats padded a four-foot high, half-diameter wheel. It was four feet wide and took up a large area. It rose up from the stone floor, ominous and imposing.

"Up," I said. "Feet near the top, head down here."

Alexi stepped up and positioned his feet at the apex of the wheel. He curved backwards and let his hands fall below his head, toward the floor. He was upside-down at a gradual slope.

Hula and Cinzia helped me tighten wide leather straps to his ankles and wrists.

I looked at him and nodded my approval.

Trapped.

Completely helpless.

Delectable.

My left hand reached up to his growing erection.

"You like this, frey?" I whispered into his ear.

"Yes, Mistress."

"You know the rule: you are not allowed to ejaculate without permission."

"Yes, Mistress."

I pulled my damp leather thong off and moved my hips toward his head, which was conveniently positioned at the right height.

"Lick, frey," I told him.

Alexi strained his neck and pressed his tongue into my wetness.

I steadied myself by extending my arms to the sides of the wheel.

Slow, long laps with his tongue brought tremors to my legs.

I could do this for hours.

I closed my eyes and let the pleasure surround my body.

After a minute or two, maybe five – who knew – I pulled away.

Alexi's mouth was wet. He moaned and extended his neck to reach me.

I laughed.

Then I pulled up onto the wheel and slowly crawled up to the top. My thighs brushed Alexi's body as I went to the top.

I nodded at Hula and Cinzia.

Hula pulled off her thong and turned away from Alexi's head. Then she moved backwards until she positioned herself over his mouth. He moaned and greedily pleased her.

Cinzia, probably cursing herself for not being closer to Alexi, walked over to the wall and removed a pair of steel thumbscrew clamps, connected by a lightweight chain.

I positioned over Alexi's full erection.

Pre-ejaculate oozed from his penis.

I took my fingers and ran them through the clear, sticky juice. Then I ran it over my lips and moaned.

Alexi tried to arch up his hips.

Instead, I grabbed onto his erection and mounted him, fully pushing down.

I was so wet that that there was no pain.

Alexi's penis shuddered. He attempted to thrust up, but the position he was in did not provide him with movement.

Cinzia took one of the clamps and quickly snapped it onto Alexi's right nipple. She immediately pressed down on his nipple, clamp attached, and listened to him groan in pain.

The sounds of his anguish inspired me further. I slammed down on him and took the full length of his erection deep inside.

Cinzia clamped the other nipple and pulled the chain up and apart from his body.

Hula reached around between her legs and took Alexi's head into her hands. She grabbed his hair and pushed his mouth harder into her.

Alexi bucked and pressed harder against my hips, thrusting deep and hard into me.

The tip of my boots pressed outward against the inside of his calves.

I slammed down onto him, again and again.

My breath sucked in and out of my lips.

"Ah!" I exclaimed.

My vision faded for a moment as the nika stole my consciousness.

I floated on the wheel.

… on my frey.

Floating…

The air was cold and rushed into my lungs.

Hula came at almost the same moment. She let out the high-pitched hum that I had long known. Her spine arched and her thighs squeezed Alexi's face.

Then, cruelly, I dismounted him without warning.

Alexi twisted his hips and pressed upward.

Hula stepped away – or, more accurately, stumbled forward. She slowly went to her hands and knees, panting.

I slapped once at Alexi's erection.

"Cinzia, your turn," I offered.

"By my heart," she said. "I thought you would never get off of him."

I carefully crawled down the wheel.

Cinzia and I kissed for a brief moment before she moved past me.

Alexi's chest heaved. I moved to his ear, "Are you well, frey?"

"Yes, Mistress," he replied, his voice half-slurred and dreamy.

"Would you tell me if you were not well?"

"Yes, Mistress."

Being inverted was new for him; no need to break my branded frey on the first night.

He raised his head off the padding and moaned.

I looked up and saw Cinzia take him into her.

"Ah!" Alexi breathed. "Ah!"

"Good frey," I pet his head. "You make my friend happy."

"Yes, Mistress!"

I ran my fingers through the chain on the nipple clamps. They were delightful toys. They caused pain and pleasure, provided control of the male, and allowed use of my hands elsewhere.

Hula crawled over to me. Her face was flush. "That was good. How did he learn to do it so well?"

"Must be a natural skill of the Earth males," I said. I yanked on the clamps and watched Alexi raise his chest. He continued to moan as Cinzia rogged him.

"We need to go on a hunt," Hula suggested.

I glanced at Alexi. He had no idea we were talking. "Yes. If only we could."

Cinzia bucked and half-shouted. She dragged her fingernails deeply across Alexi's chest. Then she pulled on the clamps before letting them drop.

She looked down at us.

Her hair was disheveled and sweat covered her face.

I smiled.

"You did not come, did you, frey?" I asked.

"No. No, Mistress. Please?"

"No."

Cinzia slowly pulled off my frey. She gingerly crawled down the other side of the wheel. Once on the ground, she pressed against the wheel with her left hand and touched herself with the right. "By my heart," she wheezed.

"Okay?" I asked.

"Oh. Yes." Cinzia looked around the dungeon. "Mermak... I need... more. Excuse me."

She found her thong and quickly pulled it up and under her skirt. She walked past me, but stopped and leaned over. "Thank you."

We kissed on the cheek. Her face was hot.

"Anytime," I said.

She nodded to Hula and then half-ran out of the dungeon.

"What do we do with him now?" Hula asked. She pulled on the clamps and stroked Alexi's left ear.

"Alexi," I said, "I am going to take you down. You will go to your knees, hands at your sides."

Hula helped me unlock him and move him to the stone floor.

We stood in front of him.

"Hand," I said.

He presented his right hand.

I moved it between my legs. "Get it all wet," I ordered. "Now, masturbate. I want you to come onto our boots. Now."

Alexi wrapped his hand around his erection and stroked. He slowed for a moment and then looked at me.

"Hand," I said.

He presented his hand again; Hula took it and rubbed it between her legs.

Alexi stroked his erection again.

There we stood, dressed in our leather uniforms and heavy black boots, with my naked, collared, and branded frey at our feet, forced to masturbate for our pleasure in our dungeon.

I felt a tingle rise along my spine.

Alexi's breathing increased and his hips thrust into his hand.

"Mistress?" he pleaded. That did not take long; he was probably close to nika for awhile.

I pushed my right boot forward. Hula moved her right boot next to mine.

"Yes, frey," I allowed.

"Thank you, Mistress!"

Alexi's hips rocked and he stopped stroking.

His penis jerked. White ejaculate spewed out onto our boots as he moved his body. He stroked again once and more oozed from the beautiful hard erection.

Surprisingly, he stroked again and produced more.

Hula looked at me with a smile. She shifted her weight to move away. I tapped her shoulder and shook my head "no."

"Clean it," I told him.

"Yes, Mistress."

His palms went to the ground and he put his face by my boot. His tongue licked the white male elixir from the leather. Then he shifted his position and cleaned Hula's boot.

I took in a long breath of air.

Hula made an approving sound. "Hmm. What now?"

Alexi moved off his hands and sat on his knees, wrists crossed at his back.

I spied a standing steel cage several feet away.

"In there," I told him.

Alexi crawled over to the cage.

"Stand."

I put him in the cage and locked his wrists above him.

Then I chained his ankles to the bottom rings of the cage.

I pushed the barred metal door shut with a metal clang and then secured it with a standard padlock.

I reached in between the bars and pulled gently on his collar. "Good frey. But now you are no good to me – for a while. We will return soon."

My fingers ran over his lips and rubbed the male elixir onto his chin.

"Yes, Mistress," he replied. His voice was forlorn.

"Poor frey," I told him.

Hula stood behind me.

"Rog?" I asked her. I already knew the answer.

"My quarters are closer," she suggested.

I stepped in front of her and pulled her hand with me.

\* \* \* \* \*

We spent the next two weeks constructing five-hundred sand spikes. Crews worked thirty hours a day to build the pieces and place them on twenty wagons for the caravan to Belenda.

We had agreed that winter was not the time to place skrow into the sea; the waves were too rough and the temperature frigid. We would set the sand spikes as the first line of defense and then put skrow into the water when the seas were at their typical summer calm. Still, Alexi desired to see the skrow farm prior to our ride to Belenda.

"Watch where you step," Lina warned us. She unlocked the metal barred gate and waved us to go inside to the first over-the-pool bridge.

Hula held onto the guard rail with both hands as she walked over the first of twenty-one brick-lined circular pools.

I turned to see if Alexi was following. He remained at the entrance, looking ahead.

"Frey?" I asked.

"This is amazing!" he said, admiring the view. "The Erskans are greater engineers and builders than anything comparable in my people's history."

The skrow farm was an indoor facility with a thirty-five foot high ceiling. Three circular pools were abreast one another and ran in seven rows away from us. Oil lamps lined the walls and ceilings. Most of the structure was comprised of brick with steel columns supporting the ceiling. Each skrow pool was about one-hundred twenty feet in diameter.

Alexi walked along the ramp until he reached where Lina, Hula, and I stood, mid-way over a pool. We could see shadowy objects moving in the water.

"How many are in there?" Alexi asked.

"This pool has twenty-six full-grown skrow," Lina looked at a cloth scroll she carried. "These are the sa doh-la."

"I've heard that word before," Alexi turned to me. "What does that mean, Mistress?"

"Breeder, a male breeder," I said.

"Follow me to the pool of young skrow," Lina told us.

We walked over four pools, sometimes passing other staff that were inspecting from above. I loosened my coat collar; it was easily fifty degrees warmer in here than outside.

A female staff member was at the pool where we stopped. "Is it feeding time?" Lina inquired of her.

"It is close enough," she replied. "Just a moment, please." She disappeared for a moment.

The staff member returned with a long wood pool.

"Watch, frey Alexi," Lina said. "Watch closely."

Attached on the end of the pole was a live erloo, what Alexi called a *bird*, suspended by its feet tied to a string. Its wings had been broken, though it continued to flap. The erloo shrieked as the end of the pole was lowered over the railing and closer to the surface of the pool.

Alexi squinted. I chuckled. Earth men were so... easily upset.

The erloo was pushed onto the surface of the water.

A small skrow, with a one-foot wide head, appeared several feet distant. Its glistening, wet, almost-clear body floated on the water for ten seconds. Then, its tentacles appeared by the erloo, reaching up around it on ten points. The erloo shrieked, broken wings splashing against the water.

The skrow's color darkened.

The erloo became motionless.

Lina released a knot at her end of the pole and the erloo slipped down into the skrow's tentacles of death.

There was the unmistakable, eerie sound of the erloo emitting a five-second long sucking, gurgling noise. Then it sank into the pool.

"Ho-lee fuk," Alexi said. I had heard him use that English phase only a few times previously. White-knuckled, his hands clutched at the railing.

Lina withdrew the pole as the ripples in the water disappeared.

The end of the pole was blackened.

"Skrow oil," Alexi said. "It is also poisonous."

"Yes," I nodded.

Hula looked at Alexi, "Would you like one for a pet?"

She was always one to find a joke.

"Thank you for your kind generosity, Mistress Hula. But I must decline."

Hula looked at me.

"Do not ask," I said, pointing a finger at her mouth.

We followed Lina to the main entrance.

"This will be another reason to not fall out of a boat," Hula said to me.

"You may look at this with optimism," I told her. "You would not have to be concerned about drowning in the sea."

"I would hate to spend much time riding to Belenda just to be eaten by a skrow," Hula replied. "Perhaps I could jump in the tank now."

# Chapter Five
## The Defense of Belenda

It was an agonizing, slow ride to Belenda, despite the road improvements. The twenty wagons were heavily loaded with sand spikes and metal fasteners. The wagons made only twenty-five miles per hour, far lower than the seventy miles per hour speed which I was accustomed by horseback alone.

This was my first field command. Cinzia was in charge of actual operations in Belenda; but the escort of the crews and materiel was my responsibility. As was typical, the kuretno in charge of the harfala reported to a jurina, or, more explicitly, she report to me. I looked over my left shoulder at Kuretno Visada. She was of medium Erskan height, long black hair, about twenty-two years of age, average build. Like all of us, she wore a heavy black leather riding coat. Her sword was cross-carried on her back, hilt above her shoulder to the right, typical of my generation of warriors.

Visada had been looking behind her, watching her warriors. She caught my eye and nodded.

My frey rode a hundred feet behind me, in the middle front of the harfala, flanked by two Elite palace guards. We were not permitted to be in an open area in close proximity to one another.

Each of the eighty-one warriors carried swords; others were also armed with a bow. Additional odd-number of people attended the column: engineers, construction crew, and frey. Visada also had two small, fast-riding teams skirting our flanks, looking for trouble. These teams were radio-equipped and reported to us on a regular basis.

"How is the pressure?" Cinzia asked, riding up through the column and coming abreast to my right.

"I intend to break under the strain and go home in tears," I told her.

"You should have thought of that before we loaded the wagons," Cinzia pointed her gloved finger at me. "I get nervous merely riding next to the wagons. I cannot see all about me."

"I will see to it that you are protected," I explained.

"Yes. Is that why you keep looking over your shoulder?"

"I am merely concerned about the safety of our senior jurina," I grinned.

"Sister, take some advice from an old woman that has done this many times in the past: do not look behind you so often. All of the warriors that are looking forward become nervous that there is something bad about to occur."

"Yes, but –"

"Visada knows her responsibilities," Cinzia cut me off. She turned her horse out.

"Netra!" I said under my breath.

"I heard you," Cinzia said, pulling to the side and letting the column move on.

*Old woman?* Cinzia was only five years senior to me. Where did that leave me if she was "old?"

Netra.

\*\*\*\*

It was an agonizing, slow, two-day ride to Belenda.

The journey normally took only four hours.

My ass needed a good rubbing with my hand. But my entire column was to the rear of me and grabbing onto oneself might appear unprofessional.

The city was quite different from my recollection. There were over six-hundred warriors already in the city with another harfala en route. We had been intercepted three times on the approach to the city by patrols that had expertly surprised Visada's scouting teams.

I could not handle it. I slid my hand to my side and up under my coat. I massaged the right buttock for a moment.

I resisted the urge to turn around to see if anyone had noticed. But that was also an improper motion.

The pressure of command.

I laughed at myself and swiveled my hip.

Several of the closest warriors looked left and right, examining the city. One warrior wiped her nose. We locked eyes. I nodded and then faced forward again.

The city walls were undergoing construction modifications to install wider gates to accommodate the passage of ships. Nine archers looked down on us as we entered the triple layer gates. Some day they would be armed with musket firearms. And later with rifles.

My right foot became numb again; I used the opportunity to take my boot out of the stirrup and curl my toes.

Alone, riding in front, I led the column into the city and toward the military post. At least, I hoped it was the proper route to our destination. It had been five years since my last visit to Belenda.

We narrowed our column and proceeded past many onlookers standing among homes and shops. I led my warriors to the front of the military post which had a separate, inner-perimeter combination stone-and-brick wall.

Visada rode up as I raised my hand for the column to stop. I returned her salute.

"Excellent work," I complimented her. "Secure the wagons and start a rotating guard."

"Understood, Jurina," Visada replied.

I turned to look at the line of warriors and wagons. The mid-afternoon gray sky threatened to drop additional snow upon us. I clenched my teeth as a gust of cold wind abused us.

There was an urge to call it a day and spend some time warming to a fire.

However...

"Visada, have the engineering crew report to the officer's cantina in two hours. Radio Jurina Sonda and advise her that we have arrived safely. Have a giracha on external patrol thirty hours a day working independently of the Belenda patrols, but advise the local commander if you see her before I do. Report to the cantina in two hours to give me an update. The remainder of your unit may fall out. We will need half of your unit before daybreak to escort the first load of sand sticks and our skiff boats. Weather permitting, we may begin assembling the sand sticks today."

"Understood, Jurina," Visada saluted and turned her horse away to begin effecting my orders.

Cinzia rode to me and stopped at my left side. "We should pre-assemble a few of the sand sticks this afternoon and night."

"Good idea," I nodded.

My frey rode to us, escorted by both Elite palace guards.

"Find quarters for yourselves," I told the guards. "Tomorrow morning we go out to set the traps and you both need to be more alert than the rest of us."

They acknowledged my instructions and rode toward the barracks.

"Where is Kendra and her crew?" I asked.

Then I saw them riding forward, navigating through the warriors that were breaking ranks. A light snow fell on us.

*Netra! More snow.*

"Only two hours of rest?" Kendra confirmed. "It took forever to get here."

"Imagine how long it would have taken on the old roads," Alexi said.

"Follow me. Let us find a warm fire," I told them. I handed my horse over to a stable frey.

* * * * *

I watched as Nerua, Kendra's most-senior engineer, marked the depth of the chain. She let out a warm puff of breath.

The waves rocked our narrow, wood skiff boat.

"It is a beautiful sunrise," Nerua observed, looking east.

"A nice view before drowning," Hula told us.

"Where is your optimism?" I chastised her.

The waves rocked us again. I clutched harder onto the two paddles.

"Oy!" Hula said, watching me.

Another set of high waves came toward us. I did *not* like being on water. Snow swirled around us, enveloping our small boat.

Hula pulled up the chain while Nerua wrote on paper.

"Do you have it?" Hula asked.

"Yes, drop it," Nerua said.

Hula released her grasp.

The chain disappeared into the water, dragged down by the iron anchor.

Nerua looked at the folded paper in her hand. "Fifteen more."

I wiped sea water from my brow. Perhaps it was also sweat.

There was no telling what the salt water and salt air was doing to my hair.

\* \* \* \* \*

"Soh-da Netra!" Cinzia exclaimed, walking in, shivering. Mermak followed her inside, quickly throwing his weight against the door.

I watched my hands and failed in my attempt to keep them from shaking. I reached out to Alexi. He pulled off the gloves, taking each frigid hand in his.

"Your hands are warm," I said.

"No, Mistress, not much."

That was disconcerting to hear.

"Thirty-one," Cinzia said, huffing. Mermak pulled off her gloves and put a blanket over her shoulders.

"Forty," I replied.

"You started a half-day before me," Cinzia countered.

"I did not work last night," I pointed out.

"Netra!" Cinzia cussed again. She kicked her boots out as snow fell from her shoulders.

My frey removed my boots and foot gloves, and then he wrapped my feet in a blanket. I sat on the dining room chair, shivering.

"Why are we doing this in the winter?" Cinzia huffed.

"Because the Treaslok are not likely to cross the sea in weather this bad," I said through chattering teeth. "The defenses need to be in place prior to warm weather."

"It is warm in here," my frey said. "Mistress."

Mermak stifled a laugh.

I glared at him.

"When I am able to move my arms," Cinzia said, shuffling over to the wood fire, "I will whip him until he is dead. And, that is not what I meant. Why are *we* doing this?"

"You have seen all of the warriors watching us from the desert?" I asked.

"Yes. The beach?" Cinzia nodded.

"We are demonstrating that the sea does not frighten us."

"It does not frighten you?" Cinzia asked, surprised.

"Of course it does. But they do not know this."

Cinzia nodded.

"And you expect offers to help tomorrow."

"Yes. But if not, I will place orders by the afternoon. *We* are not doing this tomorrow night alone."

Alexi looked like he wanted to speak. "Yes, frey?"

He took my feet in his hands and rubbed. "All of the materiel for the first caravel arrived here this afternoon. Construction can begin tomorrow morning."

"I should inspect and monitor the construction," I told Cinzia.

"No. You are *not* finding a way to avoid marking the sand sticks."

I knew that my threat was hollow. Cinzia responsibilities would change tomorrow morning.

Mermak delivered a cup of frothy rita-bean soup to Cinzia and then to me. It warmed my hands as Alexi put another blanket around my shoulders.

"Good frey," I said.

"Yes." Cinzia sipped her soup. "We have had a good three days."

\* \* \* \* \*

On the fourth day we sat on the shore as the tide went out and the water level receded. The first anchors appeared on the beach and then we mobilized two hundred construction workers. Kendra's crews drew out three massive wood stakes, held them up at about a thirty-degree angle, and then slammed them into the ground with a large fence-post impactor.

"This is our time to watch others work," Visada said.

She crouched behind us. Alexi was on my left, Cinzia to my right with Mermak.

Hula had returned to Antrana to provide escort for construction materials that required expediting.

In front of us the waves receded farther. The second row of anchors appeared and an additional hundred workers swarmed the beach, stakes in tow.

"I have never seen this many frey on a construction site," Cinzia said. "There must be thirty males here!"

"I have one in there," Visada said, looking across the beach. "He needed the exercise."

"Where is he?" I asked, peering ahead.

"Looking for another one?" Cinzia asked.

"Just to rog," I told her.

"He's is over on that crew," Visada said. "Gray-black hair. I can send him over to you tonight."

It was a nice gesture. "That is very kind of you. Perhaps another time."

"He can remain hard for quite a long time," Visada said.

"Really?" Cinzia asked. "How long?"

"About an hour."

"Tied, or without a testicles strap?" Cinzia appeared quite interested.

Mermak made a noise and looked down.

"Without a strap," Visada smiled.

Cinzia reached behind her and patted Mermak on his head. "Did you say something, frey?"

"No, Mistress."

We laughed.

"That looks like hard work," Visada said, watching the crews.

# Chapter Six
# Launch of the Normanda

Half of the construction crew and one of the senior engineers remained in Belenda to aid in ship-building. The rest of us returned to Antrana.

We hoped for a brisk ride; however, what we found were ice-covered roads that made for treacherous travel. We attempted to move along the un-paved route but the ground was too damp and soggy.

Our return travel took three days.

My oil-coated winter weather coat became as damp as the ground by the time we arrived in the palace. The coat acquired a foul odor of sweat from the inside colliding with wet from the out. Or, perhaps, more realistically, I acquired a foul odor. Oh, to reach the bath in my quarters. I was almost there.

Finally, we rode into the palace stables.

"You always enjoyed this time of year," my sister said, looking up at me.

I dismounted my horse and saluted. Then I turned to Visada, "Excellent work, again. Dismiss the harfala. We will hold here for several days. Meet me tomorrow morning at nine and we will discuss further orders."

She snapped a salute and went to break up the column.

Alexi handed the reins of my horse over to a stable frey.

"Where is Cinzia?" my sister asked.

"She met an old friend in the city – she will be here shortly."

My sister nodded. She framed the palace with her hands, palms open. "Come, frey. You may join us in your owner's room."

"Yes, Torino," Alexi bowed.

Alexi held the door open when we reached my quarters. I followed my sister inside. Alexi softly shut the door and then removed my coat. He took a whiff of it and stepped out to give it to a palace laundry frey.

My sister wore a long winter black palace-style skirt, calf-high multi-buckled boots, and starched white cloth blouse. She had a habit of touching her cut ear while talking.

"Does that hurt?" I asked.

Alexi returned and waited near the door, standing uncomfortably. Perhaps he did not want to intrude on our conversation. Several previous meetings with my sister were attended by one or more of her owned frey; this was an exception. Perhaps Alexi was unsure if he should attempt to serve my sister in a special manner.

She chuckled. "No, it does not hurt. Tell me, how was your first official command?"

"We completed all mission objectives." I pulled off my gloves and sat next to her. I nodded to Alexi and he came to his knees beside us.

"How was your first command?" she inquired again.

"It was fine. No problems. Cinzia will have nothing bad to report."

"You believe I asked her to monitor you?"

"It is possible."

My sister laughed. "There is a part truth in that. But mostly it was her request to attend. She favors you. A field mentor of her rank is a luxury that not all of us have."

"I mean no disrespect," I explained.

"You have always been the analytical member of the family," she said. "I am perhaps too emotional. You must believe me when I say that your safety is a concern of mine. But also you must believe that I know you to be a capable warrior. I have that much respect for you."

"Thank you," Sklera.

"Vercella, you are my favorite sister," she told me, looking into my eyes.

"That is kind of you to say. I am your *only* sister," I said.

"Yes. That makes it an easy decision," she grinned.

Then, uncharacteristically, she put her hands on her knees and held still. "I want you to push hard on the invasion."

"What do you mean?"

"The Korina Jurinas are in command of the invasion. But once there, you must assume a leadership role. This is your opportunity to demonstrate your ability to lead our women and frey."

"Do the Korina's know this?" I asked.

"Yes."

"Is there a set point when we will make a transition?"

"You will know when the time is appropriate. I require the absolute trust of a sister of the House Kretahla to ensure that all Treaslok warriors are executed and their frey brought here in chains"

"That is nothing you should worry about," I told her. "I lost many of my warriors."

The Torino nodded.

Then Sklera turned her gaze toward my frey. "I hear that you are quite the sex frey."

Alexi's neck turned slightly red.

Sklera laughed. "Do you recall the celebration many months ago, frey?"

"Yes, Torino."

"I enjoyed using a cane on your ass. When my sister is not so selfish of you, I will avail myself of your sex."

Wholly without merit, she taunted me in front of my frey.

"You may have him now," I offered, sweetly refusing to engage in the game she and I frequently enjoyed.

She looked at him for a moment and licked her lips. "No. There are state duties to attend this evening. The public has begun to notice increased troop movements and is asking questions. You may interpret that to mean: I must cast the first volley of disinformation."

"Look at me, Alexi," she ordered.

He looked up with those beautiful obsidian eyes.

She sighed and then stood, "I will have him soon."

Alexi rushed to open the door ahead of her brisk walk.

My sister turned and I provided a salute. She nodded before exiting.

"Sex with your sister?" Alexi said, closing the door.

"You already know she is my sister," I replied.

"I mean, uh, your sister is going to... use me?"

"Yes."

He twisted his face in the manner I understood to indicate he was confused.

"I sense your concern, but do not know what. Tell me."

Alexi's face appeared in great agony, "I know that I am not on Earth now. But we do not have sex with the sisters of someone we are seeing and – " he trailed off in his voice. "Okay, maybe it is not correct to say that I am 'seeing' you, and I know a man that has had sex with a sister, well, two sisters, and their mother too, but. But this – "

He paused and then shook his head. "It is unusual. For me."

I laughed for several seconds.

"What is it, Mistress?" he asked.

I looked down at those wide eyes. He had such a look of confusion that I felt both pity and power. "My sister did not *only* cane you at the celebration."

He continued to look helpless.

"It was not just Hula and I that you gave oral service to, prior to the first course of the celebration meal."

"Oh." He cocked his head slightly and nodded.

"Draw me a hot bath and set my bed. After you have had your bath you will pleasure me. Bring the leather hood without the eye holes, and the leather cuffs. You are going to sleep on my bed tonight and I do not want to hear metal cuffs making noise all night long."

My frey smiled. "Yes, Mistress!"

"Go," I told him.

It was unnecessary because he was already on his feet and sprinting to the bathroom.

I heard the water running. He closed the door to contain the steam of the bath.

Thanks to excellent Erskan plumbing, which was well-known to us before Earth inventions, the bath was prepared in only a few minutes.

Alexi, naked and vulnerable, opened the door. "Mistress, your bath is ready for you." He dropped to his knees and pressed his forehead to the stone floor, palms outstretched.

I hopped to my feet and walked over to the bathroom.

Alexi kissed both of my boots before he undressed me.

He held my hand as I eased into the hot bath.

Without a command, Alexi pulled my hair back and rubbed the soap into a lather. After rinsing and squeezing my hair dry, he washed my neck, back, and arms. All the while I kept my eyes closed and breathed in the hot scented vapors from the bathtub.

My breathing was slow and rhythmic as he continued the ritual.

I felt Alexi apply soap to my right leg. I did not flinch in any manner as he brought the edge of the blade to my skin and shaved.

After a few minutes he washed my legs and announced that his service was complete.

I opened my right eye.

Alexi was on his knees at the foot of the bed. He smiled.

"Are you happy, frey?"

"Yes, Mistress."

Alexi no longer asked irritating questions about his status of ownership.

"Who is your owner?" I asked him.

"Jurina Tural is my owner," he replied.

"Hold still," I told him.

"Yes, Mistress?" he asked, hesitantly.

I splashed water into his face.

He barely moved his face, but his mouth was slightly open in an expression of surprise.

A small cluster of bubbles clung to the left side of his ear. I laughed.

He laughed and bent his head down for a moment.

"Dry me and then clean yourself," I ordered. "Then...?"

"... Bring Mistress the leather hood and leather cuffs."

I stepped out of the tub and into the large towel he held for me. Then I walked into my bedroom.

I was clean and refreshed.

And now I wanted my frey.

Now.

A growl rumbled through my body when I reached my bed.

"Hurry, frey!" I shouted to him.

\* \* \* \*

"Down," I pointed.

Alexi, naked in the typical fashion in my quarters, was on his knees, facing away from me. He had his hands palm-up, resting on the top of his thighs.

I placed the leather cuffs around his wrists. They were snug. The padlocks made soft clicks and they secured my property.

I pulled the leather hood down onto his head. His breath quickened.

His cock swelled.

It was already big. I wanted to grab him and force it into me, taking it deep, and thrust –

I had to catch my own breath.

Hood. I laced the hood shut, tight, and then locked it about his head.

The ankle cuffs were locked.

Then I lifted him to his feet, and pushed him forward onto my bed, controlling his fall.

He was on his belly.

I watched the muscles ripple on his shoulders. I almost drooled. My mouth was wet.

I reached between my legs and rubbed, gyrating my hips.

"Oh," I purred.

Alexi moaned, wanting to roll over. I placed my knee in the small of his back as I continued to rock, masturbating myself.

I took my wet hand and brought it to his face, pushing two fingers into the hole in the hood. His lips greedily licked and he moaned in pleasure.

Several lengths of chain were on the bed. I grabbed a set and pulled all of his cuffs together behind his back, so that he was *kelld*-tied.

I pressed my breasts against his shoulders. My nipples tingled as they brushed his shoulders.

Involuntarily, I split my legs between his and rubbed down on the top of his right thigh. I slid my wet crotch along his leg.

This was driving him wild. He struggled.

I reached to the bed table and pulled a knife over to me.

"Roll over, frey," I told him.

Alexi struggled, with my assistance, to roll onto his back. His knees were up, but his ankles still restrained under his buttocks.

His erection was full, pointing out. Pre-ejaculate oozed from him.

I licked at the head and sucked in his taste.

He moaned loudly, thrusting his hips.

I pushed him down.

Then I crawled up and rubbed my clit against the head of his penis.

We both moaned.

I could not wait any longer. With my left hand I grabbed onto him and took it inside.

My weight pushed down onto him until his hot shaft filled me. I pressed until I felt his testicles.

"Oh, you are big," I whispered.

My hair fell over my shoulders and tantalized my hard nipples.

I shuddered.

Then I leaned forward a bit, trying to take more of him into me.

I lay the tip of the knife against his chest, above his right nipple.

He gasped as I dragged the dull edge of the knife blade over his nipple and then pressed the tip into his areola.

I pulled up a bit and then pressed down onto his hard shaft again.

The tip of the knife moved to his right nipple and I gently stabbed into him as I lifted my pelvis before pressing again.

Alexi's chest was heaving. He was unable to thrust his hips. I could see his shoulders straining to get free.

I took the tip of the blade and traced the first letter of "Frey" onto his right breast.

He squirmed and tried to shrink away from the blade while equally attempting to impale me with his hot shaft.

I pumped onto him several times as I finished the first letter.

Rivulets of blood formed the "fe" as I cut the "ra" letter.

My hips rocked onto him and my inner thighs became wetter with the passing of every wonderful, mind-searing thrust.

I could feel his cock head straining inside, the shape probing deep.

I lost my concentration and stopped only half-way carving the "yea" into his chest.

"Mistress, please, may I come?" he begged.

"No, frey. I am not finished."

I stopped rogging him and held tight.

He almost screamed in frustration.

I must finish the last letter.

Though I tried to stop completely, I was still rocking slightly on him.

"There," I said. "Do you know what I wrote?"

"'Slave?'" he pleaded.

"No. Not in English," I chided. I lightly slapped his face.

"'Frey.'"

"Yes."

I could not wait anymore.

I raised my hips and then slammed down onto him.

My frey pressed up, groaning.

"I want all of you, now!" I demanded.

"Yes, Mistress!"

I rogged him as hard as ever.

He shuddered.

"No," I said.

"Please! Please, Mistress! Please!" he begged.

I would have my nika first.

It was --

"Oh," I half-shouted.

My legs twitched, knees trembling, as my heart pounded wildly in my ears. I looked at his chest, covered lightly in blood, and pressed my palms against him.

I came again as I rubbed my hands and pushed down hard onto his chest.

"Now," I ordered.

His hips thrust a couple of times more and then he exploded.

I clenched my legs around him as his hot male juice filled me.

I came again, able only to support myself by pressing harder against his chest.

"Thank you, Mistress!" he shouted, rocking again.

I could feel his juices running down the inside of my thigh, mixing with my own.

"Thank you, Mistress," he whispered, his breathing heavy.

He thrust again.

Then he relaxed.

We remained locked into our embrace for another few minutes.

Reluctantly I pulled off.

I took a damp cloth and wiped away most of the blood.

Reluctantly, again, I unlocked the chains behind him. Then I locked everything together in front of his body. The hood remained.

I pulled the sheets of the bed around us both and settled into a wonderful, relaxing sleep.

\* \* \* \* \*

"There has been a sighting of a Treaslok ship," Visada said when I opened the door. "At Renest. Jurina Sonda requires you and the frey to the War Room."

"Free him while I hurry to get dressed," I said, allowing her inside. I rubbed my eyes, trying to wake.

Alexi was on the bed, his arms and ankles locked with leather restraints. The heavy leather hood encircled his head, only a small hole for the mouth visible.

I stepped into the bathroom to pull my hair together. I squinted in the mirror before rinsing my mouth with *seron* water to clean my teeth and freshen my breath. Then I grabbed my skirt from the wardrobe and buckled it around my waist.

I was tightening the buckles on my leather top when Alexi came in with my boots. I heard the door shut to the room as Visada left us, presumably to awaken others.

"Be quick," I ordered.

He expertly buckled my boots and then reached out to straighten my uniform.

"Are we going outside?" he asked.

"No. Wear the in-palace skirt."

I tapped my hip while he dressed. It was amazing how long it took a frey to dress. He only had shoes, a skirt, and a simple blouse to wear!

"Do not concern yourself with your hair," I told him. "Let us go now."

We ran through several corridors until reaching the War Room. Several half-awake warriors and jurinas followed Alexi and me inside.

"We will wait until Cinzia has arrived," Sonda announced.

Cinzia came in a moment later, her hair uncharacteristically untied and falling around her shoulders. She held leather hair binding straps in her hand which she tossed onto a side desk in a huff.

Sonda laid a map before the dozen-odd warriors and three frey in the room. She pointed to the Renest coastline. "Thirty minutes ago, at five-ten hours, the Renest 3rd Harfala Radio Patrol saw the outline of a ship on the morning sunrise. There was only light snow falling and the seas were calm. To be sure, they followed the ship as it moved north for approximately eight minutes. They observed it turn away and disappear."

"Who was in radio contact with the 3rd Patrol?" I asked.

"I was, Jurina Tural," acknowledged a kuretno. "They reported in for eight minutes, continuously. They were accurate in their observations."

"She dispatched a palace messenger immediately. I was able to hear the last minute of the observation," Sonda advised. "I have no doubt that it was a Treaslok ship."

"The defenses are in place at Belenda," Cinzia said. "May I suggest that we reposition a harfala from there to Renest?"

"Yes, that is what I was considering," Sonda nodded. She recognized that Jurina Yannta, responsible for home defense, had arrived to listen to the last part of our conversation.

Yannta turned to a junior officer. "Aide, dispatch an order for the 12th Harfala to deploy to Renest within the hour. I also want the 9th and 12th Mounted riding from here to Belenda to supplement the post." She looked at the clock, "What is the latest weather report on the road conditions?"

Another young aide shuffled through a traditional cloth scroll. Then she grumbled and pulled out a single sheet of paper. "Two hours ago it was light rain and snow mix between Antrana and Belenda."

The winter season was longer than in the past.

"It could merely be a reconnaissance patrol," Cinzia suggested.

"I believe it to be that," Yannta replied. "But we will prepare for the worst situation."

The aides were transmitting instructions via radio and messengers. Within a few minutes there would be nearly two-hundred warriors waking and mobilizing to Belenda.

"What is next?" Alexi asked.

"I will notify the Torino," Yannta said, walking to the door, two aides behind her. "And then we wait and learn if this is a reconnaissance, a prelude to an attack, or a decoy to draw our forces to Renest."

\* \* \* \* \*

We suffered through a nervous day and evening.

Though there had been no further enemy sightings, Cinzia and I were summoned to meet with Jurina Sonda.

."I have ordered that the completion of the first caravel become *the* number one priority," Sonda said to us. "You and your team are ordered to supervise the construction and assure its early completion and transport to the sea."

"And then?" I asked, knowing the answer.

Sonda placed her fingertips on her head, above the ears. "You and Hula will be transported to perform a reconnaissance mission. We need to know the location of the Treaslok seaport, the distance and duration of travel, their weaponry and defenses."

"Just Hula and I? Two of us?"

"We will not have a large team moving about their population. It could attract too much attention if there were several unusual people in the area."

I nodded. "We will head to Belenda at first light. What is the estimation to complete the caravel?"

"The caravel will be ready for sea trials in six days. If the crew can keep it afloat for five days beyond that, you will depart for your mission." Sonda stood, "Anything you need for the mission is at your command."

"Will my frey accompany me?"

"No. The Torino is concerned that your frey will prick his finger on a jezallo berry and become infected and then die, unable to help us with the invasion. Do you believe you can convince her to put him on unproven boat, with an inexperienced crew, and cross two-hundred miles of water? Perhaps you have been drinking too much nerlu for your evening meal." She smiled at me.

"But those conditions are suitable for us?" Cinzia pointed out, wryly.

"The frey is more valuable here than on the mission," Sonda said. "Take him to Belenda, have him supervise the final construction and perform the sea trials. Under no circumstances is he to be permitted beyond swimming distance of shore."

"Understood," I acknowledged. Cinzia and I saluted.

"Shia-talso," Sonda bid us.

\* \* \* \* \*

Two specially-trained warriors set the position of the Crest-Leeland machine gun and cycled the chamber with the deadly Earth bullets.

Alexi and I looked from the edge of the water across several hundred yards to the other machine gun on the beach. One of the women waved to us, signaling that she was ready.

"Here it comes," Cinzia observed, looking toward the shore.

There were patches of blue sky. The weather remained cold, but the wind had slowed and there had been no snow or rain for two days.

I made sure my winter uniform was straight while we waited. I ran my fingertips over the round siglet of my rank on my coat collar.

Two harfala flanked each side of the paved brick path. The moving and launch crews were comprised of many of the same women that moved the Tamagra into the palace several months previously.

"It is very big," I observed. The caravel ship slowly moved along the path, the twenty steel axles and metal-reinforced wood wheels rotating under the strain.

"I hope it floats," Cinzia said aloud.

The dozen women around me nodded in agreement.

"It will," Alexi said authoritatively. "Both of the small scale models were stable."

Jurina Iona, commander of the naval fleet – which now officially numbered as one ship – joined our group on the beach. Her boots were wet because she had been walking along the water with several aides to inspect the ramp that descended into the sea.

"Magnificent, yes?" she asked.

Several of the ship's crew looked down over the side at the swarm of people moving about them. Lines from many locations were tethered to the ship. The ground crew handled the lines as the ship inched toward the water.

"Where is the ..." I struggled for the word.

"Yes, Mistress?" Alexi asked.

I swept my hands upward, "The wood poles that hold the sails?"

"*Masts*," my frey replied. "They will be put into place before it is launched. They were too high to get under the city gates."

Of course, after he said that, the first of several wagons appeared, supporting the masts at either end.

"I hope it floats," Hula said to no one in particular.

"It will," Jurina Iona replied. She looked at Alexi.

Alexi nodded.

Then he added, "Yes."

Additional wagons appeared at the end of the road, carrying pre-assembled parts of the pier to be assembled once we knew the ship would be seaworthy.

The contingency plan was to pull everything to Belenda.

Fifty horses strained to slow the advance of the ship as the elevation of the brick path slightly steepened to the water. Engineers applied brakes to the wheels to slow the speed.

After a few minutes the ship was on the beach.

"We dug down six feet to place fifteen layers of paving bricks," one of the engineers said to us as she made another inspection. "Still, you should step back when it is here in the event the sand shifts and the ship rolls off the path."

I laughed as our group, which had grown to eight warriors, fifteen sailors, and four frey, moved twenty feet farther away.

The stacked bricks held, with only a small amount of sand being disturbed around the path. Minutes later the first part of the ship, the *bow*, touched the water. Kendra called a halt and the engineers changed positions. The launching crew lengthened their ropes as most of the horses were disconnected from the support structure.

Ground crew tied lines to wood posts that had been previously sunk into the beach. The lines were carefully measured to allow the support structure to roll only a specific distance into the water where – it was planned – the ship would lift and float on its own.

The final assembly crew took to the task of mounting both mast poles.

"Wow," Alexi said. "The Erskans are great builders." He grinned, visibly impressed. "You just need the idea – and then watch it happen."

We had used Alexi's lesson *book,* a scroll made of paper sheets, on sailing to construct as close a duplicate as we could to the caravel; we did not, however, know the weight specifications. This was a guess. Our caravel weighed one-hundred thousand pounds and was eighty-feet in length.

"Hula, you are about to have your answer," Iona said, watching the last of the preparations.

There was a flurry of activity on the ridge above us. Several Elite palace guards appeared, flanking a rider. It was my sister, arriving in a flourish. She was here to see the launch.

I had been so focused on the ship that I failed to recognize the thousand civilians that gathered to watch the spectacle.

"She had to make an entrance," Hula said softly, leaning close to my ear.

I nodded. The Torino *is* the Torino. Especially if there is a crowd of people.

The launch crew stopped, awaiting Iona's order.

Kendra stood to the side and looked in our direction. Her face had a "now?" expression to it.

"Well, she's not going to come down here, you know," Cinzia said to Iona.

The Torino dismounted.

She walked toward us.

"Oy, oy, oy," Cinzia laughed at herself.

We stood still as Iona saluted upon the Torino's approach.

"Will it float?" my sister asked.

"That is a popular question, Torino," Iona replied. She smiled, gesturing to the ship, "We await your command."

"Frey," my sister turned to a palace frey. He handed her an unopened bottle of nerlu.

It hardly seemed the place for us to drink. There was only one bottle. What was she doing?

"There is a tradition among the Earth people at the launch of a ship," she said, her voice carrying over the hundred-odd nearby people. "We will toast to the ship and give her a name. The chosen name comes from a great and successful invasion of Earth history."

We would apply a *name* to a boat? I thought we would call it the "Number One."

She walked to the front of the ship, the bow. She held firm to the bottle which was wrapped in the double blue, red, and white bold stripes of the Erskan flag.

"On behalf of the Erskan people, we name you *Normanda*. Shia-talso!" she said, crashing the bottom half of the bottle on the wood bow. Nerlu splashed out with the shards of glass.

Kendra took the cue. She touched her fingertips in front of her and then pulled her hands apart. She pointed at the launch crew with both hands.

All of us stepped back. Sklera, close by the ship, quickly distanced herself from it.

The lines were let out and the ship creaked.

The supporting structure rolled into the water. Launch crews fed the lines on either side, stabilizing the ship if needed.

The Normanda reached the water and rose off the structure, creaking even more loudly.

In twenty seconds the ship was floating about fifty feet from the beach, silent.

Lines on the left side were pulled closer and the ship slowly turned around until the bow was near the sand.

The Torino clapped her hands together nine times.

The beach roared with the sound of the crew, warriors, and civilians clapping nine times.

"It floats!" Iona said. I had never seen such a great smile from her.

"Iona, you may retain your rank, old friend," my sister leaned close, flashing her teeth.

The Torino looked at the Normanda as it rocked in the waves. Then she turned to me and pointed to the ship with her right hand. "Try not to crash, Jurina Tural. You appear to have a great number of spectators watching you."

The number of people looking down from the top of the beach had grown to over two-thousand women, children, and frey.

The crew on the Normanda carefully lowered a skiff to the water. It was pulled to the shore by lines.

I pointed to the skiff. "Here is our ride now."

\* \* \* \* \*

"No! Turn the rudder more to starboard," Alexi shouted. Then he added, "Mistress!"

A part of the mast and sail swiftly moved over my head, lines tangling, forcing me to crouch down.

"Let it go!" Alexi said to one of the sailors that had put her hands on the lines. "You'll get your hands caught in there and it will cut them off."

Water splashed from the left side... *port*, it was, and showered my oil-layered coat. My head and body was drenched and I sputtered water from my lips.

"Are you enjoying this?" Hula shouted to me. Wide-eyed, my frequent and long-time lover clutched the side railing. Her hair was soaked, covering part of her eyes. She was not presenting her most attractive face at the moment.

Neither was I. "No, I am not!"

"We need to put more iron in the keel," Alexi told Kendra. "I think it is too light!"

Kendra tried, unsuccessfully, to write a note on her paper. She folded it and stuffed the sheet into her coat. "Are we in danger?" She shook her head, trying to cast off sea water.

"We will be fine. I know it looks bad, but we are doing fine. The crew has to learn this from experience. Our models for training were not enough."

Another splash of salt water pummeled my body.

Netra! I spit water from my lips.

I shivered. Cold water ran inside my coat and down my spine.

Two sailors scurried across the bow, pulling lines. Then one of them came alongside us and did something with a pulley. The tangled mess of lines unraveled.

We rocked hard to the starboard side of the boat.

I tightened my grasp to the railing.

Then the ship held still.

We were moving!

"There! That is good! Keep doing it like that!" Alexi shouted to the captain.

I looked forward.

We were moving forward!

"Is this what it is supposed to do?" Hula asked, still holding tight.

Alexi looked up as the sails filled with air.

"Gunner, get those weapons unwrapped and see if they fit," Alexi said. "Captain Stela, turn about a quarter to port. Just about ... there! Do you notice how it feels tight, but not pushing too hard against the wheel?"

The captain nodded with the slightest smile on her tightly-drawn lips.

"How do we stop?" Hula asked.

"We are making about ten miles per hour," Alexi beamed. "Not bad for our first afternoon!"

"How do we stop?" Hula repeated.

At first I thought she was joking. However...

The Crest-Leeland machine guns were set into mounts on both sides of the ship.

The captain looked away from the wheel for a moment. "Keep the guns tied down until we are at the pier," she ordered.

We... sailed ... for a few minutes. It was brisk. Going faster was good – except that the breeze wanted to freeze my skin.

"By the numbers," Alexi said. "We are going to turn starboard. Remember which way the wind is blowing. We need enough speed to make a full turn. Or we will need to get out the oars again and row through it. I think we have done enough of that today, right?"

The captain nodded.

Alexi moved closer to the wheel and put his hands over the captain's. He said something to her. First she looked at the flat-mounted compass. Then she made a quick scan of the crew and nodded. "Now," Alexi told her.

"Prepare to come about, starboard turn!" she ordered.

Three of the senior sailors replied: "Coming about, starboard, aye!"

Alexi pointed to a sailor on the mast.

"Are you ready?" the captain asked, following Alexi's lead.

The sailor paused a moment before replying, "Aye!" She looked quite frightened. Alexi nodded.

The captain announced the turn: "Starboard turn in three, two, one, come about!"

The sail was dropped.

Two sailors grabbed the sail and held it while moving the boom.

Lines were released by other sailors.

The captain turned the wheel.

Hula made a noise as the ship jerked.

Then we turned.

"Make it! Make it!" Alexi cheered-on the ship.

The ship continued to turn.

"Perfect!" Alexi said.

"Raise sails!" the captain said. The sailors scrambled.

In another moment we were moving south along the coast.

"Did you just scream?" I asked Hula.

"No!" she replied, releasing her grasp.

I let go and walked over to the captain and Alexi.

"Have the marines prepare to practice combat boarding when we return to the pier," I told them.

Alexi blinked. "Mistress, that will not go well."

"Of course, it will not."

\* \* \* \* \*

The oil lamps brightened the maps strewn over the large tables.

"The shortest distance between two points is a straight line," Alexi said, pointing at the Belenda coastline. "We should go directly east."

Kendra chuckled. "That is an Erskan phrase."

Alexi nodded. "If we have good winds, we can make twenty miles per hour. Our distance is somewhere between two-hundred and two-hundred fifty miles. That means it will take us fifteen hours to arrive. When we find land we'll need to back off, and cruise along the coast first, mapping it."

Captain Stela swept the room of thirty warriors and sailors. "Frey, you mention yourself on the reconnaissance?"

I clenched my teeth. "I have not yet advised him," I admitted.

My frey looked directly at me. "I thought... "

Iona intercepted the conversation, "You are too important here. The Normanda is but one ship; we must build several others and develop the expertise needed for fighting on the seas."

"Oh." Alexi shrugged, "That is the reasonable decision, of course. You are correct."

"How much time until you have made the modifications?" Iona addressed Kendra.

"We counted sixteen changes this evening," she said, looking at a paper sheet. "Five more remain." She pointed out the items on her list to Uimisla.

"The rigging is the most difficult," Uimisla reported. "Either way, it will be ready in the next two or three hours."

It was oh-two hundred in the morning now.

We had worked for ten days. This involved several hours of sea trials, identifying what did not work, docking at the pier, teams effecting changes, and then taking the Normanda out. Concurrent engineers made careful notes and transferred the knowledge to the construction of the other two caravels.

An uneasy silence fell amongst us.

"Very well," I said. "Captain Stela, we set sail at daybreak."

\* \* \* \* \*

"Mistress," Alexi looked up from the floor. "I understand that it is not tradition for a frey to give orders to his mistress. However, I order you to be careful and to return."

It was the third time in the last twenty minutes that he had lost his attention.

With a heavy sigh, I coiled my whip and fastened it behind me, low on my right belt.

I entered the evening with plans to torture and rog my frey during the last hours.

It was not all his fault; I also found my mind wandering. Twice I had missed his shoulders and hit his neck.

"Clean up the blood and then lie on the bed," I told him as I released the locks from the spreader bar.

He kissed my bare feet and then went to the toilet room.

I heard the water running in the sink as I walked to the double-paned glass window, drew the curtains aside, and looked out.

The view was not notable. Five feet distant was a three-story high brick wall. Brown, barren and dormant vines were nailed to the brick. The cloudless sky allowed Netra's orphans to cast a faint blue-white light between the buildings.

The glass was cold to the touch. I ran my fingers against the smooth surface.

Someone on horseback rode past. The hoofs clapped and echoed among the deserted streets.

I heard something else.

"Mistress? Are you well?"

Alexi had called my name several times.

"Yes, my frey, I am well."

He was on the bed, kneeling. "I am sorry," he said. "I did not mean to upset you."

"No, frey, it is not you. My mind is focused on the mission. There are rare occasions when torture is not favorable."

*Did Kendra adjust the base of the compass? It had become unstable yesterday and – yes, it was on the list.*

I glanced at my bag on the table. It contained several previously-confiscated personal items from Alexi. They would prove useful on our reconnaissance mission.

I crawled into the bed and covered us both, placing my around his sides.

"Have you talked to Mermak about Jurina Cinzia?" I asked him.

"Yes, Mistress."

"Good. You know that she is stricter than I."

"Yes, Mistress. Just promise that you will return."

"Yes, frey, I will return."

# Chapter Seven
# The Execution of Cotsa

Small groups slipped out of the city on wagons before daybreak. While it was impossible to hide the fact that we constructed the first Erskan ship in history, we did not need everyone to know when we set sail.

The launch would be made with no fanfare. No celebration. No parade.

We rode in a troop wagon, enclosed, carrying half of the Normanda's crew of fourteen, and five marines. Alexi and Hula sat next to one another, opposite my seat.

Aside for the occasional word, we rode in silence. We were stopped by guards at the newly-built gate leading to the pier. Then we moved on to the beach.

Two frey met us when we exited.

"Alexi, take my bag and that of Hula's," I told him.

He reached up to take two of the bags as another frey handed them down from the top of the wagon.

Just a hint of daylight was showing over the sea. A steady breeze blew east, toward Treaslok lands.

"It is a good day for sailing," Alexi said, in an effort to be optimistic.

Several oil lamps provided dim lighting on the pier. They were shrouded on the seaside to minimize detection from Treaslok patrol ships.

We walked under another recent construction, a sixty-foot high sentry tower. One of the heavy machine guns, operated thirty hours a day, kept an eye out for intruders.

My sword rattled as I adjusted it up higher upon my back.

"Nervous?" Hula asked of me.

"All of us are nervous," I replied.

"Remember, lights can be seen for miles on the water," Alexi cautioned. "Use the special seeing-eye glasses at all times. You can see farther than the Treaslok can."

"Yes, you have said that before," I replied.

"A half-dozen times before," Hula told him. "That is enough."

We walked onto the pier. Having been designed to rise and lower with the tides, it rocked from the waves.

Sleek and mysterious in the dim light, the Normanda rocked in concert with the pier.

I stopped at the ramp leading to the ship.

Jurina Iona and Cinzia were onboard, talking to Captain Stela.

"Permission to come aboard, Captain?" I asked.

"It is your ship, Jurina Tural. Of course."

She saluted me. "Under our rules of navy, it is your ship, Captain, and we look forward to a safe and rapid journey."

"Welcome aboard. Your frey may store your items. It will be twenty minutes before the last of the crew arrives and we cast off."

Alexi moved to the aft compartment that would double as quarters for Stela, Hula, and I. He went inside to store our bags under the rope-hammocks and tie them to lines.

Iona pointed to me. "Take care of her, Hula."

"That is a task for a giracha, oy, oy oy," Hula replied.

"Try to remember how to speak Treaslok, and we will be fine," I grinned.

"Our word for 'please' is similar to the Treaslok word for 'green nipple,'" Hula laughed.

Cinzia shook her head.

However, all on board knew that Hula and I had performed many missions together. We could operate in theatre without requiring comment or even signal between us.

Iona snapped a salute to Captain Stela. "Shia-talso, Captain."

"Thank you, Jurina," Stela returned.

Cinzia nodded to us as she spun on her heels and followed Iona off the Normanda and to the pier.

Alexi returned and followed Stela, Hula, and I to the wheel of the pilot deck. We looked over the railing and watched the crew work under the increasing daylight.

I placed my hands on the machine-carved wood railing. It was coated in heavy clear lacquer.

"It is strong," Alexi commented.

I nodded and looked at the black, churning water ahead to the east.

Hula wrapped her hands on the railing and gave it a tug.

Unconvinced, she pulled it again.

Another wagon arrived and unloaded the last of the crew and our supplies. Several frey carried wood crates of food and water into the hold.

I checked the strap holding the radio to my belt. It was snug.

"It may be a custom, or not, I do not know," Alexi said, taking out a small bag and loosening the drawstring. "But it is now." He reached into the bag and withdrew three smooth-edged, small black stones. "I collected these from the River KoVer and offer them as a gift to assist with your journey."

I took one of the cold stones from his hands. Hula and Stela took the other two.

"What is done with these?" Hula asked.

Alexi reached into the bag and withdrew another stone. He pressed it against his forehead for a moment before grinning. "Mistress, you will know when and what to do."

I put the stone into my own purse and drew it closed.

One of the naval officers on the main deck turned toward us. "Captain, we are ready."

Alexi made a slow movement to his knees and then kissed my right boot. In a deliberate, slow motion he then kissed my left boot.

I reached down by his face, inside his coat and grabbed his collar. His cheek was wet with tears.

"I wish I could go with you," he mumbled, trying to stifle a sob.

"I will return when the mission is completed," I said.

Cinzia looked at us from the pier. Mermak arrived and took his position behind her. "Alexi, get off the ship," she told him, aggressively jerking her hand to point at the pier. "This is women's work. And you are delaying the mission."

With slumped shoulders, and avoiding showing his face to us, Alexi walked down the ramp to the pier. He proceeded past Mermak, wiping his face, and on to the wagon. He pulled himself up and inside.

"I shall take care of your property," Cinzia reassured me, smiling. I knew her demeanor to him was purely compassionate.

I laughed. "I am not worried. Please have Mermak teach Alexi to cook while I am gone. He is unable to prepare anything that is not blackened to a crisp."

Iona finished a conversation with two warriors and walked to the end of the ramp to address Captain Stela. "Are you ready?"

Stela nodded.

"Report in half-hour increments at first. We will adjust the timing as appropriate."

"Shia-talso," she told us all again. She and Cinzia stepped farther away and watched the shore team move about the pier.

"Nervous?" Stela asked me.

I looked at Hula. "Do I look nervous? You are the second person to ask that."

She pointed to my right hand. My fingers were rapidly tapping my hip.

"No. It is a nervous *habit*. When I do not have a sword in my hand. It is not because I *am* nervous."

Stela nodded in an exaggerated manner. She looked unconvinced. "First Officer, prepare to cast off," Stela ordered.

The naval officer on the deck surveyed the crew's positions and repeated, "Prepare to cast off!"

The ramp was withdrawn. The shore crew prepared to release the mooring lines.

I turned over my shoulder to look for the wagons. Alexi had exited and was standing tall again. He saw me and waved. I allowed him a simple nod before returning to my work. He had been at my side for more than nine months. It was understandable why this mission was hard on him. We would be gone for a month.

"Cast off in three, two, one. Cast off!" Captain Stela ordered.

The lines were pulled into the ship as both sails unfurled. With a flurry of sound and several snaps, each white sail soared up the mast.

The sails quickly filled with wind and Captain Stela turned the Normanda from the pier and toward the sea as the orange sun broke the horizon before us.

Hula shielded her eyes.

"Could not have timed that any better," I said, squinting as well, laughing at the irony.

"I doubt that we will run into anything for awhile," Stela said, trying to look slightly to the left. "Oh, yes, I remember."

Captain Stela reached into her purse and withdrew a hard non-metal case. She placed Alexi's darkened seeing eye glasses on her face and smiled. She stood tall at the ship's wheel and propped one calf-high boot against the base of the wheel. Her open full-length leather coat blew about her legs and exposed a white cloth blouse and black leather pants.

I hummed for a moment as I admired the view. I licked my lips.

My hair blew around my head as wind swept over the deck.

The Normanda increased speed and cut through the waves.

It was a perfect beginning to our mission.

* * * * *

It was horrible.

Everyone on board looked like she was dying.

I held the rail, my stomach turning over again. "Netra!" I gasped.

Gulping, Hula's nostrils flared as she spoke in a race to get the words out, "Should we turn back?" Her eyes were desperate.

Her face was green. She clenched her teeth and then she vomited onto the deck.

Captain Stela, whom had more time on the sea than any of us, clutched her abdomen, but managed to maintain position at the ship's wheel.

"Tural to Cinzia," I said, finally surrendering to the possibility of failure in our mission. I choked on bile as the radio rattled in my free hand.

It was a long delay.

"Cinzia to Tural, proceed," came the perfectly clear reply.

"I need to talk to Alexi. There is something wrong – with all of us."

There was another delay.

Then Cinzia's radio broadcast her laughing. "Your frey says to use the gifts from this morning."

Gift? What gift?

My eyes watered and mucous oozed from my nose.

The ship continued the agonizing rise and fall on the big waves. One of the sailors dropped to the main deck and vomited.

"The stones?" Hula gagged. Waves splashed over the deck and washed the contents of her stomach between my boots.

"Understood," I coughed. I placed the radio into its holder on my belt.

Stones.

I fumbled in my purse for the polished black stone.

"Is this how it is done?" Hula asked. She crouched with her hands and knees on the deck. Then she leaned her face close to the deck and held the stone to her brow.

"That is what he demonstrated," I said. I struggled to stand. Like a drunken warrior, I steadied myself with one hand on the rail and the other holding the stone to my head.

"Now what?" Hula asked after a moment.

"Keep trying," I suggested.

Stela looked port and saw us. It must have appeared comical. Except that the entire crew was barely functioning. She reached into her own purse and withdrew the stone.

I nodded when she pointed to her forehead, a quizzical expression on her face.

"Feel anything?" Hula asked.

*Maybe if I pressed the stone harder?*

*Maybe sliding the stone from side to side?*

*Too much pressure?*

*Too little?*

After a half-minute I laughed, and then stood straight.

"Is it working?" Hula asked.

"You will need to tell me," I said.

I removed the stone from my brow. I was not perfect, but I was better. At least I could stand on my feet.

"Tural to Cinzia," I said to the radio. "Thank my frey for the distraction of the gift."

"Here," I handed my stone down to Hula. "You might need two of these."

* * * * *

We gathered in our quarters, the Captain, Hula, First Officer, Marine Kuretno Leesa, and Uimisla, the engineer that was now our cartographer and navigator.

Uimisla laid the map on the small table. "If this speed holds, we could be at Treaslok shores as early as this evening."

There was a knock at the door as one of the sailors opened it simultaneously. "Captain, we have a sighting of a ship."

The sailor handed Alexi's glasses to me.

"Port, twenty degrees aft," she said.

I waited for the device to adjust.

It would be impossible for them to see us at this distance.

"Yes, it is a ship." I looked at it for a moment. It was a three-mast ship, square sails. "It appears to be headed slightly away, to port. It is one-half mile away."

"Here, Captain," I handed the glasses to her.

"I do not believe we are ready to engage," I said.

"That ship is much larger than ours," Stela said aloud. "It is your command, Tural, but my recommendation is that we turn away from it."

I agreed. "Let us turn to starboard. We cannot risk giving away the information that we now have ships."

"A suggestion first," Hula said before the Captain stepped away. "Our mission is to find the seaport, yes?"

She was correct.

We should follow the enemy ship.

"Captain?" I said.

"Prepare to turn port, eight degrees," Stela ordered.

"Make sure we move away if another ship appears," I suggested. "We have the ability to see much farther than the Treaslok. We will use that as a tactical advantage and drop back until we can barely see their ship."

\* \* \* \* \*

We followed the Treaslok ship throughout the rest of the day. We were not having any difficulty keeping pace with the ship, and had to drop one sail in order to maintain a safe distance prior to twilight.

"Contact to starboard, five degrees off the bow!" our lookout shouted from the forward mast. Her observation was repeated to the pilot deck.

"It is another ship. Crossing our path, to port, one mile distant."

"We should drop sails," I said to the Captain.

"No. Alexi's sailing book points out that a ship cannot maneuver if it has dropped its sails. We should turn away and increase our speed. We will tack southwest." She barked the orders and we made a right turn.

"Is it headed toward us?" Stela asked the lookout.

"No, Captain. It continues due north."

"Can we circle around and then continue northeast?" I asked.

"Yes."

Hula came on deck, wiping sleep from her eyes. "What have I missed?"

"Another ship. It did not see us."

"Which way is it moving?"

"North."

"Perhaps we are close to their coastline?"

"Perhaps."

"Contact! Another ship, port, fifteen degrees off the bow!"

"That is good enough for me," I said. "We cannot be observed. Head west into open water for a while. We need to wait until it is fully dark before moving closer."

\* \* \* \* \*

Even the crew had become bored. They made about thirty turns over the next three hours. The marines, Hula, and I, were accustomed to lulls between combat. We napped throughout the evening, sharpened our swords, exercised, engaged in mock sword fights, napped, ate, and exercised.

We turned toward the presumed coastline, tracking as many as three ships at once. We threaded our way between them, always maneuvering on an east, north-east course, following the closest ship until another threatened to come within range.

Captain Stela and I saw lights on the coastline at about midnight.

"It stretches for miles," I observed through the glasses. "There is a powerful light that flashes like a mirror in sunlight," I told the senior members of the ship. "It appears to be elevated."

I scanned the horizon. "I count at least fifteen ships moving about. Some are large. There are many smaller ships moving about also. All have lights upon them." I handed the glasses to the Captain.

"This is their seaport," I declared. "There are less lights south on the coastline. In seven hours, take us several miles south of the last light. We will take the skiff to shore. We will call you by radio once we are on the land."

"Understood," Stela replied.

"Stay ready," I told a sailor that maintained position at one of the two machine guns.

Hula approached and leaned on the railing. "So that is it, yes?"

"Yes."

There was a long silence as she looked to the coastline.

"My Treaslok speaking is not very good," she admitted.

"Yes," I agreed.

"Really, how good is yours? Do you have an accent?"

"When I consider that we have learned all that we know is based on a primary school teaching book, we will all sound like children."

Hula balled her fists and put them in front of me, as if to fight, "Deadly children, oy, oy, oy."

"It is time for the Treaslok to have a nightmare," I told her. "Do you remember Cotsa?"

Hula dropped her hands and frowned for a moment before nodding. "Yes, but not well."

My jaw tightened, "Cotsa was of the House Vulia. I trained her to fight. As we grew older our ways parted due to responsibilities. But we remained friends and met when we could over a glass of nerlu. She resigned her prime position in the Eighth Torino's Harfala to become a civilian. Cotsa moved to Renest."

"The Treaslok killed everyone, including civilians, at Renest," Hula recalled in hushed voice.

"Yes."

Hula and I watched the Normanda rock. Our feet had become accustomed to the motion of the sea.

"I understand," Hula told me. "No quarter."

No person would become an obstacle to our mission.

I stole another hard-eyed look at the coast. Then I lightly clapped Hula's shoulder. "I will take another nap before we kill them."

# Chapter Eight
# Reconnaissance

I signaled Hula. She moved beside me, and then a few feet ahead.

From a distance we had observed two Treaslok walking on a gravel road that ran parallel to the beach. They appeared unarmed and were casually moving north. One of them carried a lamp with a pale flame inside, barely illuminating their legs and the dirt and rock path.

We skirted the side of the path, running on the grass, to avoid the sound of crushing rock under our boots.

Hula pulled her bow and set an arrow.

To her right, I sat my arrow. She nodded.

We were thirty-six feet behind the two of them. Hula intentionally stomped on the gravel with her left boot.

The Treaslok stopped walking, which aided us in targeting.

Two arrows whistled through the darkness of the morning.

One person went down without a sound. The other made an unintelligible cry before falling, gurgling in her blood.

We ran up and cut their throats.

Two females. Civilians.

"You almost hit her clothes," I whispered.

"You got more blood on yours," Hula whispered. "It would be easier to explain this little hole than all of that blood."

We dragged the bodies to the water's side of the road and down into the high grass.

Hula went up to the road and scattered the rocks, covering our tracks and evidence of the assault.

It was the first assault, ever, of the Erskans on Treaslok land. I smiled at the significance of that.

Hula stripped the dead of their clothes.

"Tural to Torino Kretahla," I called to the radio.

"Proceed," replied my sister.

"We have taken first blood," I said. "Two civilians. We will continue on. Next radio contact in two hours."

"Understood."

She would, undoubtedly, utter a cheer amidst the Council.

I turned off the radio.

After a few minutes we wore the Treaslok clothing. Simple long flowing, light tan skirts made of thick leather. A heavy cloth long-sleeved shirt was pulled over our heads. Mine had a small blood stain on the right shoulder, so I slung my bow and sword higher on my right.

Disguised as we were, there was no sense in taking risks. We continued north on the gravel road, ready to avoid any contact.

A few minutes later we reached a small structure. It appeared to be a one-story residence. There was a solitary light inside. It had two outside doors, and steeply-slanted roof. There was an unusual, metal-shaped device in the front of the house. It had two wheels on it with metal spikes.

"What is that?" Hula whispered.

"I do not know. Try to draw a picture of it when we are on the Normanda. Maybe Alexi will know." It was not worthy of using the seeing eye glasses.

We bypassed the house and continued moving forward.

Another house. Then two. We approached the outskirts of a village. And then we encountered our first passerby.

We walked on the stone sidewalk as an adult female walked the other direction, opposite the road. She carried a small basket and was dressed similarly to us. Except she did not have two weapons.

She paid us no attention as we passed.

Hula relaxed her hand on the arrow. She had been prepared to turn about and kill the civilian if we had not been able to pass by without incident.

We turned away from what had become a main road and took the quieter side-streets. We planned to stay on the least-traveled roads lined with residential structures.

A few people looked at us as they walked outside to investigate the morning's sky. No one gave us a second glance.

The morning sun cast shadows among the rows of houses and few businesses. It looked like an Erskan village, but slightly different. It was less colorful. The Treaslok buildings were gray and dull.

The roofs were flat, unlike the steep tops of Erskan buildings.

Few outside decorations were present. Erskan homes were oftentimes buried behind colorful spring and summer flowers and green winter vines.

The houses were plain and unremarkable. Grey or dark brown drapes were the style for window coverings.

"There," Hula whispered.

Ahead, one-hundred feet, at an intersection stood two uniformed women. They were either legal officers or warriors.

They were having a conversation with a civilian woman.

We took the next right turn between houses and then turned left again, approaching the position of the three women at an angle.

"A street killing may be observed," Hula told me.

"We lure them into our opportunity," I said.

We moved to the right again, putting two roads and buildings between us and the targets.

Hula looked over into the window of the building which we pressed against. "No one is there."

We required the Treaslok uniforms.

I peeked around the corner. The three remained talking.

Hula withdrew a small mirror from her purse.

The sunlight was not perfect, but might suffice. I nodded my agreement.

She angled the mirror for a second around the corner and then retrieved it.

It would take thirty or forty seconds for them to get here – if they saw the flash of light and investigated.

I surveyed the two buildings near us. One was a closed candle shop. The other, next to us, was a two-story residence. Across on the corner was a one-story residence.

All buildings appeared to be clear of activity.

"Behind the shop," I suggested. I ran across the road and around the corner. Behind the shop was an empty field. To my surprise, small bits of debris and trash littered the ground. This would be a superior tactical location.

Silently we eased our swords from across our back and into a ready position.

"They come," Hula said, listening at the corner.

I heard two voices. One of them made a short laugh.

Careless.

I tapped on the side of the shop with the hilt of my sword, a single noise to draw their attention to our location.

Hula steadied her hand, sword unwavering and perfectly vertical.

The voices came closer.

"Wha--?" one of the women said as my sword plunged into her neck. She went down, an expression of shock on her face. Her blood spewed from an artery into the air as she collapsed. Her hands reached to the blade in desperation. Fingers were cut and dropped to the ground before her body slumped over. I pulled my sword out of her body and turned to Hula.

The other woman retreated, her hands outstretched. Hula's sword swung down and severed both arms at the elbows.

As the woman went down, trying to scream, Hula cross-cut and decapitated her. Her head rolled against the wall and came to a stop a few feet away.

I grabbed the body of my victim and pulled it to the rear of the shop, leaving a blood trail on the stones. Then I scooped the warm fingers and thumb into my hands and scattered them across the field.

Hula grabbed her body – and head – and dragged them beside me. Then she returned to the corner and peeked.

"Nothing," she grinned. She wiped her sword on the Erskan uniform skirt she wore.

The Treaslok uniforms were made of thin, medium-gray leather. We fumbled with the locations of the foreign buttons and managed to remove the uniforms. In minutes we undressed from the civilian clothes and put on the military leather. We found cloth-based documents, Treaslok money, and keys.

"Can you read this?" Hula asked. She displayed the documents to me.

I attempted to read the foreign letters. "No. I do not know most of their letters."

We dragged the corpses farther into the grass.

"Short hair," I observed. The Treaslok hair style was closely cut.

"Lean over here," I told her. I drew my knife.

Hula looked at the heads of the dead enemy and sighed. "It will take a year for my hair to grow," she said. I took a fistful of her soft hair and sawed.

A few minutes later I pulled the radio and provided an update to Iona while Hula cut my hair in the equally short and unattractive fashion.

"We need to make this look like the work of someone other than skilled fighters," I told her, nodding toward the bodies.

Hula shrugged. She handed my knife to me and took another knife from a dead warrior. She stabbed the headless body five times in the chest, then rolled it over and stabbed a few more times. Then she put it in the other corpse's hand and stabbed itself in the abdomen.

It was a confusing sight, especially with them naked.

"They will not be able to understand what happened here," Hula surveyed the scene. She stood to her feet and looked at me. She grabbed a few coins and spread them about the ground.

"Now," I said, buckling my sword on my hip, as the Treaslok did, "we can go into the city."

Hula buckled her sword and then wore her bow over the other shoulder.

At first I was concerned that the civilians would find something unusual about our appearance and look more closely at us. Contrary to that, they avoided our eyes as we walked deeper into the city.

Most of the shops we passed appeared closed or about to close. I looked in several shop windows and saw that shelves were less than half-stocked. There were hundreds of people moving about their daily business, but we observed only a few horses.

The lack of flowers complimented a rather staid, unusual odor about the city. The increasing warmth of the morning magnified the unpleasant smell.

"Keep ready," I said to Hula. Two similarly-dressed warriors crossed the street in front of us, one block ahead, and turned our direction.

"Go right," I told her.

We casually turned into the closest business. It was a food shop. I held the door and Hula walked inside.

Closest to us were rows of glass jars, all empty, with labels. Farther distant, six aisles, breast-high, contained sparsely-stocked shelves with dried meats and breads.

I shut the door behind us and faced a woman thirty feet distant behind a counter. She made a greeting in a heavily accented variation of Treaslok that approximated "Hello."

We nodded and I pulled Hula's attention to a rear aisle, pointing at nothing in particular.

We stopped and investigated a metal can with painted letters.

I squared my shoulders to the left and kept an eye on the door.

The shopkeeper moved toward us.

With a light jingle of bells the door opened. I saw a string threaded through the ceiling and to the sales counter where a couple of silver bells dangled.

I heard the snap on Hula's waist-adorned scabbard click open.

Both Treaslok warriors entered and headed left, directly to an opposite aisle holding various bread items.

"What is fresh today?" one asked. I could barely make out the language and her question.

I nodded at the warrior and turned my attention to our can of unknown contents.

Hula watched behind her via a reflection on an empty glass jar.

The shopkeeper replied with a dour face, "Nothing is fresh. This is the best." She handed a long piece of bread to the first Treaslok.

The warrior smelled the bread and squeezed the top. Satisfied, she walked to the counter and sat it down. Then she headed directly over to us.

"Is the gonu there?" she asked us.

Hula shrugged, stepping from the aisle a couple of feet. I knew Hula's movement was not out of courtesy but rather was in preparation to provide more space to draw and attack.

Neither Treaslok carried a bow.

We did.

Would they observe the obvious difference among us?

My sword was clearly a different style than what they carried.

The sword-armed Treaslok walked directly to me. Her scabbard swiveled with her hips.

"Here," I said, in my best Treaslok, handing the can toward her with my left hand. My right hand remained still and hovered near my sword.

She grinned. "No, I do not need vechit. I could never fall asleep with that." She reached to a nearby can and took it to the counter. "Ten duk shift," she added with a wink.

I tossed my can to Hula. She expertly snared it from the air and set it on its place on the shelf. She moved toward the bread aisle while I found something else equally intriguing with completely unknown contents.

The warriors paid for their purchase, nodded in my direction, and exited the store.

We waited another moment before I headed to the door.

"Wait," the shopkeeper called as I touched the latch. "Who are you?"

I paused and whirled on my heels to face her.

She was older than I, perhaps mid forties, five-foot six, heavier, wrinkled skin about her eyes. She took a deep breath. "You should leave your bows here."

Hula took my position at the door as I moved closer to the woman.

"Why?"

"Our warriors do not carry weapons such as those."

"We are from a far post," I said, fumbling for the words.

"Please, listen to me. Do not strike. I do not want to die." She placed both of her hands on the counter for us to see. She gathered her courage, "You are not Treaslok."

I moved closer to her, but kept a slight distance.

"Erskan."

Instead of looking frightened, as I expected, she appeared relieved. "Are you here to help us?"

My face betrayed the surprise I felt.

"Come away from the door, here," she said. She turned away and opened a narrow rear door.

We followed her to a small bedroom that was sparsely decorated. Several flowers were in pots about her home. Paintings were framed on the walls showing a beach dotted with colorful tents.

"We have fought small battles with the Erskans for two hundred years, you know," she said. "But we never wanted to have a war. Since the great sky fire we have made our lands better for each generation."

She pulled a painting from the wall. It was of a Treaslok warrior, young, of an indeterminate rank.

"My child," she said, holding the frame to her breast.

"I am sorry for your loss," I lied.

She looked surprised. "No. She was not killed in the Erskan battle. She was killed two years ago defending our nation from the Suir det Ineer."

"Suir det Ineer?" I asked.

"The new leaders. At first they won friends and their numbers grew by people that joined willingly. Then they threatened us – we were forced to join them. My child refused to join their new order. One night they dragged her from her room and executed her in the road as if she was a hilaj."

She looked into my eyes, "They use fear to control us. We do not want war with the Erskans. We have nothing. Our people are poor."

"What is she saying?" Hula asked in Erskan. "I understand only part of this."

"Two years ago a new regime took control. Her daughter refused to change her allegiance from the established government and they executed her. The shopkeeper believes we are here to help their people."

"I thought we were here to kill their people."

"Yes," I told her. "Perhaps the situation here is not as we believed. The people here may be unwilling participants in the war against us."

"Two years ago would be consistent with Corrigan's arrival, yes?"

"Alexi suspects that Corrigan had been to our world on earlier occasions."

Alexi would say, in English, "Once a trenama, always a trenama." Only he used a word for "trenama" that I did not understand. "Skumfukr?"

I looked at the shopkeeper. "How many Treaslok feel the way that you do?"

"Almost all Treaslok. Most of the military serves only because their family has been threatened with prison and death."

"Is there an organized resistance?"

"No," she said, warily. She was a poor liar.

"I believe you mean to say 'yes.'"

"There are a few," she acknowledged.

"We will take our leave of you now. But we shall return in eight hours to retrieve our bows. Find a leader of your resistance and have her meet us here."

"Yes, that is good." She reached into a desk drawer and withdrew a cloth scroll. "Take this."

I untied the ribbon and unrolled a map of the Treaslok city.

She pointed to a location on the southern edge, "We are here."

"Thank you for the valuable gift," I said, noting the location of the seaport. I rolled the scroll and tied the ribbon around it.

"My best," she told us. She opened a drawer and withdrew two cloth-wrapped sticks of dried meat and handed each to us. "I am Pimol."

"Tural and Hula," I said.

"Out this way," Pimol led us to a side door. She pointed at a red-flowered plant. "I will place this plant on the porch if it is safe to come in."

I handed her my bow, as did Hula.

We nodded and went outside.

Within minutes we moved at a brisk and deliberate pace toward the seaport.

"With that map we could return home now and the mission would be a complete success," Hula said.

We planned to be here for at least a month. Hula was correct; we could dramatically shorten the mission now.

"I did not want to do this where Pimol could see us," I said. "We need to make the seeing eye glasses paintings of the map."

We changed direction and moved along the back alleys of the houses and shops until we came to a corner filled knee-deep with rubbish. It was common to observe the Treaslok grounds with litter and debris scattered about, unlike the clean surroundings in an Erskan city. Here they were in a penurious state.

Hula unrolled the scroll and held it flat on the ground while I wore the seeing eye glasses and focused. I tapped the button on the right side and made the painting. Then I turned on the radio and pressed the button that would send the painting to Alexi.

"Done." I put the seeing eye glasses into the hard case. "We will take paintings of the seaport, return here early to watch the shop, meet the resistance, and then rendezvous with the Normanda. Tomorrow we can bring a couple of the Marines to shore and investigate the areas south of the landing point."

Before moving I used the radio to provide Cinzia with an update.

Then we continued walking.

We mixed well with the population, mostly because additional people jammed the streets as the day went on.

It was still not as dense as it would be in any of the larger Erskan cities. And it was dour. And smelly.

Scents from outdoor food shops mixed with the odor of exposed sewage pipes.

The neglected Treaslok infrastructure was crumbling.

We moved toward the coast and followed a wide street lined with homes above shops.

"I see few frey," Hula noted.

"One per two-hundred?" I estimated.

"If that," she replied. "There are few young girls and no young frey."

"Did you notice their defenses on the shore?" I asked.

"No," she replied, scanning the beach as we walked. "I see none."

"Yes. That is correct. There are no defenses."

The beaches were almost deserted. A handful of women sat on the sand under a multi-colored round tent. It was the first time I had seen a bold yellow color all day.

The women were a sad island of their own amongst the drab existence around us.

Hula looked at another pair of armed warriors passing slightly opposite to us, prepared to act if needed.

However we again passed without incident.

Within a half-hour we reached the south edge of the seaport.

I rest my booted foot on an iron railing and leaned slightly forward, peering at the seaport below us.

It was a curved area with the sea cut-in like a bowl into the land, much wider on our right. Eight rows of floating piers were connected via two walkways. The edges of the bowl were higher by about forty feet; we were on the south west edge of the bowl looking down.

"Let us move over behind that building. I need to use the seeing eye glasses."

Hula followed me to the back side of a building. The position afforded a good overhead view downward. She moved closer to me as I put on the glasses and made the paintings.

"We are not nearly as advanced as they. Admiral Iona would be jealous."

"I count nine large ships, probably for battle, and then those over there, the long flat ships, there are... thirteen of them," Hula counted, careful not to point with her finger.

"And fifty or more of those small boats. They are too small for war. What could they be?"

"Do you see the wood structure on the shore, south of the pier?" she asked.

It was a single wood pole at a forty-five degree angle, anchored deep into the ground. The other end of the pole was tied to a large hanging strap. Two warriors stood beside it.

"It must be a weapon," I said, focusing on the machine. I removed the seeing eye glasses and placed them in their case.

"We have been here too long, we should move," Hula stepped away.

I followed her to the street and we moved farther north, closer to the pier.

There was a single warrior guarding the walkway. We elected to turn away and follow the shore.

"Their palace is much farther east," Hula said.

"We will not go there." We had acquired a great deal of information. It was time to meet the resistance leader. "We will return to the shop and watch for several hours."

* * * * *

I put my flask of water into its thick leather pocket. We had been walking since daybreak, well over five hours and we were beginning to tire.

We completed our third safety maneuver, each time returning over our own path to ensure there was no woman following us. We came within five streets of the food shop. "I will go to the right," I told Hula.

"I will go left. We will meet at the bodies?"

"No. It is not cold enough to keep them from having a bad odor. We shall walk two blocks beyond and turn in, then one block more and shall meet. Make a rectangle around the shop."

"Understood," Hula nodded. She walked east.

I turned and walked west on the street, staying close to the shops and homes. There were fewer people here, only three or four in my immediate area. The scene appeared as dull as before. We had two hours until our scheduled meeting time and would use it to monitor the house for indication of trouble.

The afternoon sun brought the day to a mild temperature. It was surely not this warm at home, despite winter's impending retreat.

Half of the businesses appeared closed, as before.

But every store door was closed, every window shut.

This was despite the warmth of the day.

On a day like this, at least the windows should be open.

I kept walking and did not turn left to the shop, but continued strolling south an additional three blocks until coming to a stop at an intersection.

On the right were eight rider less horses, secured to three trees.

They were Treaslok military horses. A male sat cross-legged between them. He looked at the ground.

Take a deep breath.

East, toward the food shop, was an empty street.

I stepped into the shadow of an awning and concealed the small radio in my hand, bringing it to my mouth.

"Tural to Cinzia, urgent."

"Yes?" came a reply after an agonizing ten seconds.

"Hula and I have separated on our approach to meet the shopkeeper. I have found several military horses. It appears to be a trap."

There was a pause.

"You cannot be captured," she said. "Try to find her, but return to the Normanda."

I was two streets over to the west and two streets south. Hula would have gone east, then south, and look west so that she could observe the shop. The warriors must be inside the shop or south of it.

I would need to be farther south of them and then turn to approach north.

It was difficult to not run, but I continued my casual-looking stroll south by two more streets. Then I turned east and moved two blocks.

My body shuddered as I looked north on the street.

At least twelve warriors stood near the wall of a three-story building, immediately south of the shop.

Hula was on the ground, shouting and half-screaming.

They kicked her.

I instinctively reached for an arrow.

But my bow and arrows were in the shop.

I stepped forward. Then I pulled back and peeked around the corner again.

Could I cover the one-hundred foot distance undetected? If so, I could take down four of them within two seconds.

I was not as accurate with the StacGun as my arrows. But I would try. I reached to my inside thigh holster.

Three Treaslok lifted Hula to her feet. From here I could tell her face was bloodied. She was limp.

Two Treaslok pushed Hula against the wall.

One slapped her face three times until Hula moved.

Then a Treaslok lifted a wood pole that looked somewhat like an Earth handgun. It had a piece of metal running perpendicular on the barrel area. She put it against Hula's left shoulder.

I did not know this weapon.

The weapon jerked and a loud crack echoed on the street.

Hula screamed in agony.

The guards stepped away and laughed at her.

Something metal was impaled on her shoulder. It held her to the wall.

Twelve warriors. I could take down half of them and –

Then Pimol, the shopkeeper, was dragged into the street by two additional warriors.

They tossed her face-down and hard onto the gravel.

She got to her feet and made a staggering attempt to run away.

She moved almost ten feet until one of the Treaslok lifted the gun and fired.

Something hit the woman in the lower thigh.

She tumbled to the ground. She made a terrible scream.

I ran, full speed, west, and turned north. I ran north two blocks.

I could hear the echoes of the Treaslok laughing and the shopkeeper sobbing. She was pleading with them.

This should be the place.

I looked at the residence to my right.

With one kick, I broke the simple wood door and stormed inside, ready to engage anyone there.

It was a vacant building.

I ran up the stairs to the second floor.

There was a single door that was unlocked. I went in and found a few crates of clothes. Otherwise the room was empty.

I could hear Pimol crying below, begging for her life.

Light streamed in through the east pane glass window. I looked at the window frame; it was nailed shut on four sides.

I grabbed one of the wood crates. It had enough weight and it would easily fit through the window.

*I hope this goes far enough out and does not strike Hula.*

Then I heaved the crate into the glass window and followed with my head and StacGun behind it.

By luck, the crate hit two Treaslok warriors from above and knocked them to the ground, if only for a moment.

The shower of glass had everyone near Hula cover her head, which meant hands were not near the weapons.

Hula was three feet north of my position, twelve feet below.

I managed to fire into the top of the heads of six Treaslok before I took my first breath. They crouched down, which did not make my shooting any less accurate.

Blood and hair splattered the ground as their bodies fell.

That cleared anyone standing next to Hula.

I fired two shots and killed the closest Treaslok nearest the shopkeeper.

The Treaslok attempted to reorient their positions, but they continued to look at ground level.

The small room echoed as I fired three more shorts; three Treaslok down.

One Treaslok that had been hit by the crate rolled toward the building, attempting to move out of my line of fire, to my right.

I missed two shots at her.

Something flew past my ear from the left and below, and I jerked back as a foot-long, metal shaft impacted into the far-side wall of the room. Four feathers were affixed to the end.

I did not know what it was.

The Treaslok that had shot at me stood and reloaded her weapon. She pressed her boots into a stirrup of the weapon and pulled a bow-like string.

I fired, hitting the Treaslok twice in the chest. She twisted to the ground in a spiral haze of blood and flesh.

"Tural!" Hula's weak voice called from below.

I jerked my head inside just as another metal shaft brushed my face. It shattered the wood of the underside window frame.

Splinters fell onto the top of my left hand.

"Netra!" I huffed. I had felt the wind of the metal rod fly by me.

I leaned out and shot the Treaslok that had rolled against the building. She fell into the street, clutching her left shoulder. The StacGun had blown away a five-inch piece of her shoulder. She fell to the street, dead.

The remaining Treaslok warrior ran toward the shop and turned left, out of my line of fire.

I ran downstairs, three steps at a time, and burst outside to the walk.

The other Treaslok was headed my way, her hand weapon pointed in my direction.

I used the side of the building to steady my aim and as cover from her weapon.

We both fired.

My shot hit her chest. Blood and meat exploded behind her.

I was hit in my chest, full-on.

I dropped the StacGun and was thrown off my feet, my eyes tightly shut from the pain that seared my heart and lungs.

The back of my head hit the wood slats of the walkway.

Air!

I forced my mouth open and sucked in fresh air.

I was alive.

The metal shaft lay three feet in front of me.

I was flat on my back. I looked at the underside awning of the building.

"Oh," I groaned.

Above my left breast.

I gingerly touched the impact spot with my right hand.

Then I sat upright. The StacGun was a couple of feet to my right. I snatched it into my hand.

The impact hurt so much that tears welled in my eyes.

I blew snot out of my nose.

No blood.

I lifted the Treaslok cloth blouse from my body. It had a perfect circular cut-out.

Underneath was the dark blue Earth Ranger sleeveless armor shirt that Alexi gave me to wear. He said that it would stop almost anything.

He was correct. Thankfully.

And he was equally correct in saying that it would also hurt.

"Oh," I groaned again.

I steadied my hand against the wall and stood. I took five measured breaths of air.

Then I ran around the corner.

Hula had lost a great deal of blood. The metal shaft was covered with it.

"Go," she said, eyes half-open.

Her face was bruised and swollen. Her lips were split in two places and a tooth was missing. Blood dripped from her broken nose to her breast. A blue Ranger shirt was also partially exposed through the torn blouse. But the Treaslok had shot her through the unprotected shoulder.

"I will not leave you here. They will torture you."

"Then kill me," she said. Hula spit blood out of her mouth. "I cannot make it."

"Erskan," the injured shopkeeper said, rolling onto her side with a groan.

I was not going to leave Hula and walk over to her.

"I did not put the flower on my porch," she gasped. "They found the bodies. I did not betray you. I want you to know that I did not."

She closed her eyes and went limp.

I turned my attention to Tural. "This will be painful."

I grabbed deep into Hula's left shoulder and pulled her from the wall.

She screamed as I removed her from the metal shaft.

It remained embedded deep into the stone wall.

"Can you walk?" I asked.

Her rear shoulder was drenched with blood.

"No."

She was barely on her feet.

I got under her right arm and lifted her.

"Yes, you can."

"Cinzia to Tula," crackled the radio.

I reached to the button, leaving the radio low on my belt. "Not now!"

I needed to get Hula south, just a few buildings away, get inside, stop the bleeding, and then get her to the Normanda.

Two civilians walked around the corner and toward the bloody scene of the fight.

They both held their hands up, and looked nervous, but did not run.

"Erskan," one said, "we are friends of Pimol."

"She is there," I pointed with my free hand behind me.

Three other civilian females appeared.

"Kason, help her," the woman closest to me said to the new arrivals. She was taller than the others and wore a light green fabric pants and a white blouse.

"We had no way to stop the warriors," the tall woman said to us. "But we can help you now."

I had no choice but to accept their assistance. Hula would certainly die if the bleeding was not stopped within a few minutes. I nodded.

"The Treaslok will know that I was here," I said. I supported Hula's weight and moved toward the woman.

"We will hide all of the bodies. They will not know who did this."

Two additional women arrived, carrying a litter. They were assisted by another woman in dragging two of the warriors onto the litter. One woman kicked at the dead warrior twice and made a rough-sounding exclamation.

"Hurry, Kason. They will send others shortly when these do not return." Then the tall woman pointed to me, "Follow! Quick!"

"Where are we?" Hula asked. Her voice was slurred and her head slumped.

"Stay awake," I told her.

We moved south by two streets.

A woman riding a horse arrived and drew a two-axle, side panel, open-top wagon. I could not read the Treaslok writings on the side of the wagon.

She helped me pull Hula onto the empty wagon.

The tall woman and I joined Hula. We pulled a large blanket over us. "Ride!" the tall woman told the driver.

We bounced for about five minutes until we came to a stop under a covered port. I peeked through the blanket and saw that we were at the rear of a two-story building.

Hula's eyes were closed.

Her face was so beaten that I almost could not bear to look upon her.

"Stay awake!" I told her again. I pulled on her uninjured shoulder.

Two civilian women greeted us and together, the four of us carried Hula inside. The rider turned around and left, probably to secure the other Treaslok warrior bodies.

"We will clean the street," the tall woman told me. "It will not be the first time."

We carried Hula into their bottom-floor home. I swept away scrolls from a large dining table. They fell to the floor as we placed Hula on her back.

"No, roll her onto her left, in case her lung is filling with blood. I do not want her lung to fall onto her heart."

I dug into Hula's purse, still attached, and withdrew four pads of fabric treated with the Earth medicine to stop bleeding. We pulled her blouse open and I applied two of the pads. They stuck to the wound. Then I pressed the remaining pads on her shoulder blade.

The bleeding stopped.

"That may not work," Hula gasped. She looked at me. Tears ran down her cheek.

I moved over to her side and crouched near her face.

"You should go," she said.

"No, I am not leaving you."

One of the women in the room shook her head.

"Go." Her eyes fluttered, though they were nearly swollen shut.

I reached to her side and held her hand. It was cool and clammy.

One of the women from the street fight appeared and shut the door behind her. "Weko, there are no bodies on the street. We will move them far away tonight. We found all of the *bullets* and we took all of the bolts." She wiped her face. "Pimol did not survive. How is the Erskan?"

"You used a word, 'bullet,'" I said.

"Yes, Erskan. You have taken a gun from the Suir det Ineer, yes?"

"Yes," I lied.

Now there were nine civilians aware that Erskans had been here. This was not much of a covert reconnaissance mission.

"You are Hula?" Weko asked.

"No, I am Tural. This is Hula," I corrected, squeezing tighter on Hula's hands. "Stay awake. The medicine will work."

The small Earth medical treatment device was on the Normanda. It would cure Hula's wounds in a matter of minutes.

A woman gently placed a damp cloth on Hula's forehead. She returned a moment later with a light blue sheet that she draped over Hula's lower body.

"How did you arrive?" Weko asked.

I chose not to answer.

"This is the first time that all of us have gone into the daylight – we have all put our lives at risk," she told me. "You see what they did to Pimol. We all now risk that fate."

I kept my eyes on Hula.

Her breathing became rapid.

Then my lover closed her eyes.

"Hula!" I said.

Hula's hand went limp in mine and she let out a long breath of air.

I pulled her hand up to my lips, kissed her fingers, and openly wept.

\* \* \* \* \*

"Hula and I will be on the skiff at twenty-six hundred," I said to the radio.

"Understood," Cinzia replied.

"Understood. Will await your signal," Captain Stela confirmed.

I turned off the radio and put it out of sight in my purse.

Then I opened the door from the toilet room and slowly returned to the dining room.

The women sat on chairs or on the cooking counter.

The light blue sheet lay over Hula's body. Blood had soaked into part of the cloth.

I stood in the door frame and rest my hands on either side.

There was an uneasy feeling in the room.

Weko broke the silence, "Erskan, will you kill us now?"

They were afraid of me.

Did I look angry?

Yes.

I closed my eyes and shook my head in the negative.

"No." I kept my eyes closed for a moment.

Then I surveyed their faces, "No. You have risked your lives. I owe you a debt."

"Pimol said you were going to help us," Kason said after a moment, testing the waters.

"I offered nothing to her. That was her wish."

"Will you help us?" Weko asked bluntly.

"My plan was to come here and kill every single woman," I told them.

They looked at one another.

"But that plan has changed. I did not know before that the people of Treaslok are not willing in the attacks on the Erskans."

"They take everything," one woman said. "We have no food."

"The Suir det Ineer have destroyed our lives," another rushed to say. "We do not want war with the Erskans!"

I took a deep breath. Then, "The Erskans will help you. Only, and only under my conditions. This is not for debate. If you do anything other than what I say, the Erskans will follow-through with our plans to execute large portions of the Treaslok population. Does everyone understand? I will not risk the lives of... of my warriors because one of you were too excited and shared this information with your friend. This information does not go to your lover, to your neighbor, to any others in the resistance."

I had just single-handedly changed Erskan war strategy.

The Torino and the Council would probably not be pleased.

I waited for each woman to nod her head.

"I will communicate only with Weko. You will take us tonight in a wagon. I shall return at a later time. Do you have a calendar?" I did not have the Treaslok word. "A map of dates?"

Weko nodded her understanding. They produced a hand-painted calendar of the same sixteen-month year that we had. The names of the months and days were completely different. "Today?" I asked, pointed to a date.

They nodded. I selected a date, eight weeks from today. "I will return on this date, to the same place you take me tonight. At the same time as when you leave me."

"Yes, Erskan," Weko nodded.

"Good," I said. "In return for your silence and assistance, I will honor my agreement to work with you."

Kason pointed her finger. "Who are you? Why is your agreement bound?"

"I am Jurina Vercella Tural, a *Rejella* in your military rank. I am on the Erskan Council of Jurinas and I speak for the Torino, our leader."

\* \* \* \* \*

"Eight weeks, Jurina Tural," Weko said. "I will honor our agreement with my life."

Then she saluted me, in an Erskan style.

I politely nodded.

In the dim light I could read the hope of relief in her face.

"I am deeply sorry about Hula," she told me, as we sat Hula's cloth-wrapped body onto the grass.

"She will be avenged," I said, flatly. I could not allow myself to become emotional. Not of sadness; but of a rising vile and red anger that threatened to cloud my thought.

"We will collect the drawings of the palace and military ships. We will record the timing of the warriors." She closed the panel on the wagon. "I know that you will not tell me when the Erskans will come. But... it will be soon, yes?"

"I can only tell you that I will honor my agreement. We have our plans. Your information will assist in keeping civilian deaths to a minimum. The alternative is that we attack anything and everyone in our path. Instead, we can focus only on military targets. But you know there will be civilian casualties."

"Yes. I understand. Our cost for help will be hundreds of women instead of tens of thousands."

"Hundreds of thousands," I corrected her. "If either of us should miss in eight weeks then we will return five days later. If it is not us, our delegate must use the word '*wow*' to meet. Say it."

"*Wow.*"

I nodded. "Thank you for bringing Hula here."

She nodded and mounted the horse.

"Go. Do not stop riding," I told her.

"I shall not," she said. She pulled the wagon along the road and disappeared into the darkness.

After a few minutes I dragged Hula's shrouded body to the shore and placed her in the skiff.

I rowed out on the calm water for several minutes until I saw the Normanda's silhouette against the partly-cloudy night sky. I flashed an electric light to them and soon two lines were tossed down.

I secured one line to the front of the skiff and then climbed to the deck.

Captain Stela saluted. "I am sorry."

"I ask, please, that your sailors bring up Hula's body and place her on the deck until tomorrow morning."

Stela pointed to three sailors as I walked beyond her and to the cabin that the Captain, Hula... the Captain and I shared.

\* \* \* \* \*

We arrived at Belinda in the middle of the night and tied to the pier.

Cinzia kept our premature arrival secret from everyone but the shore crew.

The Normanda slid in behind the second, just-launched caravel.

Cinzia knew. But twenty hours passed since it happened. I had been unable to truly confide in anyone about my feelings.

Cinzia met me at the ramp. We stepped away from the pier, outside of the lights, and embraced. She held me for several minutes and stroked my hair while tears flowed from my eyes.

Her strong arms enveloped me and shielded the cold air.

"Hula," I whispered.

"I know. I am sorry," Cinzia whispered. She held onto me for a while. Finally, I let go and wiped the tears from my face.

Cinzia gave me strength to do the next difficult thing.

I rode with her to the post.

We were met by Mermak when we arrived at my quarters. Silently, he wiped his face with the back of his hand and then held the door open for me.

I swallowed and stepped into the room.

"Alexi," I said.

Alexi lay on a pile of pillows, on the bed, sleeping. Hula called it his "fortress of pillows."

Cinzia looked over behind me, from the doorway.

I carefully unlocked the loose chain that tethered his collar to the bedpost.

"Frey?"

His eyes popped open.

"Mistress! I thought you were returning in a month!"

"Yes. Yes, frey."

"What is going on?" He sat up and hugged me. He crawled out of the bed to kiss my boots. I gently grabbed onto his collar and held him still.

"No. Not now."

"What has happened?" he asked, frowning.

"Hula is dead," I said flatly.

"What? What happened?"

"I will tell you about it tomorrow. She died in combat. It was a warrior's death."

I willed myself to be strong. Still, my voice threatened to crack and shatter into a flood of sobs.

"But... " his voice trailed. "I... I..." Tears filled his eyes and he buried his face in my blouse.

Cinzia nodded. She closed the door and allowed me to console my frey.

*You will be avenged.*

# Chapter Nine
# Hula's Esatolo Ceremony

Seven-hundred twenty-nine warriors stood motionless on the cold and windy ceremonial field in preparation for the afternoon *esatolo*.

The ranks were comprised by the first nine of the Torino's Harfala, the Home Guard. Impeccable in their dress and demeanor, the women looked forward at the dais where I attempted to present an illusion of calm and order.

To my right and left stood the majority of the Jurina's Council. Several jurinas were out of the city on assignment.

Sklera, on my left and in the center position, spoke in a reserved tone to Sonda. Sklera's hands were fastened to one another in a stark departure from moving about as she talked.

Cinzia was on my immediate right. She glanced at me from time to time, but was otherwise silent and kept her eyes focused ahead.

The crew of the Normanda and several non-military members of Hula's House were at either end of the dais. At the farthest end Alexi and two dozen frey stood.

Alexi had cried throughout the night.

So had I.

Mermak kept an eye on him now.

A woman far on my left attempted to stifle her sobs.

Hearing another person cry was almost too much for me.

I squeezed my eyes closed and counted to five.

Then I forced my attention forward.

Between the dais and the warriors was the funeral pyre. Three massive steel beams supported the weight of various thicknesses of firewood.

A white shroud enveloped Hula's body which was elevated four feet.

I held Hula's rank bracelets in my hands because I would take part of the esatolo ceremony.

The bracelets were cold.

*As cold as Hula's hand felt in that foreign land. On the table.*

*Yesterday.*

"Tural?" Cinzia said. She pressed her left hand lightly against my right bicep.

Sklera was speaking to me.

"Are you ready?" Sklera asked. I realized she repeated the question.

"Yes, Torino."

Sklera held her gaze on me for a moment. Perhaps she wanted to know if I wanted more time?

I held her eyes until I nodded again.

More time out here was not what I wanted.

Torino Sklera Kretahla stood tall and stepped forward from our ranks.

Wind blew through my hair as I fought the tears.

The Torino kept her hands at her sides as she addressed the attendees. "Torino Morata said, two-thousand years ago, that a warrior's life is a reflection of the Erskan people she protects. Morata told us, 'Erskan warriors have faults, problems, and fears. We have all that is dark in our people. We willingly hold this in our hearts because we also carry the hope of prosperity for our people. Each woman has duty to protect the frey, preserve our way of life, and grow our knowledge. The Erskan warrior takes up arms to ensure we all prevail."

The Torino glanced at me: "And so we fight on."

I stepped forward, took a deep breath, and hoped my voice would not falter.

"The words of our first Torino have proven to be correct for the last twenty centuries," I said, my voice as loud as possible without shouting. "We have protected our people. We have brought them hope. And we have delivered prosperity out of the great flood and dark times that followed."

I clenched my teeth for a moment and paused. "And so we fight on."

The Torino made a slight nod.

I turned to face her and then presented Hula's two rank bracelets.

The Torino took one of the bracelets from my hand and lifted it to the gray sky.

"Hula, daughter of House Cala, Sixth Elite Torino's Harfala," the Torino said. "Fight on, forever."

"Fight on, forever," I said once as a crescendo of women's voices boomed across the grounds.

Three ceremonial warriors approached the dais. The Torino walked to the edge and carefully passed the bracelet to the woman in the center.

They marched to the pyre.

The bracelet was placed on the top of the shroud, in the middle of her body.

The three warriors moved to the other side of the shroud.

Korina Jurina Iona stepped forward to the edge.

Three additional ceremonial warriors approached.

Iona handed down two three-foot long red strips of cloth to the warriors on the end of the formation. "Fight on, forever," Iona said.

The ceremonial warriors marched to the pyre.

The two red strips were placed lengthwise on the shroud.

The warriors moved to the right end of Hula's body.

Korina Jurina Sonda stepped forward to the edge and she presented a single blue strip. "Fight on, forever," she said as three more warriors took the offering.

The blue strip was laid on the shroud, completing the white, blue, and red colors of the Erskan flag.

The nine ceremonial warriors formed a elliptical circle around the pyre.

I stepped to the edge.

My right hand took Hula's bracelet and pressed it firmly around my left bicep.

The first ceremonial warrior retrieved an unlit torch from the base of the pyre. She approached my position and presented the tip of the torch.

The three remaining Korina Jurinas approached me, one at a time. Each cupped a small burning candle inside a storm-lantern's case. In unison, they touched the candles to the torch.

"Fight on, forever," they said.

The torch ignited and the ceremonial warrior stepped back.

"May she fight on, forever," I said, my voice nearly gone.

The ceremonial warrior walked in a circle and ignited the other eight torches.

"Fight on, forever," they said.

Then they touched the firewood and set the pyre ablaze.

The Torino saluted.

Everyone in attendance held the salute for a long thirty seconds.

We watched as the fire rapidly blurred the lines of the shroud.

My jaw twitched.

Light gray smoke billowed from the flames, windswept at a steep angle into the sky.

The smell of the dranta wood smoke would forever be etched into my memory.

The fire raged for nearly fifteen minutes.

Blackened, steel beam supports protruded from smoldering red and fluffy white ashes.

Hula was gone.

The Torino stomped her right boot three times.

Everyone followed with six stomps.

"Shia-talso," the Torino said.

Everyone broke rank and moved about. I maintained my position.

"How are you, Jurina Tural?" Sklera asked.

"I will be fine," I replied. It was a weak attempt.

"We must talk. When?"

Jurina Iona and Sonda approached.

"Is this evening satisfactory?" I asked.

"Yes," Sklera nodded. She looked past me at Cinzia, "Eighteen thirty, at the Council chambers."

I nodded. Cinzia made a half-step toward the stairs.

"Cinzia, let us find our frey."

My eyes were drawn to the remains of the pyre.

I touched the bracelet on my left arm.

*You will be avenged.*

\* \* \* \* \*

"What did you offer?" the Torino half-shouted. Her voice echoed off the stone walls of the Council chambers.

The Korina Jurinas already stood in a half-circle beside my sister.

Sklera turned her face away from me for a moment. She pressed a single finger against the ancient Erskan stone remnant.

Her movement of turning away from me was a sure sign that she was extremely unhappy. She had never done that while in the company of others.

She faced me again.

"Why did you strike a bargain with the Treaslok?" she asked. Her voice was flat. But here eyes radiated a white-hot beam of light at me.

Cinzia's feet shuffled uncomfortably behind me.

"Torino, Jurinas," I explained, trying to stay calm as well, "the situation is much different than we thought."

"Continue," the Torino interrupted.

What did she think I was doing?

"Their story is that new leaders arrived two years ago. They call them the Suit de Ineer. That timing correlates with the dates that frey Alexi believes Corrigan first arrived to Aervanta. The new regime has been hard on the women and frey. Their society is crumbling. The Suit de Ineer forced the invasion of our lands. The civilians have formed small resistance groups and they request our help."

Sonda looked at the Torino for approval and said, "We have read your report."

Iona waved a scroll at me. "You overstepped your authority."

"I did what was needed to be done."

"And so you believe that you, alone, can decide the entire Erskan strategy?" Yannta accused. My jaw tightened in response to her acidic tone.

"'War is not brutality, rather it is the slash of the sword tempered by ethics,'" I replied.

"This is not about quoting Hisu's 'Codex of the Warrior,'" Yannta replied. She leaned her body in at me. "We lost thousands of warriors to the Treaslok last year. They killed Hula, one of our most valuable warriors. And you offer a respite simply because a few garden women assisted you?"

"Hula," I snapped at Yannta. Then I abruptly stopped and checked my voice. "Hula and I witnessed the situation. I believe the civilians we met are sincere and honest in their account."

"The question we must decide," the Torino said, "is whether we honor this Jurina's commitment and target only the military, or whether she is suspended and we target the entire female population in the tradition of two-thousand years of combat."

Iona tossed the scroll to the top of a nearby desk and shook her head. "That was a reckless decision. You had a radio. You could have called for counsel."

"You have something to contribute?" Yannta cocked her head and looked past me.

I turned my shoulders to look at Cinzia.

"Yes, Yannta," Cinzia replied, her voice contrite. "Our objectives do not change, only the strategy. Employing the civilian population may work to a tactical advantage."

I would have to thank her for attempting to help soften the beating I was taking.

"That is not the question here," Sonda told us. "You are not listening. Neither of you. You – "she pointed at me – "overstepped your authority. You put the honor and integrity of the Erskan Torinoship at risk."

I felt bile crawling up my throat.

She was correct.

"Yes. I did."

My words hung in the air for several seconds.

"I will make my decision shortly," the Torino stated. She frowned at me. "You are both dismissed."

I saluted and turned on my heels.

Cinzia marched out of the chambers and made for the closest outside door.

Mermak and Alexi knelt twenty feet distant beside a fountain in the courtyard. They moved to stand but Cinzia raised a hand to hold them still.

Cinzia crossed her scarred arms and told me, "Yannta and Iona are not pleased."

I stopped and ran my fingers along the seam of my winter skirt. I had no words to say.

"Do not worry too much," she said. "I have had my fair share of that."

"You? What did you do?" I wondered.

"That is a secret. By my heart, though it was not anywhere as big a mess as what you did," she smiled.

"I hope they have not lost confidence in me," I admitted.

"Do not discard excretions," Cinzia said.

I looked at Alexi. Concern was etched into his face.

"That is 'Don't sweat it,'" I corrected her.

"Same meaning," Cinzia laughed. She uncrossed her arms and pounded my left shoulder with her right fist.

"Yes, it is." I forced a smile to comfort Alexi. "Ah, Alexi says he needs assistance with equipment from the Tamagra for the demonstration tomorrow. Would you like to allow your frey to help him while we watch them work?"

"Of course." Cinzia touched her crotch, "I enjoy watching Mermak work hard. It gets me wet."

\* \* \* \* \*

"Have you seen this before?"

I crossed my legs under the table and looked at Cinzia. "No, he has talked about this, but I have not seen it."

"This better impress everyone, to have made the Council meet in session this early."

I sat in my place, on the outer table, in the Council chambers. My frey made final preparations at the front of the room. He focused on a small table that was not a typical part of the décor in the room.

Also not typical were the three rectangular painting frames, one at the center of the room, and one at either side. The frames displayed only a dull black.

"What does it look like?" Cinzia asked.

"He said we will know when he turns them on. It is like the radio, only not just the sound of a woman's voice."

Cinzia's constant questions were slightly irritating.

Alexi attached a metal string to the painting frame on my side and then he returned to a small Earth device on the table.

My sister, the Torino, sat on her throne, and watched this while engaged in a conversation with Iona.

Alexi stood straight and nodded to Iona.

It was the first time in our history of two-thousand years that a male had been permitted entrance into the Council of Jurinas while the council was in session.

"Your attention!" Iona addressed the Council.

The separate conversations came to an immediate halt.

"You may proceed, frey," the Torino told Alexi.

Alexi stood at attention and addressed us, "Three days ago, Jurina Tural used an Earth device, eye glasses, to gaze upon the Treaslok seaport. Last night we brought these machines here to show each of you the view that Tural had of the Treaslok."

Alexi finished his sentence with emphasis on the last word. It was almost a sneer.

"Please know that what you see will not harm you. It will look like a window, but it is not. It is a painting."

He used his fingers on the Earth device.

All three of the large painting frames became bright. Then I could see the same view I had of the Treaslok seaport three days ago!

I barely noticed the sounds of surprise throughout the Council.

My sister stood to her feet. She walked to the painting frame and touched her finger to it. Nothing happened.

The Treaslok ships were below, docked on the piers. They moved with the ebb of the waves!

Birds flew by overhead, and I realized then that I had looked up at them for merely a second.

Alexi pressed a button and the live painting got stuck.

A bird flying in the air became still.

I waited for it to drop to the ground.

But it did not.

"This is exactly what Jurina Tural saw with her eyes when she was wearing the Earth glasses." Alexi pointed to the bottom left of the painting frame, "She noticed this."

"What is that?" Yannta asked.

"That is a *catapult*," Alexi said. "Actually, there is another word for it, from a dead Earth language, *French*, but I cannot recall what."

Alexi walked to a chalkboard and removed a sheet that concealed a detailed drawing of ink on paper sheets. "The base of the catapult allows it to be rotated to point in the direction of ships approaching the seaport. The two poles on this have a sling in the middle. They use great wheels to retract the poles, loading it like an arrow in a bow. Then they put rocks or other items in the sling. An enemy ship comes up to the seaport and they fire the catapult. It could have a range of two-thousand feet."

Two-thousand feet!

"From the look of the covered area near the catapult, I would say they are throwing one-hundred pound blocks. One hit with those on the side of our own sloop-of-war will sink it."

The painting moved again as I had looked to the right of the seaport.

The bird continued flying and went out of sight!

"I have been able to count Treaslok ships and berths, or empty places in the pier. The Treaslok may have fifteen large warships similar to the sloop-of-war and thirty caravels. There are nearly seventy small ships and boats. I can move closer on the painting and we can see the small ships."

The painting moved as though we were falling into it. My hands tightened onto the table before me.

A jurina on the end knocked a glass of water from her table and apologized.

"These are boats used to hunt for fish. They appear to use nets. I do not see fish. But they do have small things in the nets. This may be like an Earth *shrimp* that can be eaten. There may be shrimp in Erskan coastal waters... we will investigate that later."

The painting moved away from the boats and then focused immediately to a sloop-of-war.

"I have looked at all of the paintings and I can find no gunpowder firearms. There is something here that looks like it was a retrofit, or something added recently. It explains what the... the Treaslok were using to attack Jurina Tural and to kill Hula."

Alexi's jaw tensed and his eyes drilled into the floor for a moment.

"On the front and side of the ship is a *crossbow*. Crossbows come in many different styles. Large ones, such as these, can puncture the wood of our ships. The tips can have knives which cut sails and lines. Small crossbows can be carried by a warrior, much like an Earth firearm. They are loaded, most of the time, with a metal shaft and a steel arrow tip."

He made the painting move to a Treaslok warrior on a pier. A crossbow hung from a strap over her shoulder.

"The crossbow bolt will fly three times farther than an arrow, and will hit up to ten times harder. It is a powerful and dangerous weapon. However, it is slower to load and less accurate than an Erskan bow and arrow. The Treaslok must step onto the front of the crossbow to hold it down while they use a ratchet to pull the bow-part. My apologies, but I do not know the names for all of these parts. Then they drop the bolt into it and it can be fired by pulling a trigger. This is consistent with Jurina Tural's description of the weapon."

"Other than the two catapults facing the sea, I was able to notice something else that Jurina Tural was not able to observe – but she captured it in the painting." Alexi moved the painting until we saw a metal fence and gates that surrounded the seaport. "Every other weapon, guard, tower, and defense on the entire seaport is aimed at the population – not at the sea. The Treaslok are more concerned with their own people rather than an invasion."

He froze the painting of a guard tower armed with crossbows and several warriors. Alexi crossed his arms in front of him and nodded, "All we need is for two advanced teams to capture the catapults and we can take the seaport. I am not a military woman, but I have an idea on how we can do this."

The Torino had been standing all this time, her mouth slightly open. "Go on."

"In the darkness, two teams use skiffs – small boats – to approach the catapults. If they can be rotated we will use them against their own ships; otherwise, we damage them.

"We build four fire ships. These are wide, flat ships that carry timber. These are set alight and we crash them into the ships docked at the entrance to the seaport; this blocks all of the ships inside. I got this idea yesterday." He referred to Hula's esatolo ceremony.

"The Treaslok ships can still fire their own catapults, but it will be nighttime and they will not be able to see us well. High-ground has the advantage, so Erskan marines will land on either side of the seaport and rush up the slight hill. We have good paintings of what is there, so we can plan each movement in advance. I suggest we build a fake seaport on the land west of here and practice in the dark.

"With all of the burning Treaslok ships, there will be chaos inside the seaport. If we can, we should load the catapults with flaming debris and shoot into the middle of the seaport. But since we cannot count on that, I propose that we construct one of our own and mount it to a sloop-of-war. We need to carry our own burning debris and boiling oil.

"Oil? Yes, we can take the lamp oil and boil it, pour it into a large spoon, and then fire it with the catapult into the middle of the seaport. It will spray onto the Treaslok below. It will burn them and they will be unable to fight.

"The flames in the seaport will attract more Treaslok warriors, most likely coming from the direction of their palace, which I believe is due-east of the seaport. The Treaslok will focus on the flames. Once our marines have secured the high-ground, our archers can fire down onto the Treaslok.

"After that," Alexi said, "I do not know. But that's what I think we could do."

My mouth was open as well.

The room was completely and utterly silent.

I looked at the Torino. She had an emotionless face.

One of the two clocks on the wall ticked for ten seconds.

Click. Clock.

Wide-eyed, Cinzia looked at me.

Click. Clock.

Jurina Sonda broke the silence: "That is a good plan."

Alexi nodded. He appeared to recognize the room's silence for the first time.

The Torino faced him. "Is there anything else you wish to share?"

She then added: "Frey?"

"I shall continue looking at the paintings for more information," he said. He sought out my attention, looking for a way out of his uncomfortable position.

It was a good plan. But it was not appropriate for any woman, and most certainly not a frey, to plan an invasion in front of everyone. Proper plans were made by close consultation with the Korina Jurinas in private.

I needed to save him. I pointed to my left side. Alexi walked toward me.

"Stop," the Torino ordered.

Alexi froze. His eyes looked into my own. He tried to appear confident, but I could read the rising panic in his eyes.

The ground at my own feet remained shaky; the decision on my actions had not been announced. It could be that my frey would share in the criticism already leveled at my direction.

The Torino walked to the painting frame again. "We will avoid a large battle on the seas if we can destroy their ships while in the seaport. It is clear that the Treaslok have superior capability to fight on the seas. We cannot afford that risk. It is to our advantage to sink their ships while they rest. This is an excellent strategy you have created."

She looked to Sonda, "Coordinate with Emla to begin construction of a training area that looks like the seaport. Hedida, you must make this secure from spies." Both Emla and Hedida nodded.

"Iona, add four fire ships to your manifest. We also need to construct a ship-borne catapult. Kendra, work with Alexi on how to build it."

"Tural, you will return to Treaslok in eight weeks to make contact with the resistance."

"Yes, Torino," I replied.

Did this mean I was no longer in trouble? No suspension of duties?

"Then you return immediately with the information."

"Yes, Torino."

"We will launch our attack in twelve weeks," my sister told everyone. "Korina Jurinas, Cinzia, Tural, Alexi, remain. All others, you have much work to do. You are dismissed."

We waited at our places while the others left the room and the door was closed.

Alexi and I were conspicuously in the rear of the room while the others were in the front center area. The six Korina Jurinas remained.

"Yannta," the Torino said, "what are your ideas beyond when the second wave of Treaslok arrive? They will observe the arrows in their dead and they should not be so careless on a counterattack."

Sonda pointed at myself and Alexi, and then to the place at the front table. We moved from the back row to the front row.

I chose to stand while Alexi went to his knees.

The Torino waved her hands in my direction. "There are strong voices regarding the attack strategy. The Korina's do not agree with the preservation of Treaslok civilians. My decision is final, however: we shall break with tradition and spare as many civilian lives as possible. Several of the Imaya Jurinas have had their work load tripled as a result of the decision. Instead of making plans for large funeral fires, they now consider how to win favor among the Treaslok civilian women."

I was unsure if saying "Thank you" was appropriate.

I settled for the neutral response: "Understood, my Torino."

Sonda nodded. "Now, the second wave of Treaslok defenders?"

We worked on the revised invasion plans for nearly five hours.

\* \* \* \* \*

"Cinzia says that you eat in your quarters all of the time for the last four days."

I walked down the ramp from the *Texana*, the second of our caravels, to the pier and saluted the Torino.

"Cinzia should pay attention to her own matters," I said.

She looked angry for a moment, and then softened her face. She brushed her cut ear with her hand and then turned her back to me.

Several warriors and shore crew moved about us.

"Follow me," she ordered.

We left the pier and walked on the beach three-hundred feet until she turned.

"Listen to you," she said. "'Cinzia should mind her matters?' That is not the sister that I know."

"I have a mission," I told her.

"This mission will not be successful with one that is blinded by anger. You will not honor her death by dereliction of your duty caused by mistakes in preparation."

It was not worth explaining.

"I have called a dining meeting of senior staff," she said. "Your attendance is required." She abruptly walked away.

I was left alone on the beach.

An insect skittered along by my boots. I kicked at it, but missed, and instead created a small shower of sand that the wind blew at my legs.

Even the wind was against me.

It was early enough that Kendra should be working. I brushed the loose sand off my heavy leather pants before trudging to the end of the beach and the beginning of the short brown winter grass.

Light illuminated from under the door as I yanked on the knob. The door, like everything else, resisted me. It took three pulls until it snapped open.

Kendra and Uimisla were hunched over a table that was illuminated by several magnified-glass oil lamps.

"Your door is broken," I told them.

Kendra looked over her shoulder. "No. It was locked. Now… it is broken."

Both of them abruptly pulled away from the table. Uimisla had an unmistakable look of nervousness about her.

"What are you doing?" I asked. I moved closer to them and looked at the table.

"We…I…" Uimisla mumbled a reply.

There were several unfamiliar metal and Earth plastic parts scattered among four Erskan ceramic bowls. I recognized a handful of Erskan screwdrivers and an additional slender metal shaft.

"What?" I asked.

"Jurina Tural, it is not as bad as it looks," Kendra told me. She stood from her stool and placed her palms out to me.

I did recognize a black rubber antenna. Now I knew what it was.

"What are you doing with this Earth radio?" I demanded.

Uimisla moved slightly behind Kendra. "I was trying to learn how it works."

"How did you even get it open?"

Kendra lifted the slender metal shaft and pointed at the tip. "She made her own tool to match it. It's called a 'fill-ips.'"

This was inexcusable. We had a limited number of the Earth radios. They were a critical part of our defense and attack strategy and they were not to be tampered with. "I do not care what you call that. Reassemble the radio. Now!"

Uimisla began to respond but Kendra cut her short: "Understood, Jurina Tural."

The door opened easily this time – before I slammed it shut behind me.

\* \* \* \* \*

I entered the banquet hall.

More than sixty warriors, a few sailors, and, surprisingly, twenty frey were in the room. Three civilian women played a lija, tolinda, and bik, in a traditional setan melody.

"Did you just wake, Tural?" Imaya Jurina Alsada asked. She pulled her frey behind her, his leash taught.

I looked down and found that my leather skirt was askew.

I straightened it and looked up, but she had moved on.

Warriors talked in small groups. They drank nerlu and other less-refined alcoholic beverages. A frey moved about serving food items.

"Jurina Tural, greetings," a senior ship-building engineer said as she approached me. She held two glasses in her hands. Then she held one out. "I released your frey five hours ago. He is not here?"

"He is with Jurina Cinzia," I replied flatly.

I did not want a drink.

"He had confided his hope to attend the celebration meal in service to you," she said. She retracted the drink and held it near her body.

"He did? Perhaps he talks too much."

She looked at me for a moment.

She had nothing interesting to say.

Thankfully, she left my presence.

Yannta saw me and maneuvered by the social groups until she reached my location.

"Follow me," she ordered.

We threaded the guests that obstructed us until we reached a large rectangular table at the front dais of the banquet hall.

"Sit," she said, indicating a chair. There were nine places at the table, none occupied.

"Are you?" I reached for my chair.

She paused. "Yes, shortly." Then she stepped away.

A scarred hand was placed on my shoulder. Cinzia sat next to me.

"You have a problem with your frey."

"I do?"

"Yes."

"What is his problem?"

"If you spent time with him you would know."

"I have been busy making preparations."

"Your frey is consumed with hatred of the Treaslok. He does not share information as he once did. The Torino is concerned that he has a plan of his own design for when we arrive. A plan that may involve the killing of their civilian population. This is contrary to the new mission objectives. The Torino is considering removing Alexi from the effort and confining him to the palace until the invasion has completed."

"I see," I said, surprised.

"There is the same perception of you. You will be reassigned to the palace and will be removed from the invasion."

I clenched my teeth.

She put her hands on my shoulder and turned me to look at her. "This cannot continue. You have been in this attitude nearly four days. It is hurting your career and your friendship. We understand your grief, but that must be let go. You have been a sothok."

"They *kicked* her to death," I explained, the words rushing out of my mouth.

The scene was burned into my eyes.

"I found your frey, last night, drawing sketches of sinking and burning ships in the War Room. He suffers also."

"He was not there," I told her. "He did not hear Hula scream. He did not see her blood covering the wall and street. He was not holding her hand when she died."

Cinzia took her hand and held my chin. She pointed my face away from the table and into her eyes. "Perhaps not being there was worse for him."

Cinzia was likely correct.

The StacGun had allowed my partial vengeance on the Treaslok. Alexi could only look to the future for his opportunity to extract his.

Just telling Cinzia, anyone, that I had seen them kicking her, released pressure from my thoughts.

I swallowed and choked on my tears.

Cinzia's hand gently slid from my chin and to my shoulder.

My feelings somehow formed into a secret, not to be shared – but only suffered.

Hula and I had been friends since the age of five.

I bit my lip and took in a deep breath.

Yannta appeared. She looked at Cinzia holding my shoulders. "Are you about to fight, or about to kiss?"

"Cinzia has been explaining that I am a moody, sothok, about to be terminated," I said.

"Sounds like fighting words, to me," Yannta said.

I grasped Cinzia's shoulders and we held at arm's length for a moment. "No. They are words of truth."

I squeezed her tightly for a moment. After another deep breath I felt that I could speak honestly again: "Thank you."

Cinzia returned my compassionate squeeze and then we released.

"No fight?" Yannta asked. "I suppose the plogos will not be needed. That means I'll have to arrange other entertainment."

"The match would not have lasted long," I said. "Cinzia is too slow."

She raised a single finger. "Only once. Not again."

Two senior officers came nearby our table. A frey carried their drinks and food on a tray. Yannta waved them to sit at our table.

"Please give my apologies to the Torino and our guests," I said. I stood and nodded at the two new arrivals. "I am going to find my frey."

"Should I hold your seat?" Cinzia asked. She stood beside me.

"No. Alexi and I both need to 'snap out of it,' as the Earth phrase is spoken. And this will require several hours." I hugged Cinzia.

"I know that I could never fill Hula's boots," Cinzia said as we embraced. "But I am here for you."

"Thank you, my friend."

She let go and slapped my ass.

"Now, go beat and rog your frey! You will both be better for it."

Yannta laughed. "Go. I will diplomatically deliver the news to the Torino."

"Yes," I smiled. "First, I need to take care of something."

I excused myself and sought out the senior ship's engineer. She was engaged in conversation with three others and I patiently waited several minutes until presented with an opportunity to approach. It was nearly impossible to hold my hands still and not tap my fingers impatiently.

The conversation among them lulled and I seized the opportunity to intervene.

"I apologize for my poor behavior," I said. "It was not proper of me, whatever the reason."

"I understand. Your apology is accepted," she replied.

The other women provided polite smiles.

"Thank you," I nodded. "Please have an enjoyable evening. I will not attend as I need to punish my frey for *allowing* me to act like a sothok."

They laughed at my joke and I walked to the door. I checked my skirt to be sure it was straight and went to my quarters.

My brisk pace never faltered until I snapped my door open.

Alexi stood on his feet, elbows on the large drawing table, his back to me. He wore an indoor, long-gray leather skirt and thin cotton blouse.

I shut the door and he turned around to look at me.

Then he looked at something on the table before going to his knees.

I walked up to him and he kissed my boots.

"You are dressed nicely, Mistress."

"I was attending the banquet. You were aware of it?"

"Yes, Mistress."

"You were given the authorization to work on your own rather than attend social activities, yes?"

"Yes, Mistress."

"I revoke that authorization now. You will attend all social activities that involve my participation."

"Yes, Mistress." His voice was flat.

"And you will be enthusiastic."

"Yes, Mistress." His voice remained flat.

I grabbed his collar and lifted his chin. His dark eyes looked past me instead of at me.

"Look at me," I ordered. I pulled up on the collar and then pressed higher until he was forced to stand on his toes.

His unfocused eyes looked down at me.

"Look at me, Alexi," I ordered again. I emphasized my point with a jerk on his collar.

He complied.

"I am guilty of the same problem as you. Our behavior has been a dishonor to her memory. We have been consumed with hate for our enemy. I was told tonight that both of us may be reassigned and removed from anything to do with the invasion."

His face frowned. "I had not thought about –"

I cut him off. "Do not interrupt me."

I leaned closer to him, "You and I have not been thinking about anything or anyone else except our own selves. I would prefer to appeal to your personality and professionalism as a trenama-hunter than simply to order or coerce you into proper behavior. Do you want to be sent to the dungeons in Ko-Ver again?"

He tensed his muscles and then relaxed.

I could see his eyes sparkle for a moment. I released his collar.

"Have you removed the snap?" I asked.

He paused for a moment. "It is not easy," he explained. "I will try... to snap out of it."

"It is not easy," I agreed. "We will try together. And if that does not work, then I shall coerce you."

He laughed, in his unusual Earth manner, "Ha, ha, ha. Yes, Mistress."

He got half-way to his feet, but I pushed his head down.

"Am I attending to you at the banquet?" he asked.

"No. We have been excused. I have other plans."

"Yes, Mistress?" he asked.

"Forehead to ground," I told him.

He responded immediately.

My frey was almost in the state of humicubation that I adored.

I walked to the chest of drawers and opened a container. I returned and positioned myself near-silently behind my frey. I paused to make him wonder what I was doing. I was intimidating.

"You talk too much," I finally told him. "Open."

He did not like gags.

But that was no matter.

I pushed the leather-ball into his mouth and pulled the straps around the back of his head. I buckled it tight.

"Yes?" I asked.

He nodded.

No sense in choking my pet to death.

I retrieved metal shackles and locked his wrists closely behind him.

The brand on his right buttock had healed nicely.

I was planning to push him down on the rug and outright rog him; but it was still too close to seeing Hula being kicked on the ground.

Different plan.

I ran my fingertip on my brand. My frey twitched.

It was only one finger. Yet it caused such a ripple in his muscular body.

His breathing escalated.

A simple finger; raw power.

What was I to do? So many options.

I glanced to the side and looked between his legs.

His penis hardened.

My eyes darted about.

A short length of chain dangled from the ceiling in the center of the room.

"Back," I told him. I reached to the wrist chain and slowly pulled his body toward the chain. I positioned him underneath the chain and lightly kicked his inner thighs to make his legs move wider apart.

I reached to the top of my toes and pulled the end of the chain. The other side of the chain spun out of the crank that was mounted to the wall.

The metal hook clicked as it fastened around the center of the manacles.

Then I stepped to the crank and turned the handle.

The metal links clinked as the slack was taken.

The wall crank made loud clicks as the ratchet pin fell.

Click.

Click.

Then I continued until my frey was forced to rise to his feet. His arms were lifted behind his back.

He groaned as the angle of his arms increased and the pain grew in his shoulders.

It looked like the right position for him.

Then I made another quarter turn on the crank.

"Ugh," escaped from his lips.

"What, frey?"

He said nothing.

"What? Frey?" I demanded.

He said nothing, but made moaning noises.

"Very well, I shall remove the gag – for now."

I popped the gag out of his mouth. Saliva dripped from his lips to the floor.

"What?" I asked again.

"Thank you, Mistress," he said.

"That is what I believed you had said," I told him. I pushed the gag into his mouth.

I walked around his body and surveyed my branded property.

Nice.

His body was bowed, his head hanging down, wrists up-stretched.

The muscles in his calves rippled.

I stood directly behind him and reached around by his forearms and to his nipples.

My fingernails were sharp.

"Ugh!" he exclaimed as I pinched the tips of his nipples with my nails. "Thank you, Mistress," he mumbled.

Drool leaked around his lips and ran along his chin.

My own breath quickened.

At first his body was tense when I squeezed his nipples. Then, after a moment, he melted in my hands. His breathing became deep. His body swayed slightly, though still chained, almost to the point of being cruel. Still, he attempted to press against my hands.

He was completely mine now.

"You are so much a sex frey," I whispered.

He half-moaned and nodded a reply.

I continued to squeeze. Harder.

I moved my head slightly to the right and saw that his erection was full.

"Ugh!" he breathed, pushing slightly into my body.

"Ask for more," I told him.

I knew it was hurting now.

"Mooor, plz, Miffstass," he mumbled through the saliva-covered gag.

"Sound like you mean it, frey!"

"Mooooorrr, pleeez, Miffstass!"

I was wet.

My frey was asking for more pain.

I gave it to him. I squeezed harder.

He pressed backwards into my body; I pushed my pelvis against his buttocks.

Then I let go and stepped away.

"Ah, ah, ah!" he exclaimed, his breath rapid.

With my right hand I reached under my skirt and rubbed. I was dripping wet.

Alexi shivered and moaned.

I must have made the growling noise that usually made him hot with lust.

The gag was in my way. I unsnapped it from his head and he spit it onto the floor.

"Taste," I said, pressing my body against his buttocks again. I reached around his head to his lips.

He greedily licked my fingers.

That inspired me.

I stepped away and lowered the chain so that he lay face-down and flat on the cold stone floor. It was sure to push against his erection.

I unsnapped the metal cuff from his left wrist, rolled him over, and locked the cuff again so that the manacles were in front of body.

This would do. Yes.

I pulled the chain again until his arms were tight in front of him and his shoulders lifted a foot from the floor.

His erection was pointing.

I looked at his eyes. They were glossy.

Then I slapped at his erection.

He yelped and buckled his hips.

I moved toward his head and faced toward his feet.

Then I unbuckled my skirt and tossed it to the floor.

I pulled my soaking wet leather thong off and tossed it in another unknown direction.

With my hands on the chain, I positioned my knees on either side of his head and lowered myself onto his face.

The height of the chain was perfect.

His mouth was positioned well.

I did not even need to give him directions; my frey serviced me immediately.

His erection had grown again. It was hard and dark red.

It was difficult, but with one hand on the chain to steady myself, my other hand slapped at his erection several times. The position forced my clit down harder onto his mouth.

His tongue stopped.

"No," I said. "Keep licking!"

His tongue moved up. It moved down.

I trained him to be – oh, he was so good.

Slapping him became secondary.

Both of my hands held onto the chain as he continued.

My pulse pounded in my ears.

Shivers ran up my spine and crashed into my thighs.

"Ah!" I half-shouted. I squeezed my legs into the side of his face as the nika blurred my vision and my fingers clutched the chain.

It was a great effort to relax my legs and not crush my frey.

His breathing was labored.

"Oh," I huffed. "Oh."

I rocked.

"Oh."

I did not see that coming so quick!

He was well trained.

Oh.

With great effort I pushed myself off of him.

He rocked his hips. His erection stabbed at the air.

For a brief moment, I thought of taking him to nika with my hands.

I lowered the chain again.

Perhaps he thought we were going to the bed.

Instead I locked the manacles behind him.

Then I brought the chain higher until the edges of his shoulders barely lifted from the stone floor.

He was mostly flat on the ground.

Except for that hard cock.

Which he could not reach with his hands.

I pulled a pillow from my bed and lifted his head.

His face was one of pity and desperation.

He wanted to ask permission for a nika.

I shook my head "no."

His eyes pleaded.

I pushed the pillow to the floor and then shoved the side of his head to it.

I blew out all ten candles and returned to the bed. Then I tossed a large-sized blanket over his body.

"Well done, frey. I will sleep well tonight."

He whimpered.

Dominated.

Used.

Helpless.

This was the proper order of things.

I fell asleep with a smile.

# Chapter Ten
## Overwhelmed on the Sea

I walked onto the ramp of the Normanda and peered over the side.

It was three weeks until the invasion. Yet there was so much to do.

"Those scare the shit out of me," Alexi said. He pointed at the water.

"I find it interesting that you have a phrase for that," I told him. For an advanced people, the Earth language had barbaric and crude words.

"Yes, Mistress. Even so..."

We walked onto the deck and again looked over the side rail.

Fluid shapes moved below, one every minute or two.

The skrow had been unleashed on the shoreline four days ago. By all accounts, they were surviving.

We prepared to sail south to Renest. Daybreak brought another sighting of a Treaslok warship. Our task was to intercept and destroy it. Coastal activity at Belenda was at a frantic pace. The risk now was too great to allow observation by the enemy.

Captain Stela discussed final instructions with her First Officer.

I glanced at the Texana, the sister caravel ship named after the home of my frey, also nearly ready to set sail. It held a select number of the original crew of the Normanda in order to share their experience and skill. Yesterday, the two ships engaged in a race and test of combat.

Crews on the beach constructed a heavier-grade launch ramp for the first sloop-of-war, the Morata, named after the first Torino of the modern age. It would be launched tomorrow morning and eventually become our flagship following successful sea trials.

Tomorrow we would cross the sea for my meeting with Weko. A single troop ship would follow us. This was to test our towing speed capabilities.

I would meet with the resistance in the hopes of acquiring information on the detailed list I left with them.

This would be sent via radio to Sonda for final strategic and tactical adjustments.

The ships would return to Belenda. Then the attack would be launched ten days later.

"Impressive," I said, looking away from the lethal animals below and instead to the top of the beach.

Our coastline had transformed in just a matter of months.

Multiple piers provided the capability to dock twenty ships.

Guard towers peppered the top of the beach.

Five platforms at the end of the piers had been constructed. Each would station a catapult within a day, to further defend our fleet of ships.

And everyone was careful not to get into the water.

Several steel cranes dotted the horizon. A replica, of sorts, of the Treaslok seaport was on final construction to the west of Belenda. Our Marines would have three weeks to practice their night-time assault.

In all, ten-thousand construction workers worked multiple shifts on Belenda's projects.

KoVer, where we had attacked and taken over, ten years ago, sent volunteer workers and engineers. They had also felt the taste of Treaslok venom on their lands and were equally inspired to extract revenge.

More striking to the Erskans was that the colder lands to the north, Helaton and Demeya, sent timber under a truce agreement. We traded road building science with them.

Their neighbors, Jinjou, supplied ore for our burgeoning steel mill. It was the first time we had peaceful relations with Jinjou in one-hundred years. We traded Alexi's vaguely-remembered cold weather agriculture techniques.

"Mistress Cinzia said that there were fifteen-thousand warriors based here now," my frey said.

"It will be twenty-thousand by tomorrow."

"Prepare to set sail," Captain Stela ordered.

The First Officer repeated the command.

My frey kissed my boots.

I grabbed onto his hair and pulled him to his feet. "Go."

"Shia-talso," he offered. He walked off the ship and snapped around to face me.

He nodded and then moved to the end of the pier to make room for the shore team.

The Normanda backed away and headed south.

The Texana drew behind us and to the left.

We signaled messages via mirrors and ordered the Texana to drop back a bit farther. I held a radio; the Texana was not equipped with one.

"If the Treaslok ship continued north, we may intercept it within the hour," Captain Stela said.

I turned my head upward to view the look-out sailor. She was, no doubt, wearing one of the three pair of seeing eye glasses available to us.

The Texana and the Normanda each held a bow-mounted Crest-Leeland machine gun. Two-woman crews could operate the weapon while protected by steel shielding, impervious to the Treaslok crossbow bolts.

Inside our ship, secured to the deck at the railings and hidden from outside view, were a dozen hand-held steel shields. These could be retrieved at a moment's notice and used to defend against Treaslok weapons.

Our compliment was ten marines, fifteen crew, two gunnery sailors, Captain Stela, and I.

Kuretno Visada was again assigned to me, beginning this afternoon, for the long-term. I was to mentor her.

She had proven herself competent in the past and I was, sincerely, looking forward to fighting with her. However, she was riding from Antrana this morning but could not make it in time for our hasty maritime operation.

The Normanda bounced as we cut through the water.

Marines peppered the ship's railing, a couple of them sharpening their swords. One was making an adjustment to her bow.

The Erskan Marines were trained to fight while hanging from rope lines. They knew how to swim and fight in the water. They were composed of many of the best Erskan warriors.

Despite our imminent engagement of the Treaslok, two marines looked bored.

Those two were the veteran fighters.

Did I look bored?

I looked about me.

This was a veteran crew; no woman appeared nervous.

We sailed for twenty minutes until I was jarred out of my thoughts.

"Enemy contact! Treaslok ship to bow, three degrees!"

"Combat stations," Captain Stela said, as she had rehearsed two dozen times.

"Combat stations, combat stations!" the First Officer repeated.

"Signal Captain Olssa," Captain Stela ordered. "What is the Treaslok distance and direction?"

The lookout gazed ahead. "Three quarters of a mile, direction appears to be toward us."

"Signal the Texana to turn port, five degrees, for one minute, then resume parallel course."

One of the sailors flashed the beginning of the message, but Stela held her hand out to stop. "Disregard. Put the Texana directly behind us. I want the enemy ship to believe there is only one of us until the moment we engage. Then, the Texana will go port if it makes sense from their point. Send it."

The crew shifted positions. Metal-plated wood doors were pulled over sensitive or vulnerable parts the ship. Swords and other weapons were placed in strategic areas of the ship.

"Tural to Iona," I said to the radio. "We are preparing to engage the Treaslok war ship."

"Understood," was her reply.

"I do not recall us preparing for a head-on attack," I said to Stela.

"We did not."

That was not the answer I had hoped to hear.

"One half-mile!" the lookout shouted down to us.

My hand went above my shoulders. My fingers wrapped around the hilt of my sword for a moment. The tightly-wrapped leather handle was warm and felt solid.

"Have they changed course?" I asked. I pulled my hand down.

"Their direction remains to – disregard, Captain. Now they have turned slightly west."

"Change course seventy degrees!" Stela told everyone. She turned the wheel.

Two sailors quickly made adjustments to the lines.

"They had to tack," Stela said. "They will tack again, turn starboard, upon approach so that they have the coastal wind and power."

"Then we should turn also."

"I believe so. This is not part of the strategy that your frey shared with me; we did not have time to go into details for all situations. For this… for this, we will learn as we go."

Stela looked at the sailor with the mirror.

"Signal the Texana of the Treaslok maneuver and our intent to tack west, to starboard, as well. The Texana should follow."

I looked behind us. Captain Olssa already made the course change. The Texana fell into our wake.

"One quarter mile!" the lookout shouted.

I could see the mast and sails of the Treaslok ship.

Stela faced me. She looked concerned.

"What is it?" I asked.

"It is much larger than our Normanda."

The Texana completed maneuvers and positioned our ship between her and the Treaslok.

"Captain?" the First Officer asked, with obvious stress in her voice.

"Prepare to make for starboard turn!" Stela announced. The command was relayed by the First Officer.

"Starboard turn on the count of three. In three, two, one! Turn."

The Normanda leaned as the crew expertly negotiated the turn.

The Texana was slightly behind us, but not quite as efficient. She lagged when her turn failed.

"She's losing momentum, Captain!" the First Officer observed.

"Netra!" Stela said. She turned her attention forward.

The Treaslok ship was more than twice our size. Three masts. She was tacking into the wind.

And then she turned, hard and fast.

"Prepare to fire!" Stela ordered.

The Treaslok ship came at us with full wind in her three large sails.

We had been absolutely outmaneuvered.

Stela did not panic.

"Hard to port!" she shouted. She cranked the wheel of the Normanda.

The sails were partially let down as the forward boom swung wide. Sailors scrambled over the lines and rushed to tie them.

Now our aft, starboard side was exposed to the advance of the enemy.

Our main gun was up front, useless against the Treaslok approaching from the rear.

The Treaslok ship was close enough that I could see their crew at the rails.

Farther behind us the Texana floundered, wind completely lost.

We regained moderate speed again, but the Treaslok ship would overtake us in less than a minute.

"Prepare to come about to port, on a count of ten!" Stela announced.

We had to get our bow gun into them.

"We'll lose all momentum," the First Officer warned.

"I know." Stella looked toward the Texana. "They are about to regain wind."

I heard a tap at the stern of the Normanda.

"They are firing bolts," Stela advised.

There was another tap.

"On five!" Stela counted. "Set us for thirty degrees!"

A bolt went over our heads and hit the aft sail. It cut a three-inch slice into the cloth.

"Three, two, one: come about!"

The Normanda turned.

Two more bolts cut through the sails before arcing silently into the sea.

I retrieved a shield as a volley of bolts hit the deck, our port broadside now exposed as we turned.

Again, we had been outmaneuvered.

Frustrated, I clenched my teeth and cursed aloud, "Netra!"

The Treaslok ship turned as well, and bore down on the aft port side.

"Cover!" Stela warned.

Dozens of bolts sprayed us. My wrist was jarred when two bolts impacted my shield. I watched one of the bolts bounce on the deck and then roll out of sight.

I heard a scream on the main deck as our lookout sailor fell, a bolt in her abdomen.

She tumbled, her body catching in the lines, until hitting the deck with a thud.

The Treaslok ship moved parallel to us, approximately one-hundred feet behind.

"They are much higher than us," I warned as several bolts flew. "They will be able to fire down on our deck and we cannot return fire!"

"Netra!" Stela said. Her face showed panic. "Soh de Netra! Their sails will block our wind and then they can continue firing as we sit idle. We must turn again, or we are lost!"

She looked at the crouching sailors and gave the orders, "Protect the crew with your shields! Prepare to turn hard to starboard. Drop sails only and turn!"

The First Officer looked up at us as though we had lost our minds. She knew anyone on the deck would be targeted.

"Come about, hard to starboard, in three, two, one!" Stela shouted.

Bolts continued to fly around us. The bottom right half of the aft sail had several tears and was in danger of letting out all of the wind.

I covered Stela with a shield in my left hand while my right hand protected my body with a second shield.

She cranked the wheel counter-clockwise.

Sailors moved about, crouching.

Two sailors were moving the boom when a rapid-fire volley of bolts flashed around them. They both went down, hit multiple times, several pieces of their body ripped and strewn about the deck.

Another sailor protected her comrada with a shield as they attempted to move the boom.

The first sailor untied the lines and pulled it across. The sailor guarding her was hit in her right shoulder blade. She spun in a half-circle until she hit the railing and tumbled over the side into the sea.

The Normanda turned.

We were more agile than the large ship; it passed by behind us. Our stern gave the crew protection against the deadly rain of metal.

A barrage of bolts flew overhead and ripped a great tear into the aft sail. It collapsed into a heap.

Two sailors raised the forward sail and we moved again, albeit slowly and crippled.

The Treaslok ship executed a starboard turn.

"They are going to come around for the kill!" Stela said. "From the stern again!"

We would be annihilated.

Then the Texana cruised before us, moving at full speed. We slowly came out of our turn.

We watched as the Texana aimed directly mid-ship of the Treaslok vessel. We heard the staccato sound of bullets firing from the machine gun.

It was a beautiful sound. "Yes!" I shouted.

"Forward two-hundred feet, then port!" Stela ordered.

"Forward two-hundred, then prepare for port turn!" the First Officer repeated.

"Prepare to fire!" Stela told the gunner. Her comrada had moved to take the place of one of our lost sailors.

The Texana adjusted course to remain dead-aim on the Treaslok ship.

Tracer bullets from the Texana arced toward the ship and sprayed the railing. Then the gunner aimed at the water line.

Chunks of wood exploded. Five-inch wide holes dotted the body as splinters flew out into the sea on the starboard side of the Treaslok warship.

The Texana caught the enemy ship in the middle of her starboard arc, underside exposed.

The bullets ripped at the heart of the enemy.

We finished our turn and came hard onto the outside of the Treaslok ship, to its port side.

Captain Stela kicked at a crossbow bolt. She looked at me and placed a satisfied order: "Fire!"

Our own heavy machine gun leapt into action. Empty casings flew into the air and dropped onto our deck.

Dual streaks of tracer fire raked the Treaslok warship.

"Fire only at the water line as it goes between us!" Stela shouted to the gunner.

I wasn't sure she heard that.

The First Officer, also not sure, ran to the gunner to pass on the order.

It would not do well for us to fire on the Texana in the cross-fire.

"Prepare to go straight after she passes!" Stela said. "We will let the Texana pursue because she is faster with both sails."

The Treaslok ship slowly moved between us.

Our machine gun raked the waterline of the ship.

"Cover!" someone warned.

A few bolts landed around us, much less than previously.

I stole a look under my shield and saw a number of Treaslok crew running about, changing positions.

Then we saw the Texana. She turned to pursue the Treaslok ship. We held fire until the Texana passed, and then we turned to follow.

Debris from the Treaslok ship trailed its wake.

She turned to starboard. But it was a slow, languid movement. As she turned I noticed that she was leaning starboard, opposite of what normally happened. Water was likely rushing into the bowels of the ship.

The Texana positioned herself directly behind the Treaslok ship and fired the machine gun again. They aimed at the rear of the Treaslok ship.

They were targeting the rudder! That would keep the enemy from turning. It was a brilliant tactical idea.

I looked at Stela. She flashed a solid white smile. "Die!" she said, looking ahead. She adjusted the Normanda's wheel.

The Treaslok ship slowed. With our one sail we would overtake the two ships.

They headed for the coastline.

I grabbed my radio. "Tural to Iona!"

"Speak!"

"We have them retreating and under fire. They are attempting to make for the shore."

"The Sixteenth Harfala is en route. How goes it?"

"We have taken losses, but it turns in our favor now."

"Fire!" Stela ordered.

I stopped talking when our own machine gun fired and targeted the rear deck house of the ship. The sound of the Earth bullets filled the air.

The Texana focused their fire onto the center mast. Our gunner swept the deck with suppression fire. Several enemy sailors were cut into pieces as the explosive bullets tore through their bodies.

I watched as bullets split a metal shield and then disintegrated the body of a stunned Treaslok warrior.

The center mast collapsed. With a loud and prolonged cracking sound, the wood splintered and the mast fell into the forward mast. The lines were hopelessly tangled.

Our gunner killed half a dozen Treaslok sailors when they attempted to untangle the ropes.

The wounded ship decelerated.

The Treaslok ship listed to starboard at nearly ten degrees.

The Texana slowed, matched speed and eventually came to a stop. The gunner continued firing in bursts and picked off any movement.

We stopped. But continued firing at the front of the enemy ship. Our gunner carved a foot-wide hole in the bow.

Water rushed into the jagged hole.

Two lifeless bodies were propelled through another tear in the ship.

Stela signaled the Texana and they came alongside the listing enemy ship. Our gunner maintained firing bursts until the Texana's Marines threw grappling hooks to the side rails.

Ten Marines climbed the lines, swords cross-carried on their back.

We banged into the side of the Treaslok ship as well, our ship creaking from the impact. Our Marines tossed the grappling hooks and climbed aboard.

No more guns.

Traditional fighting now.

I heard the sounds of combat and greedily rushed to it like a hiraj to a bone.

"Come here if she starts to sink!" Stela cautioned.

It was an easy climb to the deck.

I came over the railing and cross-drew my sword.

Treaslok bodies and parts littered the deck.

I stepped over a web of downed lines and debris.

Blood was splattered everywhere.

Two Marines were engaged with three Treaslok on my right. I assessed and joined them.

The Treaslok closest to me went down in a half-second as I brushed her sword aside and cut into her left bicep. A spray of blood hit my face. I licked the warmth of it from my lips and then cut down the second Treaslok when I split her head.

My precision had never been better.

A Marine killed the third Treaslok.

The three of us looked for more.

My eyes swept the deck.

I pointed to the other side of the ship deck where two Treaslok were holding off three Marines.

The three of us moved in and within a moment the Treaslok were dead, one by my hand.

Then, unexpectedly, the fighting was over.

Six of our Marines encircled two Treaslok at mid-ship. One wore a rijella's uniform, while the other was apparently a sailor. They held swords and swept the blades around them.

"Rijella, drop your weapons," I said, in their language.

"Never, Erskan dog."

I drew the StacGun and, in one fluid movement, fired at her left knee.

I missed, but did hit her thigh. She went down in a scream. Her sword fell from her hands when she reached to the ripple-wood deck to break her fall.

My second shot hit the sailor in the lower abdomen. She mouthed a word before collapsing to the deck and fell onto her own intestines.

"Treat her wounds and take her to the Normanda," I told the senior Marine. "Find anything of value, confiscate some of their weapons, and then get off the ship. It is sinking."

The machine guns ignited a fire in the stern of the ship. Smoke obscured the stern.

"Make it quick!" I told them.

I helped two of our wounded Marines over the side and into the Normanda.

In another five minutes we disengaged. Soon the Normanda and Texana were a hundred feet distant of the demolished ship.

We collected two-hundred or more bolts on the deck of the Normanda.

The aft sail was ruined.

The starboard side of our ship looked like a needle pin cushion.

"Hard to believe, by looking at us," I told Captain Stela and her First Officer. "But this is our first victory at sea. Congratulations, Captain."

The Treaslok ship was engulfed in flames and heavy black smoke as it sank into the water.

We were less than two-thousand feet from shore.

The eighty-one riders of the Sixteenth Harfala appeared onto the rocky shore, no doubt guided to our location by the billowing smoke.

"I almost cost us this battle, and perhaps the invasion," Captain Stela admitted. She shook her head and then wiped her face of sweat and soot.

Several sailors stood nearby and paused to look.

I gave Stela a reassuring smile. "Do not second guess yourself. This was a learning experience for us all. I will contact Iona and advise her that we are returning to the pier. Signal the Sixteenth Harfala to return as well. There will be no need for them to assist with Treaslok survivors."

The First Officer appeared to be at an impasse as well. "Tend to the injured and start making repairs," I told her.

"Understood, jurina," she said.

The entire crew, including the Captain, returned to their posts.

\* \* \* \* \*

The evening victory celebration was attended by none other than the Torino herself. She announced the official transfer of duties of Iona as our Admirala of the Navy, a new title. The Torino also made note that the completed number of troop ships were doubled from original plan.

After the meal a select group of senior officers were called together for a separate meeting.

"The Treaslok prisoner," the Torino told us, "is not cooperating. This type of interrogation is your skill, Jurina Tural."

"Now?" I asked.

"You are to set sail tomorrow morning, yes? Now would be appropriate."

Jurina Iona, Yannta, and Cinzia were also in attendance, as were two Elite guards.

"I am always ready for an interrogation," I said. "I have been thinking about this for eight weeks."

I pointed to one of the guards, "Bring the Treaslok to the pier. I will be waiting."

\* \* \* \* \*

Her leg was tied off to prevent the blood from flowing. Without treatment from Earth medicine, she would eventually require having her leg amputated.

She would not live that long.

Of this fact she knew.

Guards held her face down on the deck, naked except for a crude iron collar around her neck and manacles holding her wrists closely behind the small of her back.

I pulled a line under her armpit on both sides and tied it near the back of her neck.

She struggled and cursed.

One of the guards helped herself with a kick to the Treaslok's left hip.

"Again," I said, quite satisfied.

The guard kicked again.

I secured the line to a post on the pier.

"You will tell me about the Suir det Ineer and about the coastal defenses," I said in the Treaslok language.

"Never!"

"I offer you a quick, painless death for the information. Otherwise you shall regret your decision."

"Never!"

On the pier were more than two dozen warriors, Iona, Yannta, Cinzia, and Netratoh Visada. My frey sat cross-legged by Mermak. He had been duly warned about what would occur and had rather aggressively insisted that he be present.

Ample light was provided by two of the portable electric lamps.

"How many Earth humans are leading the Suir det Ineer?"

"No!"

"What are the number of raa sticks they possess?"

"No!"

"What are their plans to attack us?"

"No!"

I sat on her ass, taking her head in my hands. Then I lifted her head and banged her forehead to the wood pier.

Then I hit her face onto the pier five additional times.

"No!" she spat blood.

"This is your last opportunity," I told her. I dropped the line from her restraints down into the water.

"Drowning does not frighten me!"

Alexi chuckled.

I looked at the assembled Erskans. Only a few of those present could easily translate the Treaslok words. I helped: "She says that she is not afraid to drown."

Several women laughed.

"Drowning should not be your concern."

I stood and then nodded.

Two guards grabbed her body and then shoved her over the edge of the pier.

She splashed into the cold water, on her side.

She yelped when the rope cut into her arms and held her vertical.

I shone a light down at her. It was low tide and the pier was five feet distant from the top of her head.

The line was taut and kept her neck above calm evening sea.

"How many Earth humans are leading the Suir det Ineer?"

She did not reply.

"How many Earth humans are leading the Suir det Ineer?"

"Never," she shouted, craning her neck to look at me.

I shone the bright light directly into her face.

Then I shone the light to her left, toward the sea.

"You have about five seconds to tell me what I want to know and die quickly – or ... "

She followed the light with her head and then shuddered and made a sound.

The jelly body reflected the light to the gentle waves as it circled around the Treaslok.

"What? What is that?" she exclaimed. She kicked the water with her feet.

I pressed again, "How many Earth humans are leading the Suir det Ineer?"

"Never!" she replied, but with fear in her voice this time.

We watched the jelly body move under the enemy, drawing its green-glowing tentacles behind.

The woman kicked her feet, splashing. "What?"

She cursed.

The tentacles went deeper and out of sight.

"The skrow knows where you are, Treaslok. Next it will attack."

I turned off the light.

By the indirect lighting from the pier we watched the Treaslok bob in the water.

I paused.

"How many Earth humans are leading the Suir det Ineer?"

She did not reply.

I activated my light and illuminated the Treaslok.

Then we saw it, four feet to her right, when its glistening jelly head rose to the top of the water, still and motionless as small waves brushed by. Below its wispy white head was the green mass of tentacles.

The skrow moved several inches closer to the woman.

"Wait," the Treaslok said.

"How many Earth humans are leading the Suir det Ineer?"

She did not answer.

The skrow dropped down out of sight again. My light could not find it.

The Treaslok cursed.

Then she shattered the night's calm with an agonizing scream.

My jaw tightened at the sound of horror.

The woman screamed again, less loudly, and puffed out rapid breaths.

"Ahhh, ahhh, ahh," she moaned and kicked out with her feet.

The skrow surfaced a few feet away and watched her. It floated.

"Now it knows you can not harm it. It also knows that it can harm you."

She shouted something at me, most likely a Treaslok curse.

I deactivated the lighting.

"How many Earth humans are leading the Suir det Ineer?"

She did not reply.

I twisted the light in my hand and again brightened the area below us.

The skrow dropped down again.

The woman kicked furiously.

The next sting would be significantly different from the first.

She looked wildly about her until suddenly she let out a horrendous shriek.

A dozen green tentacles wrapped around her waist. The jelly head floated below her breasts and gave an illusion that it was looking at her face.

She screamed and screamed. It was a high pitched wail that was louder than any I ever heard from a frey during a punishment whipping.

"How many Earth humans are leading the Suir det Ineer?"

She continued screaming.

"How many Earth humans are leading the Suir det Ineer?"

"Three! One woman, six men!"

She sobbed and then howled again.

"What is the number of raaa sticks that they possess?"

"Only a few." She sobbed. She shook so violently that I thought the line may break. Her body was bucking into and up from the water.

"Pull her up two or three feet," I said to the guards. Then, "What are their plans to attack us?"

Her body was pale. Her skin was turning a dark grey beside the tentacles which remained wrapped around her waist.

She screamed again. I saw her cough out blood.

"Attack in the spring!" she spat. "Please, kill me! Please!"

"Look," I told Iona, whom along with many others peered over the side of the pier.

The skrow had massed a number of tentacles at her vagina.

"By my heart, I did not know they would do that," Cinzia said from over my shoulder.

"It's inside of her," Iona observed. "Ew."

"How many warriors is the Treaslok?"

"Sixty thousand. Please kill me!" She sobbed and screamed. "Please!"

The Treaslok spit blood again. She babbled while her legs flailed.

"That's about all we can get out of her," Yannta noted.

"Sorry, Lady Skrow," I apologized to the creature.

I took the StacGun and fired a single shot into the top of the Treaslok's head.

The shot echoed about the pier as the screams fell silent.

"I wish I could have done that," Alexi said under his breath.

He was beside Cinzia.

The skrow continued thrashing about the body.

I cut the line.

The body rolled over, and sank, the metal restraints dragging it down.

"I need to take rest before sailing," I said.

"Sixty thousand?" Yannta repeated.

"Who is with Corrigan?" I asked Alexi.

"I have no idea," he replied, shrugging his shoulders in the Earth expression that meant he was not knowing.

"With a female. An Earth female?" Iona asked. "That could explain his ability, at first, to take control of the population."

Yannta grasped my shoulder. "Excellent, Tural. I would have never thought of that. It is a wonderful interrogation tool you have found."

I turned off the light and left the skrow to its feast.

# Chapter Eleven
## Vengeance Delivered

The invasion would begin in fifteen days.

My frey gave me a somber morning farewell. But his face brightened when told that he would be in the rear wave of the invasion.

I looked behind at Port Belenda as it receded from view.

"Already I miss the feel of my horse," Kuretno Visada confided. "Women were not meant to be on the water."

"At least Erskan women. Not yet. We almost proved that yesterday," I said.

"It was a victory," Visada said.

"We have not released all of the facts of the sea battle."

"Oh? Why is that?"

"The appropriate use of information is a key element in our strategy. The population will hear that we were victorious in our first battle, and that we did indeed sink a Treaslok warship twice our size. But you may know, Kuretno, that we came within an inch of losing."

"Ah," she replied, surprised.

"War is like that," I told her.

"I was on the Luchian battlefield," she said. "I saw you kill the Treaslok decoy and then I saw how we almost lost the battle."

"Then you know."

"Yes, I suppose that I did."

"Be glad you are on the Texana rather than the troop ship. It looks cramped onboard."

The Normanda required major repairs. We towed a single-mast flat, long troop ship that carried two Harfala: Visada's eighty-one unit, plus another of equal strength. Our speed was respectable.

Captain Stela transferred her command to the Texana. It was slightly faster than the

Normanda, having benefited from many modifications.

"How do you stand the boredom on the ship?" Visada asked.

"At this rate, you only have to wait about twelve hours," I wryly told her.

"Only twelve. Thank you."

\* \* \* \* \*

We surveyed the coast for movement and observed a solitary horse and rider at the rendezvous point. The heat-looking mode of the seeing eye glasses made the darkened coast appear as though it was daylight.

I climbed down the line into the troop ship and then extended my hands to Visada.

She descended and then stood next to me. She steadied herself in the dim light of the Orphans above us.

We pushed off from the Texana and paddled. We had removed the sail and dismantled the mast. The wide, flat design of this ship would allow us to float onto the shore itself.

And with a scraping sound we slid onto the narrow beach.

Marines exited and took positions on either side.

Visada and I moved forward to the road.

"She is five-hundred feet north," I told Visada. "Just three of us."

Visada picked a woman from her group and nodded.

Weko stood in the approximate location we planned eight weeks earlier. She held the reins of her horse in hand.

It was a matter of professional pride that the three of us managed to approach Weko and her horse without either suspecting our presence.

"Oh!" Weko whispered, startled.

"What information do you have?"

She retrieved several scrolls from her saddle bag and offered them to me. I nodded to Visada, whom took them.

"We have maps of the streets, guard patrols and times, and the palace defenses – but only the outer wall. We have been unable to get inside."

"Good. Has anything happened?"

"Yes. I do not believe the warriors tied their missing officers to you – but they thought it was the resistance." She looked down for a moment. "They burned every home and shop within two blocks of where they killed Pimol and your comrada."

"We will meet again so that I may ask final questions. You must come here at this time and report in exactly fourteen days. Can you do this?"

"Yes."

"Thank you, Weko."

"Thank you, Jurina Tural."

She mounted her horse and rode north.

"How well do you trust her?" Visada asked me.

"If possible we will attempt to validate part of the information with our own observations," I explained.

We moved two miles south and inland a few thousand feet. It appeared to be a perfect for our needs.

It was heavily wooded. Unusually-shaped trees filled the area. It was mostly made of bark until the top where the wide green leaves spread out.

Warriors swept our perimeter.

The Texana and the empty troop ship sailed to Port Belenda.

We were on our own until fourteen days' time.

Visada held the edges of the final map. I looked straight down at it with the seeing eye glasses.

I pressed another button on the radio, "I am sending the paintings now."

There was a pause.

"We have it," Alexi replied. "Just a moment, Mistress. Yannta has a question."

"Tural. We see only three roads leading to the palace. Do you believe that is correct?"

Visada pointed at the map.

"That is what we see."

"You will need to confirm this."

"Yes, I shall."

There was a pause before Yannta spoke again. "Tural, move to a secure location. I want only you to hear."

I stood and walked into an isolated location. "I am secure."

"About your decision to preserve the lives of the civilians," she said.

"Yes?"

"You may believe that all of the Korinas are against you on this."

"Yes, I do."

"Only two are. The others, myself included, desired to know if you have strength behind your decisions. I am pleased."

"Thank you."

"You may yet have more decisions to make. At some point the campaign will become solely yours."

"After the ground forces land?" I asked.

"Yes, that is true. I mean to say, Tural, in the greater concept of the campaign."

Oh?

She continued: "Also, if there are indeed sixty-thousand Treaslok warriors. If that is true, then you will face another decision. Your answer could be extremely unpopular here at home."

"Sparing Treaslok warriors' lives," I stated. Yes, that had consumed part of my consciousness.

"Yes. The Council is sharply divided on this potential issue. You may discuss it with the Torino, but I do not believe she is interested in taking any prisoners."

"Where do you stand, Yannta?" I asked. I needed to know.

"If there truly is a core faction that is responsible for the attacks on us… then we could be lenient. I suggest that you consider alternate plans for the occupation should you decide to spare lives. That is not the traditional approach."

Was Yannta encouraging me to work around official channels? To work around my sister?

"I understand," I said. Though not entirely.

"I have resources available to you. Decide what your plans are, and I will make preparations here. Decide soon."

"I will contact you within fifteen hours," I said.

"A half-day is good. Yannta out."

I walked to the camp area.

"Two harfala is many warriors to keep out of sight," Visada said.

"I heard you the first time," I told her.

Then, in a soft, encouraging voice I tapped her shoulder and said, "I am confident you can accomplish this. Avoid contact, but do not allow anyone to escape. Make rounds and then return to me. We have to work on an additional attack strategy."

"Yes, understood." Visada waved two warriors over to her position. "Follow me. I want to check our perimeter again."

\* \* \* \* \*

"Tural, the armada has set sail," Iona said. That meant the attack would begin in four days.

I placed the radio near my mouth. "I would like to see that," I admitted.

"Your frey is making eye paintings of it."

That was of little surprise.

"Eight ships have failed to function safely, troop ships. The other fifty-nine are working."

I did the calculation in my head. Fifty-nine at three harfala each was fourteen-thousand, three-hundred thirty-seven on the first wave.

"You are on the Morata?" I asked.

"Yes. This ship is fast."

The ships would unload on the south here and return for the second wave. Those troops would be deposited north of the seaport.

"We have encountered no patrols," Visada said, as she impatiently sharpened her sword. "We are ready."

\* \* \* \* \*

Fourteen thousand warriors unloaded and staged in camps throughout the area.

It was two days until the attack.

The armada returned to Belenda to acquire the second wave. This would be attended by the rest of the fleet, specifically the slower-moving artillery ships.

The result of a half-year of furious construction provided us with five sloop-of-war, four caravel, one catapulter, and seven fire ships.

An additional eighteen troop ships came available as well, due to cannibalization of other ship parts.

Our second wave contained twenty-thousand warriors and marines.

I ate cold meat for my meal and then sharpened my sword.

Visada and her top-level warriors stretched out on the grass.

Shamed by my inactivity, I joined them as they began the first set of one hundred push-ups.

My patience was nearly exhausted.

And there were no frey to rog. That added to my tension.

Next time we stage a major invasion, we will bring a couple of pleasure frey.

\* \* \* \* \*

"Weko," I said.

Surprised, again, she spun around and faced Visada and I.

"How do you manage that?" she asked. "Woah." She tapped her breast.

"How many members of your resistance do you have? How many close family?"

"Uh. Why? Is something wrong?"

"Answer the question," Visada told her.

"Uh. Twenty, maybe thirty."

"We can handle that," Visada replied.

I nodded.

Visada turned and made a sign to one of her officers.

Ten warriors appeared from the darkness and approached.

"Woah," Weko said. "What is happening?"

"Provide Kuretno Visada with a detailed list. We will escort each person within the hour to this location."

"Why?"

"To move them from harm's way," I said.

"What harm?"

"The invasion begins in two hours. This officer will go with you, home to home, and extract the names from your list. You must accompany her to ensure that there is no resistance among your friends."

Though poorly illuminated, Weko's face betrayed her surprise. "Yes, I understand. Thank you."

"Any person we contact will not have an option. They must leave with us immediately, or die."

"The women of Treaslok will welcome the liberation."

My Treaslok was good enough to detect that contrary to Weko's definition, I called this an 'invasion.'

"How will we load all of them into my wagon?" Weko asked.

Visada nodded. Two troop wagons, each drawn by two-horse teams, appeared and came astride us.

"Go. Time is running short," I ordered.

Remaining motionless was one of the most difficult things I had done. But I remained in my position and watched Visada take control of the mission.

Cinzia came beside me.

She did not need to speak.

"Yes," I said my voice barely a whisper.

"Oy, oy, oy," she laughed.

We walked a few hundred feet into the third perimeter line. Weko was unaware that she met us within two other perimeters and that she had been under constant surveillance for the last half-mile.

Spread out in carefully arranged patterns, and divided into harfala and giracha, were approximately fourteen thousand warriors. Half of them would be shuttled via troop ships under sail to the south end of the seaport. The other half would advance by ground north.

The same would occur north of the seaport.

Officers surveyed the ranks and looked for any exposed metal that would reflect the dim light.

Fourteen thousand warriors.

Cinzia and I approached the shore.

"Shia-talso, my friend," I hugged Cinzia.

"Shia-talso."

I boarded the skiff. The two woman crew paddled to the Morata.

\* \* \* \* \*

"Welcome aboard," Jurina Yannta said.

"This is so big," I admitted.

The deck of the Morata was longer than the entire length of the Normanda.

Jurina Iona talked on the radio.

Several jurinas and aides surrounded a table in the rear deck house.

"Cinzia reported in," Iona turned to me. "Your resistance leaders have all been retrieved without incident."

"Good."

The lights in the room were brilliant. Outside they could not be seen.

Aides moved small figurines about on the large map.

Two clocks sat on the table, tracking the time of the operation.

"Kuretno Enda reporting. Our position is set."

"Understood, Enda," Iona replied to the radio.

Iona surveyed the room. "We are ready?"

Yannta nodded.

I nodded.

Iona took the radio into her hand. "Iona to Torino Kretahla."

"This is Kretahla," my sister replied.

"We are ready."

"Shia-talso," was the simple command.

A sheet of paper identified each military unit with a corresponding attack and movement time. Eight copies of this were laid on the table at different locations.

"There are two warships headed out from the seaport," came a rushed voice.

"Identify yourself," Iona said.

"Kuretno Casa, position eighteen, Jurina."

I looked at the map. "They will run directly into the pre-positioned fire ships."

"Captain," Iona said to the ship's captain. "Notify all sloops and caravels to accompany us. We will engage the warships immediately." Iona took up her radio. "All units. Prepare for countdown orders."

I moved close to Iona. "Admiral. We should allow the other sloops to engage. As our only command and control center, we take great risk if we are disabled."

She clenched her teeth.

"Captain, we will fall back."

"Jurina?" she asked.

"Send the other ships to engage. We will move in according to original plan."

An aide looked at the clock and the sheet of paper. Then she looked to Iona for confirmation.

"Yes. Begin the count."

The aide held the radio. "Unit one, this is your one minute notice."

"Understood."

Our balance shifted as the Morata moved.

Yannta waved at me to follow.

We went beyond the triple doors to the pilot deck.

The Morata followed two other sloop-of-war ships. I also recognized the silhouette of the Texana to our starboard, ahead by one-hundred feet.

To port, a thousand feet distant, were the lights of two departing Treaslok ships.

Surely by this point they observed our fleet.

I heard a horn blow in the distance.

Our three closest ships continued to advance on the two Treaslok ships.

It would be a head-on engagement.

Simultaneously, three arcs of tracers shot out from our ships.

The horn stopped.

The sound of machine gun fire reached us.

A few lamps at the seaport were lit.

The surprise invasion would not be a *complete* surprise.

Another horn, from the shore, sounded the alarm.

Additional lamps at the seaport appeared.

It would be a race to the port.

Yannta turned to advise Iona to begin the next step.

After a few seconds, all eight of our fire ships became alight. They had coasted to within merely a few hundred feet of the seaport.

The Normanda swept by to retrieve the crews from the fire ships.

In the middle of our panoramic view the night time battle among three Erskan ships and two Treaslok ships proceeded.

Machine gun fire continued.

Three ribbons of light touched the enemy ships.

We watched as both Treaslok ships caught on fire. Bright yellow and orange flames flickered across the waves.

Our ship moved closer to the port.

I looked over my shoulder

Alexi was on the Hios, the caravel protecting our rear flank. We thought it would be unneeded.

Several horns wailed from the direction of the seaport.

Even more lights dotted the shore. Several lamps moved toward the pier.

"This is a good view, yes?" a sailor said, pausing for a moment beside me.

"Yes, it is."

The first of the fire ships entered the southern mouth of the seaport.

A Treaslok ship made for the port exit. One sail was unfurled. Lamps onboard indicated the crew was working to get the second sail up.

However, they collided in a tremendous fireball that brightened the entire seaport.

Everyone within miles would know something was happening.

The white-hot ball blossomed a hundred feet into the air.

A rumble from the explosion washed over us.

A second fire ship, on the north entrance, crashed into the pier.

The third fire ship crashed into the second at almost the same time.

A double ball of fire rose and illuminated the pier and several ships.

I turned to the sailor and smiled, "Yes, a good view. I've been waiting a long time for this."

I could see dozens of Treaslok running about on the pier.

On our ship the wood slats around the command deck were dropped by several aides to expose the strategy table.

There would be no need to conceal our presence now.

"Unit twelve, proceed," an order was given via radio.

The Morata's sister ship, the Gitana, disengaged the two damaged Treaslok ships and made a pass alongside the seaport.

She fired her machine guns and swept the piers and buildings to clear out anyone standing in the area.

One of the two Treaslok warships was fully engulfed in flames. All three of its sails burned. Tendrils of fire licked the night sky.

Dark clouds of smoke boiled upwards.

The other ship was bow-up and was sinking rapidly into the sea. It would block the southern seaport exit.

We passed both ships to port by about two-hundred feet. Treaslok sailors splashed into the water.

A number of our marines took the opportunity to fire volleys of arrows at the survivors.

"Unit thirteen, proceed," another order was made.

Fire ship number four crashed into the seaport, in the middle. The pier exploded, and scattered burning slats of wood into the air.

The fireball explosion illuminated two girachas of Erskan marines that stormed the enemy catapults.

Our own catapult ship moved into position and set three anchors.

Our responsibility was to provide cover for it while we controlled the invasion.

Then the ammunition ship docked to the stern of the anchored catapult ship.

The first of twenty one-hundred pound blocks were loaded into the sling.

The calm naval officer continued to give commands into the radio: "Unit fourteen, fifteen, sixteen, proceed."

This last order would order the ground troops to attack from both directions.

Fire ship number five plowed into the seaport on the south entrance.

We were close enough now that the explosion lit up the deck of our own ship. Shadows of our crew betrayed their positions for a moment.

In the rear of the pier, several enemy ships attempted to maneuver in order to put their broadside toward us. Their crews dodged our gunfire as they pulled ships lines in a vain attempt to rotate.

I heard a loud *clap* to the left.

Our catapult launched its first missile.

The burning pier and at least four burning Treaslok ships provided more than enough light to allow accurate targeting. But the block landed harmlessly into the channel of the seaport.

They would make an adjustment.

*Clap*!

Another block sailed overhead into the seaport.

It collided with a section of the pier and carved a thirty-foot wide gap. Treaslok sailors were struck down. Several sailors disappeared under the block as it splintered wood and crushed bodies.

Erskan ammunition ships pulled to the seaport's side catapults. A small fire had already been burning underneath the cauldrons of these ammunition ships.

Treaslok warriors, now mobilized, appeared on the perimeter of the seaport, and at the shoreline.

The captured southern catapult was ready first. It launched a load of boiling oil into the center of the seaport.

Erskan warriors defended the positions as well, firing arrows when needed.

The Treaslok were caught by surprise.

Hundreds fell and screamed as they were struck with scorching hot oil.

The oil doused wide areas of the pier.

Black smoke from the fires obscured my view at times.

Screams became frequent.

Wood was crackling everywhere.

Sails burned.

The entire port was ablaze.

A sinking Treaslok ship pulled apart the pier with a great crashing sound.

Treaslok warriors fell into the water, either shot by arrow or in a vain attempt to soothe their burns.

The ship-mounted catapult switched to launching flame bombs. A cluster of logs and coal, bailed together with wire, arced skyward to the center of the seaport. It crashed into a Treaslok warship. Several crew jumped into the water, crying in agony.

The catapult fired every thirty seconds.

A third ammunition ship tied up to the rear while crews maintained a steady feed of the flame bombs.

The last of our fire ships crashed into the northern outlet. The fireball was almost irrelevant compared to the wide swath of fires already consuming the seaport.

"Oy, oy, oy," Yannta said. "It is beautiful."

I had been staring. I was completely mesmerized by the sight and sounds. I could feel the heat from the flames.

"This is my vengeance," I told her.

"There remains the palace," Yannta said.

"That shall be my vengeance as well."

"Look," she pointed to the south end.

We could see the first wave of Erskan marines taking the high ground.

"Our turn," Yannta said.

"Yes, our turn," I replied, unsnapping the strap of my sword.

The Morata came alongside the south end of the pier, by the catapult crew. They fired missiles and picked off surviving Treaslok by laying waste to twenty-foot swaths of the pier.

Every ship in the seaport was either burning or lay at the bottom of the channel.

The pier was in shambles.

There was hardly a single piece of wood that was horizontal.

I climbed over the rail and went down to the edge of the catapult pier. I was followed by thirty of our marines.

Yannta led our unit up the hill to the right, where our forces had established positions.

She stopped at the door of one building we commandeered. It would be the first of several field command posts. "Good hunting, Tural."

Visada met me. Her entire unit was present. No casualties.

"Kuretno," I said, "Let us go."

\* \* \* \* \*

Any preconceived thoughts I had about engaging in sword-to-sword combat were quickly dispelled.

As expected, the Treaslok ground forces moved toward the seaport.

We launched waves of arrows upon them from our superior positions above.

Then, the next attacking group of Treaslok moved further south in an attempt to surround us.

Cinzia's eight-thousand-strong force instead flanked the enemy within the city.

It was a rout.

Cinzia's forces killed two- or three-thousand warriors and suffered only a hundred casualties. Her forces had attacked the rear of the Treaslok and caught them by complete surprise.

Using the maps from the resistance we also identified individual reserve units and captured thousands more with only marginal Erskan casualties.

The same occurred on the northern end of the seaport and city.

Our forces moved east through the city until we encircled the outer wall of the palace.

We were twenty-two thousand strong.

The Treaslok suffered ten thousand dead, with eight thousand captured. We demolished a third of their forces. It was believed another third were scattered throughout the continent and would, of course, be recalled.

Less than a third, approximately ten thousand warriors, remained inside the palace walls.

We fought and moved systematically through the large city.

Seven hours into the invasion Visada handed a flask of water to me.

"Thank you."

"Siege catapults will be here in an hour," she advised.

The morning sun cast long shadows on the deserted street.

There was no civilian population outside; they were ordered to remain indoors or face execution.

We dismantled most of the catapults in order to move them along the road to the Treaslok palace. We waited for the arrival.

I straightened my skirt and stood tall.

"Where did you get that?" Visada asked.

I looked over my left shoulder and could see dried blood. I shrugged. "I do not know."

Visada poured water onto a cloth and wiped my shoulder clean. "It is not deep." She waved to a field medic.

"Iona to Tural."

I took the radio in hand.

The medic applied salve from an Erskan medicine plant onto the slight wound.

"Yes, this is Tural." I winced as my shoulder stung.

"Please move to a secure location for a message."

"I am secure now."

"I have bad news about the Hios."

The Hios was the caravel guarding our rear flank.

Alexi was on that ship!

"We have found the floating remains of two ships, one Treaslok. The other is clearly from the Hios." She paused for an eternity. "Tural, I am sorry."

"Jurina?" Visada asked. She reached across to touch me.

I staggered. I took her hand and went to my left knee.

Visada took the radio from my hand. "Visada to Jurina Iona. We have received the message."

"Understood, Iona off."

"Aaaarrrrgggghhhhhh!" I shouted. I pushed the medic aside.

"Jurina?"

I turned away from Visada.

I walked to the closest door of a house and drew my sword.

My blade shattered the small glass window.

I hacked at the frame.

Again.

And again.

And again.

Over again.

I hacked at the wood.

Splinters flew.

Again.

My sword was wedged in the frame.

I let go and shouted again at the ground.

First Hula.

Now my frey.

I huffed for a moment and rest my hands on my knees.

Several warriors stopped what they were doing and looked at me.

Then I looked through the broken glass and torn door.

Ten feet inside, half-hidden in the shadow, were three people. A very young woman, perhaps sixteen years old stood in front of two children, a girl and a male.

The children, about eight or nine years old, were wide-eyed and they cowered behind the older one.

The young woman held a knife in her hand, shoulder-high with the hilt pointed toward me. It was a throwing knife and her arm was cocked.

My sword was stuck in the door.

I held no shield.

I had put the Ranger blouse away when we launched the actual invasion.

And I was framed by the broken door.

A perfect target.

We looked at one another for a moment as these thoughts raced through my head and I came to the realization that I was defenseless.

"Go away!" she said.

"Yes, I will. I am sorry," I told her.

"Stop hurting us. There's nothing else for you to take."

I slowly put my hands toward her, my palms open.

"I mean you no harm," I said.

She did not lower her weapon.

Obviously, she watched as I broke a three-foot hole into her front door. It probably looked like "harm."

"This has nothing to do with you," I explained. "I was angry. Not at you."

"You are different," she said. "Are you Busai?"

"No. I am Tural. Who are you?"

"Yuso."

"Yuso, are you here alone?"

"No."

"There is no need to hide the truth. You are here alone, yes?"

"Yes."

"Where is your mother?"

"The Suit de Ineer took her. A long time ago."

I heard boots shuffling to my sides.

"Yuso, will you put your knife down? I will have your door repaired and we will leave you alone. Or, we have food with us."

"What food?" she asked.

"Drop the knife!" Visada ordered from my right side.

Visada pointed an arrow past my right shoulder. It was aimed at the girl.

Another archer placed an arrow on my left shoulder and pointed in.

"Yuso, put your knife down. Please. These women will not ask a second time."

The knife harmlessly bounced across the wood floor toward my feet.

"Thank you," I said.

I let a long breath of air out of my chest.

"Visada, see to it that they have all the food they want. And we need to find out how many other homes have children running the house. This is inexcusable."

The arrows were lowered.

"Understood," Visada replied.

"Yuso, this is Visada," I said. "She will help you."

Visada pulled on my hilt and extracted the sword from the door. She handed my weapon to me and then reached around and opened what remained of door.

I straightened and rubbed my right shoulder as Visada carefully entered and knelt down to talk to Yuso.

I slowly put my sword back into the scabbard. I left the front porch of the building and stepped into the road.

The other warriors returned to their tasks.

It occurred to me that the oldest among the warriors might have mistaken my actions for those of my sister.

Visada came outside with the three children. Their clothes were threadbare. Their hair was unkempt and they were pale. But smiles broke their faces when Visada turned them over to a quartermistress that presented them with bowls of hot greintol.

Visada walked over to me.

"Netra," I cursed. "Find out what is delaying the catapults."

"You could have been killed," she said.

"By a child, yes." I looked at the children as they attacked their bowls of food. "The Treaslok are not our enemy."

"The Suit de Ineer," Visada nodded.

"Thank you for saving me," I said to her.

"You went from mad to calm – and held your hands up. It was an easy guess to know you were in trouble."

"Yes," I agreed. "Catapults?" I asked.

"I will investigate," she replied.

\* \* \* \* \*

Clap!

Clap!

Clap!

Three catapults launched in succession and sent blocks of steel-reinforced concrete crashing into the outer wall of the palace.

Then we experienced the first encounter with a firearm.

A Treaslok appeared on the top of the wall and fired several shots at our catapults and crew.

We were prepared.

The Crest-Leeland machine guns had been removed from all but one ship and were mounted under cover with each of the three siege emplacements.

The Treaslok was mowed down when two of our heavy guns fired.

We continued to hurl one-hundred pound missiles.

Clap!

Clap!

Clap!

"Visada, ready your warriors," I said.

I took the radio, "Tural to Yannta, we will breach the outer wall in a moment."

"Almost there ourselves," Cinzia added from her location.

Yannta replied, "Understood. I will be there shortly."

If Cinzia wanted a race to the palace, then so be it.

Large sprays of stone and mortar exploded from the wall.

The all-morning pounding caused a headache. I pressed my fingertips against my forehead.

I looked at the base of the wall and estimated the growing pile of broken stone to be about six feet high.

The wall would be breached within a minute or two.

Erskan Kuretno officers, each commanding a harfala of warriors, prepared their lines for the impending assault through the outer wall.

Clap!

Clap!

Clap!

Crash!

Twelve thousand Erskans readied to enter.

Swords were drawn.

Razor-tipped pikes intermittently pierced the sky.

Steel plated shields glistened in the sun.

The Erkans held fast.

Approximately two-thousand Treaslok defenders burst through the hole while we held our position.

Clap!

Clap!

Clap!

The spoons of the catapults were reloaded and instead launched buckets of boiling oil.

Treaslok warriors were caught off guard. Hundreds of swords were forgotten as hands went up to protect against the searing liquid.

They were burned alive.

Screams

The others stalled in their outward advance as the bodies piled in front of them.

Clap!

Clap!

Clap!

The catapults launched the blocks again, low, at ground level.

The first massive stone rolled haphazardly, tumbling, until it colliding with the few surviving, screaming and burned warriors. The second stone approximated the same route and cleared the path of bodies. The third stone crashed into the wall.

"Netra!" Asada exclaimed. Her mouth gaped.

She was correct.

The scene before us was one of total carnage.

Approximately twelve-hundred Treaslok warriors were dead or dying. Body parts were smashed into one another and then melted by the oil.

Erskan casualties: zero.

"Yes," I told Asada. "This is war. We keep going now and we think about this later."

I made sure the catapults were disarmed. Then I gave the signal.

With minor difficulty, Erskan warriors found a trail through the bodies and then raced into breach to confront the remaining Treaslok.

We swiftly overwhelmed their broken defenses.

By the hour we found ourselves at a heavily fortified inner wall.

Afternoon arrived and we moved the siege weapons in, positioned our warriors, and extracted our casualties.

All surviving Treaslok warriors were executed.

Yannta appeared on site as we fired our tenth volley of missiles to the wall.

The solitary Treaslok gate was shielded with metal.

Our missiles barely scratched it.

"Earth metal," Yannta observed. "It will take a day to break the wall around it."

"The wall must be fifteen feet thick," Visada said. "We have hit one area four times and it has done little damage."

A Treaslok catapult, or catapults, on the other side made a noise.

Visada crouched as a block flew over our heads.

Yannta and I both remained standing tall. I laughed.

The block landed about one-hundred feet behind us. It nearly struck a supply cart.

Yannta faced me. "Are you well, Tural?"

I knew her concern was about Alexi.

"I will deal with that later," I replied, honestly.

Yannta nodded and faced the wall. "We have no idea what is on the other side?"

"None," I admitted. "The information from the resistance was incomplete beyond this point."

"That is good, you see?" Yannta said.

Visada shook her head. "I don't understand."

"Information that was 'too complete' would be suspicious," I explained.

Clap!

Clap!

Clap!

Two of our missiles crashed into the wall. The third flew over the top of the wall.

Metal rods twisted like worms from the damage.

"Look at that!" I said. I pointed at the steel reinforced wall.

Yannta was correct; the siege would take an entire day.

Acrid, nauseating smoke billowed past us from the fires used to burn the dead Treaslok. Ten years ago I learned to tolerate the smells of combat and death. Tolerate it – not enjoy it.

I turned and observed several masked Erskans dragging the dead by the use of meat hooks and cargo net.

"Put out the fires," I told Visada.

"Understood," she said, her voice questioning.

"I have an idea."

* * * *

"I cannot believe we are doing this," Visada confided.

Eight dead Treaslok were loaded per sling.

A charred hand fell off the sling and to the ground.

One of the gun crew gingerly picked it off the ground and tossed it onto a different body.

"Are you sure about this?" Visada asked.

"Yes," Yannta replied for me.

Clap!

Clap!

Clap!

Twenty four bodies, or parts of bodies, flew up and over the wall.

"Load one and two with bodies," I told the woman in charge of the catapults. "We have two-thousand more."

We watched as several Erskans heaped one corpse after another onto the slings.

"Now, load the missiles into the third catapult. We have to find where they have positioned their catapults."

We then launched sixteen bodies over the wall. Torsos and limbs spiraled as they dropped from our view.

A pair of blocks came hurtling over us, landing far to the left. They rolled and took out the wall of a guard building.

An observer ran to us from the left.

"About eight degrees," she said.

"Range?" I asked.

"Sixty feet."

Visada relayed the order.

Clap!

Our block flew over the top of the wall.

We waited for the return volley.

Nothing.

"Got it," Visada said.

Now we could aggressively intimidate them.

"More bodies," I said. "And raid a few of the food shops. Bring butter, honey, anything sticky that we can pour on the bodies."

Visada stood beside me. She bit her lip and watched another eight Treaslok bodies launch over the wall.

"Yes, Kuretno?" I asked.

"I cannot say that I've seen or heard of doing this before. Sending the dead to the enemy."

"I have never had a machine such as a catapult to use before this," I told her.

"There is *that*," she nodded. "It should encourage the Treaslok to make a quick decision. And the dead are not feeling anything."

"My thoughts, as well," I said.

Visada moved away to find additional ingredients to our experiment in biological warfare.

Yannta reached down to adjust the laces on her boot. "How is she?"

"Visada?" I asked. "She will be fine. She is learning."

We continued firing. We moved our catapults about in order to target other areas inside the palace.

In three hours we exhausted our supply of two-thousand bodies.

Treaslok will plead for surrender by the heat of tomorrow's sun.

Tough luck, Cinzia.

"Get rest when Visada returns," Yannta told me. "You have been on the advance for almost a full thirty hours."

I offered no resistance. "Understood," I thankfully replied.

\* \* \* \* \*

In the morning we slowed our rate of missile fire because we were running out of large blocks of stone and other heavy items. Construction crews repositioned to the front lines and destroyed sections of the outer walls in order to supply ammunition for the catapults. We fired faster than they could give us materiel.

One of our catapults failed shortly after noon. One of the five-woman crew was injured when it snapped.

We stopped using the other two catapults and ordered safety inspections while an engineering crew scoured the city for replacement timber.

I sat under a colorful field tent, my legs crossed under me. My sword lay across the blanket.

I held a sketch drawn on paper by Alexi. It depicted the seaport and the movement of warriors up to the palace.

Only the west walls of the palace had been known at that time; I added lines around the side to represent what we knew about it now.

About two months ago, Alexi drew a picture of the Antrana palace and gave it to me as a gift.

I teased and told him that first-level children in art class made better drawings.

I folded the paper and put it into my pouch, hoping that doing so would also put away my feelings of guilt.

Subsequent searches on the sea failed to find survivors of the ship wreck.

I could not allow myself time to grieve. Not now.

Yannta seemingly relinquished more of her command to me.

I could not yet grieve.

I heard a commotion on the other side of the wall. It continued for several minutes.

Then a solitary Treaslok warrior appeared at the top of the wall with hands outstretched.

I leapt to my feet, snatched my sword, and found Visada within a few seconds. "Hold fire!" I ordered.

Visada passed my order down the lines to our warriors.

"Come with me," I told her.

We mounted three horses and rode to within fifty feet of the wall.

"Do you understand me?" the warrior shouted. Her face was dirty and she looked haggard. I could barely identify Treaslok rank on her uniform collar.

"Yes, we do."

"I am Rijella Monu. I want to discuss the terms of our surrender."

"There are no terms," I told her.

"Many of my warriors have not wanted to fight you, Erskan. We had no choice. Now, we have turned inside and fought. The Suir det Ineer have retreated to the inside of the palace itself. We have you on our west flank, and they are on our east. We do not want war with your people."

"How many are the Suir det Ineer?" I asked.

"One thousand loyal to the Suir det Ineer."

"How many of you are?"

"Three thousand."

"I am Jurina Tural. You will provide me escort and information into the palace."

I looked at Netratoh Visada. She agreed to share in the risk with me. She nodded.

"Monu," I shouted. "In exchange for your cooperation, your warriors will not be killed if they surrender now."

She leaned away and had a brief discussion with someone. "I accept those terms. We will come out."

We turned about and returned to the ranks.

I rode my horse along the front lines of our warriors and stopped at each Netratoh officer and told them to not permit any execution of the prisoners. This was met by quizzical expressions.

Then I stopped by Yannta.

"They will surrender?" she asked.

"Yes. No killing."

"The Torino will love this," Yannta grinned.

I shrugged.

We both dismounted the horses and faced the inner wall.

"All is ready," she told me.

Handling large numbers of enemy prisoners was new to us. Unmarked crates of supplies arrived this morning and were nearby.

The sound of metal grinding came from behind the gate. It moved to the left side until all ten feet was open.

The first of many weary-looking warriors came out, in two columns. They placed their swords and crossbows and bolts on the ground and walked to my left, toward several Erskans warriors. The Erskan warriors quickly performed a search for additional weapons and then secured the prisoners with steel collars and chain.

The last to come out was Rijella Monu. She made an Erskan salute and went to her knees.

Visada snapped shackles onto her wrists and ankles, and stripped her of any personal items.

Yannta stood behind us and chuckled. She brought her radio up. "Yannta to Cinzia."

"Cinzia, yes?"

"Tural has breached the inner wall on this side. Send two-thirds of your forces here to proceed with the attack."

There was a pause.

I would wager that she stomped the ground with her boot.

"Understood," was the evenly measured reply.

I looked up and around us. Thousands of Erskan warriors stood at attention, all eyes riveted on the surrender of the Treaslok Rijella, still kneeling at our feet.

Yannta nodded her head, ever so slightly.

This was not planned.

I stepped a couple of paces away from the Treaslok prisoner and drew my sword from across my back.

This was not choreographed.

I turned to face the brave Erskan fighters and thrust my sword into the sky.

It was the right thing to do.

I stomped the ground with my right foot.

The ground trembled as four-thousand boots beat the ground eight times in succession.

Visada wiped grime from her face and saluted to me.

Then Yannta nodded my direction.

The Erskan force was silent and poised to make the final assault on the palace.

I slid my sword into its scabbard.

"You are familiar with the palace, yes?" I asked our prisoner.

Visada lifted the Treaslok Rijella to her feet.

"Yes."

"Good. I want to know the weakest point in the palace wall. And then, then you will tell me where Louis Corrigan is hiding."

# Chapter Twelve
## To the Victora Go the Spoils

"How much will this cost me?" Cinzia asked. She rode to my position. There were approximately three-thousand warriors behind her. They positioned into columns in the yard.

"We will determine that later," I replied. "But you can expect a hefty price."

"Sonda to Tural."

I took the radio, "Yes, this is Tural."

"Where is your position?"

"We are within the main yard of the palace. We are making final plans."

"Keep us informed. Sonda, out."

Kendra, the chief engineer, walked to our position. We nodded in acknowledgement.

"There are five entrances to the palace," Cinzia said, climbing off her horse.

Yannta looked across the five-hundred foot distance to the stout wall.

We could see Treaslok guards peering out through broken windows. They occasionally fired a bolt from any of the nine floors of the palace.

"What is keeping you from firing missiles?" Kendra asked.

"I am not concerned about the structure," Yannta replied. "We have information from a prisoner that there are prisoners in the dungeons. There may be Erskans in there."

"Corrigan is inside," I added. "While the Torino does not want him alive, she will require proof of his death."

"Why does it smell so bad here?" Kendra asked. She turned her head to survey the damage-littered palace grounds.

Most of the bodies had finally been burned. Just out of our view, around the left side remained one of three piles of corpses.

"You do not want to know," Cinzia replied. "I wish I did not know," she added.

Yannta placed a stone on the map to hold it down from the breeze. Our map now depicted the far side of the palace since we knew its complete shape.

"When are you allowing your frey to come up here?" Kendra asked. She kept her eyes on the map.

I shuddered. Then I faced her until she looked at me. "Alexi's ship was sunk."

Kendra's face turned white. "I am sorry, Tural."

"You did not tell me this?" Cinzia inquired.

"No. We have a mission," I said. My voice trembled.

"Alexi was on the Hios, yes?" Kendra asked.

"Yes. He was," I replied.

Kendra looked at Cinzia, "Jurina, Mermak was on the Hios."

Cinzia's head snapped around. Her face turned red and she practically spit the words from her mouth, "That is impossible. I ordered him to stay in Belenda!"

"He passed me at Port Belenda. He said you requested his presence."

Without a radio, Alexi knew there would be no way to communicate from the Hios to expose the ruse.

"What happened to the Hios?" Cinzia asked.

I blinked before answering: "It looks like it collided with a Treaslok ship. There were no survivors."

"He was told to wait for my signal!" Cinzia said. Her voice was half-anger and half-despair.

"It is most likely my frey encouraged Mermak to disobey," I said.

Cinzia looked toward the west, where trails of smoke continued into the sky. Then she looked at the palace and shook her head.

We had more important duties at hand.

"Yes," I agreed.

Yannta pointed at the map, "The prisons are here... and here. We could enter on this side, as a decoy, and move small numbers of units here."

"They will be able to fire down upon our warriors," Cinzia said.

"We would take too many casualties," I agreed. "We need another option."

"Has there been any gunfire?" Kendra asked.

"None," I answered.

"They may be low on ammunition," Kendra continued. "We are down to twenty percent bullets on the heavy machine guns."

Once depleted, the ammunition would be gone. The elusive ingredient for gunpowder, saltpeter, continued to evade our grasp. Still, to manufacture high-performance ammunition for the big guns would be years distant.

Several of us faced the palace and contemplated the next move.

I tapped my hip.

"This looks like a soft side," I pointed to our right. "It is not directly over the prisons. Kendra, can you dismantle the Earth metal gate from the wall?"

"Yes."

"How many wagons would it take to support the weight of it?"

"We could draw one of the catapult carriers up here. That should be good. They have six axles to distribute the load."

"What are you thinking?" Yannta asked.

\* \* \* \* \*

The Earth gate was lowered by two dozen lines of chain until it lay flat atop a steel-framed, twelve-wheel transport carrier.

Fifty feet wide, twenty-feet high, and four inches thick, we estimated the weight at over four tons.

The lines were removed. Twelve lines then were affixed to either front corner of the carrier.

Two horses assisted us with positioning the carrier and gate. We pointed it to one particular section of the palace wall, five-hundred feet distant.

"Will this roll on the grass?" Cinzia wondered.

"Yes, no problems," Kendra replied.

Yannta flashed a great smile. "This will be a sight."

Our warriors encircled the palace, ready to attack.

The lines were then connected to eight horses, four on the right, four on the left. The horses were positioned at a slight angle and pointed slightly outward.

Kendra contacted the single riders at both teams of horses for final instructions before she returned to our location. We waited behind the carrier.

Treaslok loyalists in the tower appeared to finally comprehend what was going to happen.

I pointed to the catapult firing officer.

Clap!

Clap!

Clap!

Clap!

Clap!

Five missiles plowed into the side of the palace and scattered the Treaslok from their windows. It provided covering fire for our riders.

"Now," I told Kendra.

She signaled both riders. They charged, riding forward, their direction just passing the sides of the castle.

Ten warriors pushed on the rear of the carrier.

The carrier rolled.

Slowly at first, then it was at four-hundred feet from impact.

Three-hundred feet.

A Treaslok appeared at a window, crossbow ready. One of our armed Elite guards fired her StacGun at the Treaslok and forced her to retreat.

The carrier reached two-hundred feet from impact.

The carrier wobbled at one hundred feet to target.

"By my heart!" Cinzia urged. "Go!"

The riders cut the lines and broke their horses away.

The carrier was on the verge of toppling.

Then the gate and carrier crashed into the palace wall.

The earth shook beneath my feet and I laughed.

A fifty-foot wide, one-hundred foot high section of the wall collapsed amid a great pile of stone and dust. The impact hurled pieces of rock two hundred feet from the wall.

Now that the wall was weakened, we launched five volleys of missiles at the edge of damage to widen the hole.

We could see several demolished rooms, five floors, and a few bodies.

We were presented with a one-hundred foot wide breach.

"How is that?" I asked.

Cinzia crossed her scarred arms and laughed.

"By all means," Yannta smiled. She nodded in the direction of the Kuretno Visada, who was in the front and in charge of the first harfala to attack.

I waved my hand at Visada and then pointed forward.

With a shout of "Shia!" the first wave of seven-thousand Erksan warriors stormed the demolished wall and poured into the palace.

\* \* \* \* \*

There had only been thirty minutes of fighting until we took control.

I followed three officers down two flights of stairs to the palace dungeon.

Yannta and Cinzia waited as I struck the padlock several times with a blacksmith's hammer borrowed from Kendra. Visada and ten warriors accompanied us.

I pulled the broken, heavy door open.

Visada's warriors entered and flanked the corridors.

I followed, sword in right hand at the ready, my left hand holding a torch.

Twenty cells per side, forty in all. Each had a wood door, a metal slide window at the top and a metal feeding slot at the bottom. They were closed and pinned.

A single torch was used to light the room.

Shuffling noises came from the cell closest to us.

I broke the lock and Visada pulled the door open.

I almost dropped the hammer in surprise.

On his knees, naked, collared, and shackled hands and feet, facing away, was unmistakably an Earth male.

His body shook. There were hundreds of scars on his torso and thighs.

A chain led from his collar to the top of the small cell, which measured less than four-feet square and six-feet high. The smell of urine and feces was overpowering.

"Mistress?" he asked in Treaslok.

"Turn around," I told him in Treaslok.

He rotated slowly, shuffling the dingy barn straw around his legs.

His face was gaunt, eyes barely visible in the dark. He squinted as Visada moved the torch closer.

"Can you stand?"

"No, Mistress," he replied, his voice cracking.

"Cut that," I told Visada, pointing to the ceiling chain.

She struck it with her sword thrice until it broke. I caught the links.

"Out," I said. "Slow."

In obvious pain the male moved out and stretched out onto the dirty floor. He moved to kiss my boots.

I stepped away from him. "No."

Cinzia and Visada broke open another door while Yannta watched.

"Another one," Iona said. "He's dead."

They opened a third cell.

The Earth man lay on the floor near my boots.

Cinzia flashed two fingers to me and shook her head.

We broke into all cells and found only the three Earth males, two deceased. Both had died recently and had unmistakable signs of severe torture.

"Take him up to a room," I said.

Visada and two of her warriors lifted the Earth male from the ground and carried him out.

"What was going on here?" Cinzia asked. "To treat a male like this... it is not rational."

A messenger appeared. "We have a prisoner with information."

I followed her to a main hall strewn with several overturned tables. Three dead Treaslok lay in the corner.

In the centre were several Erskan warriors surrounding a Treaslok sitting on a table.

She had been stripped of her clothes and a chain locked around her neck. A bandage was wrapped around her left hand where it appeared that she had lost one or more fingers.

"Who are you?" I demanded, speaking in Treaslok.

"I am not of the Suir det Ineer," she replied.

"We will see about that. I will spare your life if you cooperate."

She looked at Visada and Cinzia. Among the assembled warriors, the three of us wore the only significant uniform decorations of rank. Perhaps she felt that was sufficient. "They left when the first report came in about the attack on the seaport."

"'They'?" I asked.

"The Earth woman and her Earth frey."

Yannta, Visada, and Cinzia faced me with equally stunned expressions.

"Is the Earth frey named 'Corrigan?'" I asked.

"That is his name."

"What is the name of the Earth woman?"

"Her name is 'Ineer.'"

"Where did they go?"

"There is a fortress in the mountains."

"How far away is this?"

"The mountains are five day's ride. That is to the base. Then one day to climb the road." She rubbed her hand. "The fortress is well protected. There will be no way to assault it."

Cinzia crossed her arms before her, "We will see about that."

"How many warriors defend the fortress?" I asked.

"Perhaps only two-thousand. It does not require a large contingent."

"What do you want in return for leading us there?" I asked.

"You would make an offer?" she asked, surprised.

"The Treaslok are defeated," I explained. "The Erskans have nothing to gain by killing you or your warriors. I need your help in finding Corrigan ... and Ineer."

"I would gladly help you find them," she said. "But first, I would like to see my family."

This was unexpected.

"How long has it been since?" Cinzia asked.

"Two years," she replied, tears welling in her eyes. "If they are still alive."

"Remain here," I said.

Yannta, Cinzia, Visada, and I moved to a corner of the room while others watched the prisoner.

"Five days," I repeated.

"That is too far in our present condition," Visada said.

True. Our forces required time to recover.

"For a large force, yes," Cinzia added. "As we know from prior experience, the occupation of Treaslok will be complicated and require a great number of warriors."

"I believe we will have less resistance than in the past," I told them. "They have been crushed by the Earth people."

"Perhaps," Yannta said.

Yannta surveyed the room, "This is large enough to suffice. You need to establish your command center here and begin directing all operations to this location."

"Understood," I replied.

Yannta looked at Visada. "Have all of the bodies removed. Separate the survivors as those that are definitely loyalists and those that are not. Any doubts, put them in a third group. Isolate them. A fourth group will be those of civilians and frey, if there are any of them. Move the Third Harfala to begin sweeping patrols in a five-hundred foot radius of the palace's outer wall. Report when these are complete. We will make the command center operational at that time. Say about two hours?"

Visada nodded.

"Aide!" Yannta waved over a junior officer. "This room will be our command center. We need Kuretno officers from the Prima Harfala assembled here in two hours, unless they are engaged in actual combat."

The aide scurried off to relay the orders.

Yannta turned to face me directly. "Please join me for a private conversation."

I followed her to a small office. Inside were a small desk, single chair, and dozens of scrolls with unintelligible Treaslok script. Yannta adjusted the oil lamp and brightened the room. She pointed to the door.

I closed it as she sat in the chair.

She withdrew her Earth radio, "Your sister and I, as do all the Korina Jurinas, believe it is time. Yannta to Sklera."

My sister replied, "Is she there?"

"Yes."

"Tural. Reports are that the Treaslok population is approximately the size of our own. The Treaslok have been oppressed, their economy is in disarray, their social structure weakened, and their leadership destroyed. There are great problems to solve. We do not have the willingness to execute four million. We need a long time solution.

"The Treaslok land is much distant from Antrana. It is therefore ideal for an extension of power. In our tradition, only the bloodline may rule. As you have proven yourself these last months, the decision has been made that you assume command of the Treaslok Empire with the title of Torino Secera."

My fingers stopped tapping my hip.

*What?*

"Only Mranda, of the Elite guards, and the six Korina Jurinas are aware of your bloodline relationship to the House Kretahla. You will have the assistance of Jurina Yannta for the duration of two months to establish your own Council of Jurinas. You may choose any six Jurinas from my council as permanent officers. I recommend Jurina Cinzia as a member of your Korina staff. The Erskan Council has twenty five jurinas, I expect that you will manage with a staff of fifteen for the first year.

"Kendra will stay in Treaslok until Yannta returns.

"Yannta will assist you with the plans for occupation and conversion. She has extensive experience in this area. Foremost among your priorities is to establish communications with the civilian population. They are likely anticipating mass executions and are considering an escape or revolt.

"Do you have questions?"

I had a thousand questions.

They would wait.

It was apparent that Yannta's covert effort at an alternate plan was not much of a secret.

"Understood. You will make the announcement in two hours?"

"That is correct. With great power comes great responsibility. You can no longer place yourself at risk of injury or death in combat. You have been afforded a great level of freedom in the past, allowing you to move about at will. That luxury ends in two hours. Though you are widely regarded as the best Erskan swordswoman in many years, I strongly recommend that you identify competent officers to engage in direct combat."

My emotions were running from elation and honor in taking the family title to those of disappointment in the realization that the impending change in my life was about to limit me. Limit me in ways that I had seen often trouble my sister during the last two decades.

"Half of the navy is yours," Sklera offered. "You will retain one-half of the warriors for now; I expect that you will find those that want to relocate to Treaslok and those that you will need to acquire from the defeated Treaslok warriors. We have never acquired warriors from the enemy, but it is impossible that we will execute the remaining thirty-thousand warriors. This would surely have a damaging effect on our relations with the civilian population. We must find –" she paused. "*You* must find other options."

"Understood. Thank you."

"Congratulations, Vercella," she said.

Yannta snapped her radio into her belt pouch and then saluted me, "Congratulations, Torino Secera Vercella Tural."

I returned the salute.

"We should draw your list of names now. The announcement will cause unease among the ranks. You must immediately identify primary command officers essential to the current operations."

Yannta looked out the door for her aide and waved her over. The woman brought her a black lacquered box, which Yannta handed to me.

I snapped the catch and looked. Inside were the silver siglet rings of Erskan military rank affixed to the red cloth backing.

"There are two sets of four rings," I noted.

"Those are yours. Sklera will add a siglet to her, making five." She pointed at one of the rows of three siglets. "Those will, I expect, belong to Cinzia."

"Is she aware?"

"No. This has been closely held. Only the Korinas, your sister's frey, and my frey know about this."

"I will be passing over twenty-three jurinas," I noted, closing the box. "Thank you."

"You are welcome. You could have passed them over when you were eighteen years old," she replied. "I will be here for a time to help."

"That means a great deal to me, Jurina Yannta."

She chuckled. "I shall not call you Torino Secera Tural in private if you agree to call me Yannta."

Though she had just used that title a moment ago.

"Agreed, Yannta. Let us learn the progress of the Earth man. He may have valuable information."

Yannta followed me into the main hall, which was quickly being transformed into our Command Center.

We moved to the table and observed that his condition was worse. Two of our – two of *my* – best medical doctors attended to him. He lay on his side, half-curled into a ball. A blanket covered his body except for his head.

"Jurina Tural," one doctor approached me. "Much of his skin peeled away as we cleaned him. It is – " she shook her head. "It appears they have tortured him for a long time. We cannot speak words with him."

I placed my right hand on her shoulder, "Thank you for trying. How much longer do you believe he has to live?"

"I am surprised he is alive now."

I moved to where several senior warriors stood nearby the table. I crouched down to his face. His body experienced minor trembles and his breathing was short.

It reminded me all-too-much of being at Hula's side when she died.

Cognizant of the others around me – my soon-to-be-staff – I swallowed once and then placed my hand on his bruised shoulder.

His eyes opened.

"Are you in comfort?" I asked in English.

"You speak English," he said, his voice cracking.

"Yes, I can talk in Earthspeak. I is Tural. Are you in comfort?"

"Yes, I am. Thank you." He closed his eyes for a moment. I almost gasped, but held my breath. He looked at me again, "Tural. I know that name."

"Why are you in this here, in here place?" I asked.

He paused. Then tears ran down his face. "I was on Louis' team. We all were. But when we were lost here and could not leave, Louis sold us to them. He left us to die. Carson. How is Carson?

"You are the one to be living," I said.

"Oh, god," he said, more tears flowed. "My brother." He cried for a moment.

"My medical woman says you are hurt bad," I told him.

"I know," he said. "I cannot feel the hurt anymore. I..."

He closed his eyes.

Then, "Please find Louis. Kill him."

"I will," I said. "Who did this to you?"

"We never wanted to hurt anyone," he cried. "I am sorry for what we did to your people. All of the people. It was only the money. Not to hurt anyone."

His eyes fluttered. "Who did this? All of them. No. Some helped us when they could. Not all were the same. Not all. Louis made them. He killed many of them that did not go along with him."

His body shook.

"I don't want to die," he said.

I took his hand and held onto it. "I am here to be beside you," I said, trying to soothe him.

My emotions were about to get to me. I closed my eyes for a moment and saw a flash of Hula.

"Thank you for being kind to me," he whispered.

"Shhhh," I said. "We will take care of you and –"

He stopped breathing.

My fingers on his neck found no sign of life.

I pulled the blanket over his head.

The room was quiet.

"I caught only part of that," Cinzia said.

There were more than thirty warriors in the room. I was sure that many felt the revulsion that I did at the way of the Treaslok mistreatment of the frey.

"Corrigan betrayed the other trenama with him. This one wants us to kill Corrigan for revenge."

Yannta nodded. "Everyone wants Corrigan dead."

I looked to an aide, "Have his body and those of the other Earth men removed and placed into the outside. I want their bodies burned separately from the Treaslok dead."

I said to another aide, "Bring Rijella Monu here."

\* \* \* \* \*

I lay a map down to where we had pushed together several tables. I pointed at the center. "Monu, tell me about these positions on the border."

She had been permitted to retain her Treaslok uniform, though the rank had been removed and she had her wrists manacled together in front of her. Considering the traditional Erskan procedure called for execution of all military personnel, this was a significant development that Monu recognized in her favor.

"These walls border Dola,"

"Dola?" I asked.

She blinked. "Yes. Dola. The city. The name of our city. There are five-thousand warriors on the wall. There are only three gates, here and here and south here."

Yannta, in broken Treaslok, faced her, "Why? Why are there so many warriors there?"

"For defense," Monu replied, another surprised expression on her face.

"Defense? Defense from whom?" I asked, trying to hide my concern.

Monu squared her shoulders and looked at me. "The Ineer and her frey Corrigan did not only wage war against you Erskans." She pointed to a half-dozen other cities to the northeast, east, and southeast of Dola, "These are not Treaslok lands."

"Netra!" Cinzia exclaimed in Erskan. She looked at me, "Do I understand this correctly? They are fighting all of these others? Why?"

"Yes." I looked at Monu, "Why do you have this many wars?"

"The Ineer felt confident to make war when she had the great weapons. Much land was taken and then the weapons were moved to the attack on your land. But the great weapons were lost in the fighting with you. After that the other nations fought against us and we had to retreat to the barrier wall."

"We need to contact them and advise that the Treaslok have been defeated," Yannta told the assembled room.

"Monu, will they listen?" I asked.

"The Ineer ordered us to do – to do actions we never did before. I do not believe it is likely the other nations will accept anything other than you giving all Treaslok warriors to them – for executions. And they will want our males."

The realization of this situation formed in my head. I inherited a catastrophe.

"What are the Treaslok warriors on the barrier wall doing now?" I demanded.

"I do not know."

"Are they aware of the collapse of your military?"

"I do not know. Probably. This was so... so sudden." She shook her head.

"Are you in active combat anywhere along here?" Yannta asked.

"Yes," Monu replied. "The Busai, here, are the greatest concern. We have repelled their attacks three times in the last four months. I expect another attack soon."

"'Soon' meaning...?" I asked.

I heard that name before, "Busai." Where?

"Today. Next week. Any time."

"The smoke from the fires at the seaport – it is a long distance, but we must expect it can be seen from the border wall," I noted. "The Busai could sense an opportunity."

Kendra was joined by Uimisla. They listened to our conversation.

Yannta, across the table from me, took her hands off the map and stood straight, about to speak. Her lips moved, but then she smiled.

"Yes, Jurina Yannta?" I asked.

"Shall we contact the Torino and ask her to delay her congratulatory message to the warriors on our great Erskan victory?"

Two Erskan clocks had been laid on the map. I looked at the time.

"With your permission," I said, "we shall provide the Torino with an update and submit a request to retain the bulk of the forces that she was prepared to receive home. And then we may continue with the congratulatory message, as planned, in thirty minutes."

Her smile grew. "I concur."

"Aide," I waved a teenaged warrior over to me. "Find the location of the civilians that Jurina Cinzia repositioned two days ago and bring them here – politely. No. Instead," I pointed to Visada, "I want you to personally see to Weko's safe arrival here. Inform her that she and another woman of her choosing will meet with me – that should limit their resistance, if any. I want them here within two hours. We will establish communications with the civilian population today."

I pointed to Monu, "Provide this aide here with the names of your former council and known living rijellas. Also, I want the names of senior officers on the barrier wall. We will dispatch Erskan warriors to take over control of the defenses."

"Uimisla," I said, looking to the woman that was, unknown to her, soon to be my senior engineer, "when can you have the first bulk food shipments delivered here?"

"Now, Jurina Tural."

"Wait. We will begin the operation after Weko, the civilian, and Monu can agree to make a public announcement.

I looked at Yannta and nodded.

"Your attention," she said. She waited until the thirty-plus women in the room were looking at her. "The Torino will deliver a congratulatory message by the radio in twenty-five minutes. It is mandatory that all senior staff listed here attend a station equipped with a radio." Yannta handed several sheets of printed names around. "Aides, see to it that the names on this list are contacted immediately."

Six women took the sheets and left the room.

I looked at Monu. "Are there other rijella officers that have survived and should be here?"

She looked down at the floor for a moment, then toward at the force of over thirty Erskans that surrounded her and the table in her former palace. "No others here in the palace. As you may know when you were outside of our gate, that I led a rebellion against the loyalists to Ineer. Those of us true to our – our now-dead Torino – executed them. You will find that most of the rijellas on the great wall were sent to that dangerous frontier because their loyalty to the Ineer was suspect. Most, if not all, of the warriors on the borders do not support the Ineer."

"And you?" Cinzia asked. "Without other Treaslok here, we are unable to know what your role has been over the last two years."

"I have done what I could to help," Monu said. "I will admit to my actions, and I am prepared to face the consequences. In my defense, in many times I made adjustments to the orders."

"Explain," I told her.

"I positioned myself to be in charge of civilian security. Two months ago we had a rebellion in the south of the city. A team of Ineer loyalists disappeared. My orders were to raze a ten-square block around the area, without regard to civilian lives. Instead, I sent two trusted officers to warn the civilians to evacuate. We torched a two-square block area to give the appearance we had followed orders. No one was injured or killed. But I am guilty of committing aggression against my own people's lives, yes."

"You will shortly have an opportunity to respond to accusations of your people," I said. "If this is true, perhaps you will find them conciliatory."

Monu nodded.

"We will assemble here in fifteen minutes," I instructed the officers and aides. "Monu, you must remain under guard by that warrior and shackled until later today. You understand, yes?"

"Yes," she nodded.

Yannta moved her head in the direction of our small office and I followed.

Once inside the room, she pressed her buttocks against the edge of the small desk and crossed her arms before her. Then she laughed.

I tapped my hip for a moment. Then I laughed as well.

"I am sure your sister would rescind the promotion," she wiped a tear from her eye.

I shook my head. "No. I am prepared to do this. It is my responsibility and my duty to see this through."

Yannta ran her fingers along the seam of her black leather skirt. Then she looked at her gray-painted fingernails for a moment. "In all honesty, Tural, I do not envy you. But I admire your dedication. I will stand by as your counsel until you are ready to release me."

She laughed again, and then stood near me. "It was never intended for you to be in this situation."

"I know. I will handle it."

"Hmm. Do you intend to be promoted to Torino Secera wearing such a dirty field uniform?

I looked at my slightly worn and faded top and short combat skirt. One of the strips had been torn. At least it was straight.

"No. Thank you."

"After the announcement, who do you desire to pin the siglets upon you?"

"It would be an honor for you to do so," I replied.

"It is an honor," she smiled. "I recommend that you then immediately make a statement by promoting Cinzia."

"Yes."

"You have less than fifteen minutes," she noted, taking her radio from its holder and placing it near her face. "In the meantime, I have to talk with your sister."

"I should participate," I protested.

"Tural, I will see to it. Oh, do you know what will happen at the ceremony?"

"Yes." I had been prepared for this on several occasions during the last ten years.

"It is not customary for the new Torino to make a speech. Choose your words carefully if you should decide. Now, get dressed."

# Chapter Thirteen
## Coronation of Blood

"Thank you," I told the aide. I closed the door and laid the new uniform onto the bed.

Alexi should be here.

He would bathe me.

He would dress me.

He would set my hair.

He would attend the announcement and ceremony.

He would participate in the celebration of the victory, however short-lived, and help us plan to deal with our new problems.

And he ...

I had commandeered the closest officer's quarters to be found. Later I would move into Ineer's spacious rooms.

All drawers had been emptied onto the floor. All sheets turned over. All paintings examined. The search had been made to ensure that weapons were confiscated.

It was quiet.

My stomach felt somewhat unsettled. This happened a couple of times this week.

I took a sip of water from a flask, and then I stripped off my field uniform and gently laid it on the bed. I pulled off the cloth thong and replaced it with a clean one. The black, well-oiled and shiny floor-length skirt buckled around my waist. I pulled on my leather bra and then partially covered it with a pressed sleeveless white blouse. I repositioned the StacGun in my right thigh boot and resisted the urge to buckle my sword behind my back. A Torino rarely carried a sword, and even then it was for ceremonial purposes. After the announcement it would be prohibitive for me to engage in actual combat.

"I shall not carry you often again," I said to it.

Alexi would have held it up behind me until I fixed the buckles across my breasts.

"Thirteen years of field combat," I said. I held my scabbard and sword in my outstretched hands. It had never felt so heavy. Thirteen years

It was sixty-seven years old. It was my grandmother's weapon.

I used my sword to kill more than four-hundred women.

It was a bloody journey.

A knock at the door startled me.

"Jurina Tural?" said a young woman's voice.

"Come," I said.

It was an aide. "Jurina Yannta advises there are two minutes until the radio celebration."

I sat my sword on the bed and then walked into the hallway.

My stomach remained unsettled. I tried to tell myself that I was nervous from the ceremony.

\* \* \* \* \*

More than sixty women stood in columns, according to rank and position, in the room. A handful of Treaslok prisoners, led by Rijella Monu, stood at the rear corner, each manacled unobtrusively with their hands before them. This was a stark departure from traditional Erskan protocol in that they were alive, much less permitted to attend an important state ceremony.

A platform had been placed at the front of the room. Yannta, Kendra, Cinzia, and eight of the Kuretno-grade senior officers were present on the first row. They faced the rest of the attendees in the room.

A senior aide placed Yannta's radio onto the lacquered box which contained the siglets. Another table on the back row had our third radio. These three radios would remain here so that we could communicate with Antrana and with our own field operations.

I would try to obtain a fourth and fifth radio, considering our new circumstances. Surely a debate about resources would soon occur. It would be to my advantage to find the right opportunity to engage my sister in an analytical debate rather than one of passion.

On the negative side was that we now had one less functioning radio to use.

And no one to repair it.

I strode to Yannta's side, nearest the platform. I was the last person to enter the room. Our Elite guards blocked the three entrances to the room.

Several Erskan flags were displayed on the walls. The bold double-blue and red colors added life to the room. I allowed myself a smile for a moment or two.

"Your attention," Yannta ordered.

All present stood straight.

Yannta approached the table and pressed the "talk" button on the radio.

"My Torino, we are assembled and we await your message."

"Thank you, Jurina Yannta," replied my sister, her voice strong and clear.

Yannta faced the radio toward the attendees and then she stepped back a few feet. The aide crouched near the floor and monitored the radio.

"Today we celebrate our victory. Foremost, we have defeated a hated enemy. I commend and honor all Erskan women that have made this invasion the most successful operation in the history of all Aervanta. Erskan civilians made great sacrifices in their livelihood to provide materiel and women for our cause. Many Erskan warriors have paid the ultimate sacrifice in order to protect ourselves from future hostility. We have crossed the seas. Antrana is victorious."

She paused. Then, "No one will dispute that it is the tradition of all our cultures for the victora to capture and assimilate the civilian population, enslave the frey, and execute all enemy warriors. We shall not take this course of action."

There was a noticeable relief on the faces of the Treaslok officers in the rear of the room.

"Yes, we have defeated our enemy. We have also liberated an oppressed population that has been subjected to tyranny and terror by an unnatural, alien influence. In this we may afford sympathy with the Treaslok and grant a level of leniency rarely demonstrated in the past.

"It is important for the Treaslok to not misunderstand our generosity for weakness. Make no mistake that Treaslok lands are now and will firmly be under the control of the Erskan military and shall be assimilated to the Erskan culture. Resistance will be dealt with swiftly and effectively. In this I will reserve the ultimate decision to unilaterally rescind peaceful efforts to accommodate and encourage development of Treaslok life and prosperity in the Erksan tradition.

"I shall repeat my last statement again. I reserve the ultimate decision to unilaterally rescind peaceful efforts to accommodate and encourage development of Erskan culture and prosperity. This is important for all to understand in light of my next statement."

I stiffened my shoulders and looked dead-straight at the farthest point on the wall. In a moment all eyes would be riveted upon me.

I resisted the urge to run my fingertips upon my hip.

My shoulders felt light, unburdened by my sword.

"Torino Hirlana Kretahla, my mother, ruled Erskan lands for thirty-nine years until, as her daughter, I succeeded her. The truth has been long concealed that Hirlana had two daughters of the House Kretahla. It was our mother's desire that my young sister earn her right to join in the twenty-century-long Torino lineage."

Dozens of warriors looked from side to side, first surprised to learn there was a sister. And then in an attempt to guess who that was.

On my right peripheral vision I could see Cinzia lean slightly forward. It must have been torture for her to resist turning her head in my direction.

"We are now aware that our expectations for a conclusive victory here is no longer realistic. As they had done to us, the former Treaslok regime instigated multiple wars on their own land. Now, Treaslok forces are defeated. They are ineffective at providing defense to the Treaslok civilian population. We Erskans find ourselves in the unenviable position of having to provide support and defense, while engaging in diplomatic or military actions at the borders. This is a dangerous situation. This situation requires the attention of an Erskan warrior that has proven herself time and again. This Erskan warrior has earned the right to lead Erskan interests abroad and command as a daughter of the House Kretahla.

"It is a great honor that I announce the rightful appointment to Torino Secera of my sister, Vercella Tural Kretahla."

I failed in my attempt to hold my breath so that it would be timed with her announcement. Instead, I gradually let out air as my sister's words hung in the air for a moment.

It was one of those instances where you felt time had stopped. But you knew otherwise.

"Korina Jurina Yannta," my sister said, "I request that you perform the ceremony on my behalf."

"Understood," Yannta replied. She stepped forward, made a sword's sharp left turn, and stopped before me.

The aide stood, lifted the box in her hands to Yannta, and presented it with the lid open.

Yannta removed a two-thousand year-old dagger. It had a twisted, four-inch blade on a leather-wrapped hilt. The ancient blade was marked by three chips on the edge. Though it was well-used in its day, Sklera earlier warned me about the sharpness of the blade.

Yannta placed the dagger into her right hand, laying the blade across the palm of her left. "Torino, I am ready," Yannta said.

"From the blood of one woman," Sklera's voice addressed us all by radio.

Yannta closed her left hand and slowly drew the blade out.

I heard her breathe in as her blood dripped down the blade and onto the floor.

Yannta handed the dagger to me, hilt-first.

I took the dagger into my right hand and laid the blade into my left.

"To the blood of another," Sklera said.

That was my cue. I closed my left hand and slowly pulled the blade through.

Sharp and cold, the blade burned as I tried to balance the importance of the ceremonial act against the possibility of rendering my hand useless for the rest of my life.

My blood dripped down the blade and blended with Yannta's own.

Yannta and I held our bloodied hands toward one another in the air for a moment before we pressed the palms against each. Our fingers intertwined.

The Torino continued speaking: "We find strength in each of our hearts for the future to rule with honor, honesty, and valor. We find strength to protect our people and ensure prosperity."

I felt blood dripping down my wrist and to the underside of my forearm. Had I cut too deep?

Yannta and I locked eyes, unblinking. I was unable to read her expression.

"We find strength to fight into the dark of night and the light of day for what we are sworn to protect."

Yannta squeezed her fingers tight and pressed the back of my knuckles.

I returned the pressure in-kind.

We continued to lock eyes.

"We find strength in the rule of Torino Secera Vercella Tural Kretahla."

Yannta, maintaining her vise-like grasp, stomped her right boot once onto the stone floor.

The room boomed as the Erskans stomped their boots eight successive times on the floor.

"Shia-talso," my sister said.

"Shia-talso," Yannta told me. Her painted lips pressed into a slight smile.

"Shia-talso," the women in the room repeated, their words reverberating off the stone walls.

The aide stood between us and held out a red cloth. I lay the dagger onto it and waited as she wiped the blade clean and then placed it into the box.

Yannta and I released the other's hand.

The aide handed red cloths to me and to Yannta. We wrapped the cloth around our palms and the aide tied a knot on the back of each hand.

Yannta snapped an Erskan salute to me.

All Erskan warriors saluted.

I returned the salute and faced the room.

"Torino Primera Sklera Kretahla," Yannta said, "I present you with Torino Secera Tural Kretahla."

"Thank you, Korina Jurina Yannta," my sister replied, her voice somewhat lighter than previously.

"Thank you, Torino Sklera Kretahla," I told her. I was pleased that my voice was strong and did not crack. "Thank you, Korina Jurina Yannta."

I stole a glance at Cinzia. Her eyes were as wide as I had ever seen.

I took one step forward to address the room.

"The strength of an Erskan warrior comes from inside her heart. Strength also comes from years of training and education. Finally, strength comes from having courageous and dedicated women with us when we engage the enemy and confront the unknown. It has been my good fortune to learn from the greatest warriors of our time. I will assemble a Council of Jurinas to rule the Treaslok lands, and I have been granted the option to appoint jurina officers from the Erskan Torino Council."

I nodded to the aide. She held the box open for me and I withdrew two pair of three-circle siglets. The aide stepped back.

"Jurina Ecorse Cinzia, approach," I told her.

Cinzia stiffened for a moment, surprised. She composed herself in a half-second and marched to my presence.

She saluted.

Perhaps Cinzia felt awkward saluting me.

But I was already comfortable with it.

"Jurina Ecorse Cinzia, you are promoted to the rank of Korina Jurina and chief counsel of the Torino Secera."

I removed the one-circle siglets from her blouse collar and snapped on the three-ring siglets.

"Thank you, Torino," she said. Her eyes sparkled.

I nodded.

Cinzia saluted again and then moved to her place in line when I acknowledged her.

"Other assignments will be made in rapid succession over the next several days," I addressed the room. "We are each aware that there will be no respite from combat at this time. Orders have already been given to secure control of the city and outlaying lands. There is an imminent threat of attack from several bordering nations. And we have not fully accomplished our mission until we have seen to it that the off-worlder Louis Corrigan has been executed for his trespasses against all of our people. Senior officers are to remain here. All others are dismissed to attend to your duties. Shia-talso."

"Dismissed," Cinzia said, after the briefest pause. She had quickly recognized her new role in effecting my orders.

Most of the room disbursed.

Yannta handed the radio to me.

"Contact me when you need assistance," my sister said.

"Did Yannta advise of our request to maintain present warrior forces?" I asked.

Yannta nodded.

"Yes. I am recalling only a quarter of the forces now instead of half."

"Thank you. We shall talk again this evening?"

"Yes." She paused, "Contact me if you need anything, sister."

"I will."

"Sklera, out."

Cinzia approached and stood beside Yannta and I. Her mouth opened, but then shut.

I smiled. "I would value your suggestions at any time. That is your job and I also expect it as a friend."

"This is a great honor I never expected," she said. "I do not have the words to show my gratitude."

"There will be plenty of time for you to hug one another later, but we have two pressing matters," Yannta said, sternly, but with a grin of her own.

"The border and internal security, yes?" Cinzia stated.

"Yes," Yannta nodded. "Aide, pull those tables over and set out our maps."

We stood as the tables were moved.

"Monu," I pointed to the Treaslok that stood at the rear wall. "Here, with your colleague."

The Treaslok rijella approached, a junior officer, also shackled at the wrists, was beside her.

"Who are you?" I asked.

"First Legion Commander Lendon," she replied. "Torino," she added.

"What is the 'First Legion?'" I inquired.

"Our internal security," Monu explained. "This is one of the two officers I sent to warn the civilians."

Visada came into the room, leading Weko and another civilian that I recognized from the home where Hula had died. I nodded at Visada, and then she and two warriors escorted the civilians to our table.

Weko bowed her head to me.

"It is good to see you are alive," I told her.

"Yes, thank you, Torino Tural. May I ask of your plans for our people?"

"As I had promised you, we will stay executions of civilians and most of the military. You had told me that you were part of an organized resistance."

"Yes, Torino."

"I have assumed that there are, in fact, numerous resistance units within the city. I want you to issue a call for leaders of resistance areas to identify themselves to my block commanders. We will meet in one hour with these leaders to begin the process of identifying those in the Treaslok military that have committed atrocities against the civilians versus those that attempted to minimize their role. For this I need civilian assistance."

Weko's face brightened. "Yes, Torino. I relish the opportunity to do this."

"Do you recognize either of these two Treaslok officers?" I asked.

"No," Weko said.

The other civilian stared at Monu and Lendon.

"Well?" I asked.

"That one," she pointed at Lendon. "We have met before. Where?"

"In the rear of the shoe store on Garneth of the Way," Lendon reminded her.

"Yes. She warned us about the warriors coming to burn our homes."

"Much of a coincidence," Cinzia pointed out.

"All of this did happen in one small area," I noted.

"It is the truth," Lendon turned to face me. "I could have been executed for my action."

"I need the names of Treaslok officers on the border at the great wall. Monu, you will accompany us in two hours to the border."

Cinzia looked at Visada. "Kuretno Visada, make sure the route to the border has been secured."

The aide holding the siglets was standing a few feet away. I waved at her and opened the box.

"As senior Kuretno, and for having proved yourself in battle," I reached into the box and removed the circles that Cinzia had worn, "you are promoted to the rank of Jurina, effective immediately."

I handed the two siglets to Cinzia. "Would you do the honors, Korina Jurina Cinzia?"

Cinzia nodded. Visada stood at attention while Cinzia removed the three silver bars and replaced them with the circles.

They exchanged salutes.

"Thank you," Visada said.

Cinzia waited four seconds, then, "About that security sweep?"

Visada smiled and saluted again. She moved backwards, turned smartly on her heels, and approached a group of seven Kuretno officers.

"Cinzia," I said, "mobilize forty harfala to head to the border, to the center gate. We need to be moving in three hours. I am concerned about the risk of an attack."

"You are going yourself?" Yannta asked.

"I am not going on the other side of the wall," I said. "I appreciate the warning. Thank you."

"It is not good for morale for the Torino to be killed in combat on her first day," Yannta said.

I laughed. "It is not good for my morale."

Cinzia nodded.

"Kendra, Uimisla," I said, "pre-position the first food shipments at these locations in two hours. When will you have the first pier constructed?"

"Tonight," Kendra said. "We will be able to unload two ships per hour."

"Quite a good job of destroying everything," Uimisla said. "We cannot get a single ship into their port."

"Thank you," I replied.

I had a sheet of carefully-written tasks handed to me by an aide.

Alexi called it a *to-do* list.

"We will make announcements to the civilian population in two hours. I will answer questions of up to thirty representatives of city zones. You will see on this map how we have drawn these zones. We have an Erskan officer appointed and stationed now at each of these zones. Weko, it is your responsibility to assure that we have a Treaslok civilian contact the zone leader within one hour and thirty minutes. They will be transported here.

"I can tell you now what the primary message will be. First, repeating the edict of the Torino Primera that we may activate immediate force as needed. Second, that we will protect the Treaslok from her enemies. Third, that we will seek and punish Treaslok that willingly collaborated with Ineer and Corrigan. And fourth, that this is not an occupation of Treaslok lands but a cultural adaptation. We will become one Erskan people."

"There will be those that resist, of course," Weko said. She squared her shoulders to me.

I could feel Cinzia tense.

"Then they shall be executed. There is no other option."

"How is this different than the Suir det Ineer?" Weko asked.

"Your people lived under arbitrary laws. You lived without prosperity. Little food. Few opportunities. Whereas the women of Antrana have more food than we can eat. We have more natural resources than we can use. We will share these techniques with our Treaslok sisters. In short time we will enhance your living conditions. I believe you will be thankful."

"Thankful through force," Weko said.

"That is another way of explanation," I nodded. "Other differences you may find from Ineer and Corrigan are that the civilian and Erskan officer in each zone will meet me each week so that I may hear about problems and find ways to address them. We will also conscript former members of the Treaslok military into the forces here. And – well, you shall hear about these in less than two hours."

"And what of our males?" she asked.

"That has not yet been determined," I lied.

"I see. You have everything else 'determined' except for this?"

"There are differences of opinion among my staff. I continue to take the issue under advisement. For the time being, we will not take your frey. Now, you should go."

Weko nodded. Cinzia pointed to a Kuretno officer that had been listening. The two of them walked out of the room.

"Monu," I addressed the Treaslok officer, "we shall ride to the border following the meeting with the civilians. We have your list of names?"

Monu looked at an aide who then nodded.

"Jurina Cinzia. Assure that we are treating the captured Treaslok warriors well. Have Kuretno Fyana, here, address the senior prisoners in the presence of Lendon. You will find a pre-written statement in here," I handed her a scroll. "The most important part is to advise them that we will begin releasing military prisoners in five days, after they have been documented."

"Understood," Cinzia nodded.

"Jurina Yannta," I asked, "Do you have suggestions?"

She shook her head no.

Either I was on the correct path or she would wait for a private opportunity to correct me.

"Very well, thank you." I looked at another aide. "I have not received any situation reports within the last half-hour. I need to know what is happening."

"Yes, Torino. We will have the information in one minute." She stepped away to consult with other messengers.

I barely overheard Monu whispering words to Lendon.

"You have words to say to us?" I demanded.

"Only that we were once this efficient," Monu said.

"Guard," I said, "take four guards and escort these prisoners to their rooms for a half-hour of personal time. Then return here. We will eat before our civilian meeting and then the ride to the border."

"Thank you, Torino," Monu said.

They were escorted away.

It was then just a dozen Erskan warriors.

"Well done," Yannta said, touching the right side of her forehead. "Lay the facts of their situation, warn them of the penalties, and then offer conciliation on a few items."

"The highest potential for resistance will happen in two days when every Treaslok begins Erskan language classes," Kendra smiled.

# Chapter Fourteen
## A Disagreement with Kale

The civilian meeting went better than planned. I established the conditions of the occupation and listened to the civilian representatives for twenty minutes.

Months of planning for this did not only include the military conquest. We had planned to the minute detail of the civilian conversion. And the script was being well-followed.

It was the non-execution of captured warriors that was hastily planned.

The civilians asked about their imprisoned warriors. We advised that Treaslok military liaisons were already meeting with the prisoners. We advised that they would not be executed, but would be identified and documented, and that we would begin releasing them in five days.

In fact, we secretly planned to release the lowest-rank warriors in thirty-hours. They would spread the news that they were being treated well, fed, and so on. We carefully choreographed the balance of where they were released so that we did not face concentrations of warriors from the same military units.

An abundance of food was already positioned. Each zone civilian would return to their area with a message about the Erskan warnings and promises. They would already have food to provide to the civilians. Thousands of flowers were crated-in. And we gave them pallets of new, colorful material for clothing.

It was also noted that the Erskans were assuming the task of protecting the Treaslok from further attack.

Yet there hung over them the thin threat that Treaslok frey would be captured and taken to Antrana.

It was not the threat of execution that would stay the thoughts of a Treaslok revolt; it was the loss of their males.

I understood this personally.

I stepped out of my room and into the hall. Two aides stood by. An Elite guard followed the three of us to the palace courtyard.

The afternoon waned; the sun cast long shadows about the palace grounds. Deep ruts cut through the grass in a hundred places.

Parts of the palace wall lay scattered about.

Cinzia stood beside her horse. Visada was to her right, standing.

Behind both of them were two harfala, one-hundred sixty-two warriors, mounted and ready. Beyond the remnants of the palace outer wall were another three-thousand seventy-eight warriors, plus support teams.

In the middle were Monu and Lendon. Both were dressed in clean Treaslok uniforms, still shackled, although loosely.

A stable frey crouched to his hands and knees and I used his back to lift myself onto my horse.

Cinzia and Monu followed suit.

The wind was still. Clouds formed in the east.

Yannta appeared at the damaged door to the palace, flanked by several aides and her own frey, Tekor, just arrived from Antrana.

"Wait here," I said. I rode the fifty foot distance to Yannta.

She saluted. "Remember, do not get killed."

"That is not on my to-do-it list."

"Then why do you carry your sword?"

"I would tend to ride to the right without the weight to balance me."

"Yes, of course." She moved closer to me, out of hearing range of the others. "Be more careful now."

"I will."

She saluted again and stepped back.

I turned about and nodded to Cinzia.

Cinzia ordered the twelve escort riders to begin. They rode first from the harfala, six to each side, and monitored our flank.

I rode behind them, to the left of Cinzia and left of Visada, as we headed toward the eastern wall.

\* \* \* \* \*

The ride took two hours to leave the city of Dola. Then farther we rode, overnight, occasionally encountering a Treaslok check-point which was typically provisioned with a dozen warriors.

They saw the four-thousand-strong invasion force of Erskans and immediately surrendered. Monu and Lendon assured them of their safety before they were returned to the city. Erskan warriors took their place.

We posted notices, written in Treaslok, at the town centre of eight Treaslok villages, to advise them of the Erskan occupation.

We reached the great wall at ten in the morning.

It was true to its name. Easily fifty feet high, with guard columns spaced evenly at five-hundred feet. It was constructed of stone and more of the brick-like material that likely had bars of metal inside.

The road rose up to a crest and then dropped gradually for about two-thousand feet before us, where the road terminated through a military camp and to a sturdy gate.

Several camp fires created thin trails of smoke that drifted to the cloudy sky.

"A storm is building," Cinzia said as we came over the hill.

"Bring the column to a halt," I said, "before the Treaslok can view the size of our force. Then go over the other side and have them spread out a bit."

Cinzia raised her left hand and then turned to pass the orders onto Visada.

"Yes, it looks like a good one is coming," I agreed, looking skyward.

"Monu?" Cinzia asked.

"Yes, bring her here." I looked down at the camp, which was now alerted to our presence and was mobilizing about a thousand warriors.

Cinzia pressed an order to a field aide to retrieve Monu. Then, "This is shameful. We caught them completely unprepared."

I nodded. "I count only one-hundred horses, several wagons, twelve catapults. How many warriors do you believe are on the top of the wall?"

"A couple hundred, here alone," Cinzia replied. "Two-thousand total?"

The Treaslok likely observed only thirty Erskans.

Visada rode to us. "Ready."

"I will back my horse two steps when you should have the entire column come over the hill. Pause. And then you decide whether to come in for combat or rather to form into camp."

"Understood," Visada said.

Monu reached us with her Erskan guard.

Two-thousand feet ahead, four Treaslok warriors gathered together on horses and rode toward us.

I moved forward, Cinzia, an Elite guard, Monu, her guard, and one of Visada's best archers with me.

We rode about half-way and I stopped.

"Recognize anyone?" I asked Monu.

"Yes."

"Is this good or bad?" Cinzia asked.

"Good."

The Treaslok came within twenty feet of us and stopped.

"It is true," the closest Treaslok said. She shook her head. She did not try to conceal her disappointment.

"Greetings, Peto," Monu said, her own face strained. "It is."

"The last message we received was that the port was under attack," Peto admitted.

"I am Tural," I told her. "Order your warriors to stand-down. Those that surrender will not be harmed."

A warrior near Peto clenched her teeth. Then, "We will surrender to... all forty of you?"

"No. More than forty," I replied. "This is a courtesy I am offering you. And this is because we intend to replace your warriors and defend the wall. Treaslok warriors will eventually be integrated within the Erskan forces. For now, you are to stand down. Senior officers that desire to remain on an advisory role are welcome."

"Peto," Monu said, "it is a complete loss. The Suit det Ineer and the Louis fled to the mountain fortress. The Erskans have not performed executions. Stand down. That is an order."

I moved my horse back two steps.

"I swore an oath to never surrender. I swore – " Peto was speaking. Her eyes widened.

The other Treaslok officers looked behind me.

"Stand down," I repeated. "But keep one quarter of your forces on the wall for now."

Peto sat higher in the saddle for a moment while she looked right and left. Then she sighed. "Kedo, stand-down."

A different Treaslok shook her head, but turned about and rode quickly to the front of the column of Treaslok warriors.

Cinzia flashed three fingers to Visada.

Visada sent on two lightly armed warriors.

"These warriors will take your weapons," Cinzia told them.

We waited a moment until the Treaslok removed their swords and knives. One crossbow was surrendered. They were handed to the two Erskan warriors.

An Erskan wagon came over the hill and was escorted by a dozen Erskans. Then the first of several hundred Erskans, led by Visada, rode down and headed toward the dejected Treaslok.

"How is the Anela Betel?" Peto asked Monu.

"It is fine," she replied. "All are fine. There is minimal damage to the city. The Erskans only attacked the seaport and military targets."

Peto frowned. "The Erskans did less harm to the civilians than the Ineer did to us."

We watched the Treaslok dismount. Weapons were confiscated and placed into the wagon.

Other Erskans relieved the Treaslok of catapult duty

Another wave of Erskans relieved the Treaslok warriors on the walls.

After ten minutes an Erskan messenger rode to us. "Jurina Visada advises the area is secure."

"Who are you, again?" Peto asked. "Your Treaslok is very good. I almost cannot hear an accent."

"Torino Secera Tural. And, thank you. Your Erskan will be perfect someday as well."

"'Torino,'" she said, twisting her lips thoughtfully. "I know that Erskan word."

"She is the Erskan leader over all of Treaslok," Monu said.

"I want a situation report," I told Peto. "Where is your command post?"

"Follow me, Torino," she said, turning about.

\* \* \* \* \*

"Busai forces are about three-thousand," Peto told us. She pointed over the side of the wall to a table-flat expanse of waist-high grasslands that stretched for at least twenty miles in all directions. "We placed the wall here to take advantage of the grounds. Behind us are the hills. This makes an enemy approach easily visible."

"In the daylight," Cinzia observed.

"Yes," Peto admitted. "Each guard column has a wall-mounted rapid-fire crossbow that is armed with at least five-hundred bolts. Each warrior has five flame-arrows that she can fire into the air and the ground to signal a night attack and light the target area. Mounted warriors in reserve can ride to active areas. Catapults are spaced a couple of miles apart so that they may be used against siege weapons."

"Well done," Cinzia admitted.

"The Great Wall is two-hundred years old," she said. "It has never been breached."

"When was the last attack?" I asked.

"Eight days ago," Peto replied.

"Do you have talk with them?"

"Not in a few months. We retreated to the wall. We have fought since then."

"What did they want?"

"All of our males."

"I will remain here for two days. Then I will return to Dola," I said. "I will leave three-thousand Erskans here to relieve your warriors. You may stay here or return with me. Senior Treaslok warriors will be held for a week in custody. Then they will be released. They can return home or to restricted duty. Erskan language, military protocol, and other training for officers will begin in one week."

"You intend to defend all of Treaslok now?" Peto asked.

"No. We will defend Erskan lands now," I corrected.

\* \* \* \* \*

"You look tired," Cinzia said.

"None of us have had much sleep," I replied.

Visada lifted a cup of wadu soup to her lips and nodded. "This will keep me awake. I should not be drinking it."

I put my bowl onto the small knee-high table. We sat around a small fire, outside of the few buildings.

The wind shifted direction in the last half-hour. The Orphans were low on the horizon and were barely visible through the clouds overhead.

Earlier, Visada moved our warriors to camp beside the Great Wall for protection against the threatening weather.

"This would be a perfect time for an attack," Visada said.

"Yes," Cinzia nodded. "I have been thinking about that for the last few hours."

"Yes," I agreed.

"What do you think of Monu?" I asked them.

"We keep her," Cinzia replied, without hesitation.

"I agree," Visada told me. "She has agreed to everything so far."

"True. That might be a problem," I said. "If she is too agreeable that may signal she's got other plans. We need to throw something at her soon that we expect she will fight. If she doesn't, then we have to worry."

"Are you asking for ideas?" Cinzia wondered.

"Yes."

"Tell her we will take all of the frey from senior officers to Antrana... as spoils of war," Visada offered.

"Does she have her own frey?" I asked them.

They both shrugged their shoulders.

"What was the name of the place they asked about earlier?" I inquired, trying to remember.

"Anela Betel," Cinzia answered.

"Let us find out if that is a residential area or a what. We could say we are going to destroy it and make room for a new Erskan cultural training center."

"And take their frey," Visada added.

I laughed. "And take their frey."

We were silent for a while.

I listened to the sounds of our warriors moving about. Horses made noise. Wind carried waves of different odors to us.

The flames of our small fire were pushed down by a short-lived gust of wind.

"The Treaslok probably think we are crazy, sitting out here," Visada noted.

"We'll go inside when it starts to rain," I told her. "I want to get a feel for the air here."

We were silent for a while longer.

My thoughts drifted to Alexi.

My frey.

I knew that soon I would have to face his death.

Keep moving now.

Do not think about it.

Not now.

Cinzia's face was only partially lit by the flames; was she thinking about Mermak?

I heard the Elite palace guard shift her feet. She was about fifteen feet behind us, armed with a StacGun.

"I have talked with several Treaslok warriors," Visada told us. "They are not happy that we defeated them. On the other hand, they are pleased to be rid of the Suit de Ineer. One warrior told me that they have had three-hundred per cent price increases over the last year."

"The warriors stationed here are those that the regime did not want," Cinzia noted.

"This could be the core group we use to rebuild the military," Visada suggested.

"Possibly," I nodded.

I could smell rain.

Cinzia and Visada stood. I got to my feet.

"I will take care of it," Visada said. She lifted a bucket of water toward the fire.

Cinzia and I headed to the heavily guarded commander's quarters for a restless night's sleep.

\* \* \* \* \*

I listened to the rain fall on the clay tiled roof.

The scent of the extinguished candles had long-since left the room.

"I miss him," Cinzia confided.

She lay on her sleeper, on the floor, a few feet to my left.

All of my warrior's tricks to fall asleep had failed.

My eyes stared at black shadows of the unfamiliar room.

I felt a tear drop onto my lip. "I know."

\* \* \* \* \*

"Two-thousand, perhaps three," Visada counted. She placed her fingertips on either side of the Earth seeing eye glasses.

It was mid-afternoon and the rain continued at a steady pace.

My coat barely kept my body dry. My hair, on the other hand, was soaked.

"What is that?" Peto asked.

Monu was also interested.

"We can see long distances with it," Cinzia told her.

Visada looked to her right. "No. There are more. Now six-thousand."

Monu frowned. "This is not normal."

Visada looked to her left. She shook her head and then looked at me, "We may want to re-arm the Treaslok. Quickly."

"What do you see?" I asked her as I uselessly looked eastward and squinted.

"Another three on the left."

"For those of you keeping a score," I said, "that is nine-thousand warriors." I looked at Monu and contemplated how to form a question of her.

She sensed my thoughts. "We will fight with you, not against you."

Cinzia nodded when I turned the other way and looked at her.

"Distribute their weapons immediately," I said to Visada. "And bring up the wagon with the Crest-Leeland."

I unsnapped my radio. It was the first time that the Treaslok would see it. "Tural to Yannta."

"Stand by for Yannta," an aide's voice replied.

Monu and Peto stared wide-eyed at the Earth device.

I wiped rain water from my brow.

"Yannta here."

"We are facing nine-thousand Busai forces. I need the first reserve to ride here. And prepare the second reserve."

"Please repeat. Did you say 'nine-thousand'? Nine, zero, zero, zero?"

"Correct, nine-thousand."

There was a pause.

A broad dotted line filled the horizon as the enemy approached our position.

"It will be no less than eight hours until the first reserve can arrive."

"We can defend for that," Peto said, still looking at the radio.

"You may consider the help of the Treaslok," Yannta suggested.

I saw weapons handed out below.

"Yes, good idea," I replied.

There was a pause. "You already did that, did not you?"

I laughed. "I appreciate your advice."

Yannta chuckled, "You are too polite to be a Torino."

Several Busai riders broke from the expansive line of warriors and headed toward our gate, avoiding but closely following the muddy path.

"I need to go," I said. "It looks like a meeting."

"Shia-talso," Yannta bade us.

I replaced the radio.

"Who is going with me?" I asked.

Cinzia shook her head. "You are not going anywhere... Torino."

I began to protest; however I was surprised when Monu also stepped in front of me. "Let us do this, please."

Her hair, though tied in the back, was strung out straight on the side of her head while water poured down onto her oil-rubbed coat. "Besides, none of you speak Busai."

"Very well," I relented.

Monu pointed to Belo, the assistant to Peto, "Get their horses and meet us at the gate."

Monu then turned to Cinzia and tipped her chin in a question.

"Yes," Cinzia said. "We go now."

With a sigh, I watched them hurry down the steps and mount the horses.

The heavy-machine gun was brought up to my position, mounted on the wall, and armed by its two-woman Erskan crew.

Assured by a heavy defensive presence on the wall, the gate was opened. Large metal-plated wood girders were removed from the base of the gate by an eight-woman Treaslok team. The metal-reinforced wood doors swung inside.

Cinzia, Monu, Belo, Visada, and an expert Erskan archer rode to meet the Busai, approximately one-thousand feet distant.

Their horses kicked up mud and wet grass behind them.

"Radio test," I heard Cinzia's voice over the sound of their horses splashing in the field.

"Good," I replied. Then I pressed the muted sound button.

"This will allow us to listen?" Peto said.

"Yes. We will also be able to talk here and this will not be known to the Busai."

The Erskan Elite guard smiled and kept her hand at-the-ready of her own StacGun. Other Erskan senior officers were at my side as well.

After another ten seconds the Erskans and Treasloks approached the five Busai on the field. They were about a thousand-feet distant; close enough to see, but not to pick out the details.

The two groups of five faced one another, horses still.

The rain was falling in waves which made visibility difficult, even with the use of the seeing-eye glasses which were perched on my nose.

"They are meeting now," I told everyone.

"Yeeduk beya torok," we heard through the radio.

"That is the Busai greeting," Peto told us.

"Yeeduk beya torok," Monu replied. Then, in Treaslok, "Kale, what do you want? This is not good weather for a battle."

"Are you the Erskan leader?" Kale asked.

"I am not. I speak for her," Cinzia replied in her best attempt at Treaslok.

"What did she say?" Kale demanded.

"She is not the Erskan leader, but she does speak for the Erskan leader," Monu replied in her perfect native Treaslok language.

"I will talk to the Erskan leader only," Kale demanded.

"No," Cinzia replied.

The Busai apparently understood that.

"Is she a coward?" Kale asked.

The rain was slowing and afforded us a better view.

To my right and left the great wall was lined with thousands of Erskan and Treaslok warriors.

The long line of Busai warriors remained stationary on the wet grassy plains.

"If fighting broke out now... there, a thousand feet away," I said to Pewa, a Kuretno junior grade officer.

Pewa frowned. "The Busai mounted warriors will get there before we could."

Our tactical position was unacceptable.

"Hurry!" I barked.

She excused herself from the wall and ran down to the ground. She and other officers pulled together a mounted force of a thousand warriors near the gate. Several dozen Treaslok joined in the formation.

"No. She is the bravest woman in all the world," Cinzia told her.

Monu translated, "Kale, fed ontoh, gal te ren brek stel to ne net."

"Is the brave woman there?" Kale asked.

"Yes," Cinzia replied.

There was a pause. I could see a slight movement of one Busai horse toward Cinzia. Cinzia's horse moved back.

"Where did you get this?" Cinzia demanded. Her voice was harsh.

"Kale, juut gene de nad daeo?" Monu translated.

"I will only speak with Tural," Kale said.

"Then you will wait here," Cinzia snapped.

Cinzia turned about and rode hard toward us.

Mud and water splashed in the air behind her horse.

Cinzia slapped the flanks of the horse with the loose end of the reins. She shouted at the horse to go faster.

The guards at the gate were nearly run down when Cinzia flew in. Her horse stumbled upon the mud and soggy grass and she came to an abrupt stop at the foot of the steps.

She looked up at me as light rain pelted her face. She was clearly distressed.

"What?" I asked, looking once over the wall. I hurried down the steps and met her.

She dismounted and came around to me.

In her hand was a polished steel collar.

I sucked in a breath as I took it from her hands. I rolled it over to read what I already knew would be there. "Property of Jurina Tural."

"What is that?" Peto asked, appearing by my side.

"Stay here," I told Cinzia. I stripped the reins from her hand, pulling them from her fingers.

"You cannot go out there," Cinzia said.

The Elite palace guard reached to take the reins from my hands.

"Do. Not. Interfere," I warned the guard. My voice was ice cold and as threatening as never before.

"My Torino," the guard protested.

"Okay," Cinzia told me.

She raised her hands before her and faced the Elite guard, "You heard your orders."

The guard retreated.

I mounted Cinzia's horse. I handed Alexi's collar down to Cinzia.

"Change your radio," Cinzia said as she reached to her own.

There were nearly a thousand mounted Erskan and Treaslok warriors ready to file through the gate if necessary. Three Erskans in the front lines were equipped with Earth weapons. The war wagon was positioned to the side by the gate.

I pressed the button on the radio, tossed the seeing-eye glasses to Cinzia, and then turned the horse about.

I rode beyond the gate at a moderate pace.

The image I would present would not be one of haste or recklessness.

"Radio test," I said.

"Good," Cinzia replied.

"Good." I told her.

The nine warriors faced one another in the gray-green, rain-streaked field. They were silent as I approached.

Visada, Monu, Belo, and the Erskan archer separated for me.

"You are Kale?" I demanded in Treaslok and eyed the woman at the forefront of the Busai.

"I am. You are Tural?"

She was shorter than I. She had a dark, ankle-length coat that hung down on both sides of her horse. A sword was plainly belted to her right hip; a couple of knife handles became visible on her outer left thigh when her horse shifted. She had blond hair, cut short, and displayed several metal piercings on her ears and nose.

"I am Tural. State your intentions."

"You know Treaslok well," she said.

I brushed aside the false compliment. "State your intentions."

"Good, straight to the point. I also do not enjoy the games of hidden politics. I will tell you what I want and why I want it." She pointed behind me. "The Treaslok attacked my people after many years of peace. Tens of thousands Busai were murdered by their sudden attacks. They used weapons, fire sticks, that we could not defeat. Ten of our twenty cities fell to the Treaslok. They burned our capital city and executed all those that could not escape."

Kale pointed at Monu, "Then *they* stopped. We learned that they also attacked the Erskans, you, as well. And the Treaslok lost their war with you."

She continued, "We repelled the Treaslok until they returned to the original border. Here, at this wall. Others have also been the victims of the Treaslok and they are coming to fight. But now the Erskans have defeated the Treaslok."

Kale stabbed her finger at me, "Now that you are here, you believe that we shall change our minds and simply go home?"

"I know all of this," I told her. "I have more warriors than the Treaslok did. I have many fire sticks and other weapons you have never seen. You shall not be successful in any attack. The Treaslok are under our protection because this is Erskan land now."

Kale laughed and crossed her arms before her. Her expression was of an asop that just ate a guuna.

"I received an emissary from the Suit de Ineer," she said. "The offer is simple. I return Treaslok lands to her. She gives the Earth frey and the Erskan frey to me."

Alexi and Mermak.

I did not pause. "These are Erskan lands. You will never have them."

Kale nodded smugly.

"I will make you a better offer," I told her as I leaned forward. "You deliver both *Erskan* frey to me, healthy and alive, and I will not burn your remaining ten cities to the ground."

Kale frowned.

One of her four warriors gradually moved her hand to pull open her coat.

I looked at the tall, wet grass several feet to my right and noticed a two-foot wide area that did not sway with the wind and light rain.

There were Busai warriors lying on the ground, covered with grass to conceal their presence.

Likewise, I concealed my detection of their trap.

"But that is not the best way to make friends with our new neighbors," I said.

I looked directly at Visada and asked, "What else can the Erskan Empire offer to the Busai in exchange for our frey?"

She paused for a moment. She did not expect me to include her in the negotiations.

"She does not understand Treaslok well," I said to Kale. Then in Erskan, I said, "Do not look about. There are Busai hiding in the grass?"

I made it sound like a question.

"I see," Visada replied, looking directly at me. "It is my hope that your radio is working."

"One would hope," I said.

Wary, Kale cocked her head.

"Tia!" the closest Busai shouted, looking behind me.

Help was, no doubt, riding toward us.

At least ten Busai warriors rose from the grass all about us. We were outnumbered three-to-one.

I lunged forward to Kale. My sword sang as I cross drew it from my back. The steel blade glinted as it rose in the air.

She backed her horse a couple of feet and brought her own sword up to counter my downward strike.

Steel collided between us. Sparks flew.

My hand vibrated as the sound of steel-on-steel rang.

Our horses, trained in combat, held fast.

My left hand brushed my coat to the side as my sword blocked Kale's counter-strike. Then I attacked with an upward strike.

Kale was slow.

I caught her blade close to the hilt, which pushed her right arm open and exposed her. I followed my attack by spurring my horse closer.

Then my sword found its way to the soft, inner-side of Kale's right forearm. Blood splattered as I pushed the blade a few inches into the flesh.

She dropped the sword and maneuvered her horse away. She shrieked.

I heard the whisk of an arrow.

Kale continued turning away. Her coat swept over my blade and she used it with her left hand to push my sword from her.

She continued turning and then fully disengaged.

I saw motion on my left and barely managed to deflect a killing blow to my head. I ducked, turned my horse clockwise, and leveled my bloody sword.

The Busai attacker tried to recover; however my sword cut across her belly, spraying blood into the rain. She fell over the side of her horse with her boots tangled in the stirrups. She screamed when her head hit the mud and her intestines poured to the ground.

The clash of swords continued.

Another arrow flew by my head.

I whirled around and saw that Kale was escaping. An Erskan arrow protruded from her upper right shoulder.

The arrows were not aimed at me; they were defensive.

Less than a thousand feet distant charged thousands of mounted Busai warriors.

On the other side, Erskan and Treaslok warriors funneled through the gate and headed to our rescue.

I had not enough time to estimate which force would arrive first; a sword flashed before my eyes and I raised mine in the last moment.

Sparks flew at my breasts as both swords crossed.

Our horses crashed into one another. We both fell inward, the Busai warrior and I.

We grappled, clutching for the other's uniform with our left hand while trying to keep the swords outstretched.

I slipped my boots out of the stirrups as we collapsed onto the wet and bloody grass with a hard impact that jarred my teeth.

She grabbed a handful of my coat and raised her sword.

We crossed blades. With my left hand I punched her face and struck at her mouth and eyes. It disoriented her and I was able to force her body down into the water.

I dodged a sword blade that took a swipe at my head from above when a rider went past us.

The Busai and I continued to wrestle for our lives.

Our swords locked above our heads, slicing blades of grass. I gained leverage and pushed her forearm down. Then I pummeled her eyes with the hilt of my sword. Her right eyeball exploded. She screamed as my knee kicked her at the stomach a couple of times.

She was blinded when I quickly gained control of my sword. I pressed the blade against her throat and first cut through the skin and then the windpipe. She gurgled blood and air through the gaping wound below her chin.

Dead.

I got to my knee and immediately engaged another.

It was the Busai that had swiped at me, riding a horse. I chopped at her knee as she rode toward me.

My first hit did not cut through the leather armor around her legs; but my second strike severed her kneecap. She howled and clutched onto the horse, which turned and rode away.

Another Busai, on foot, appeared at my side.

We crossed blades twice.

Thrice.

Swords sang around us.

Screams.

We crossed blades four times.

She was good.

The grass was slippery.

Blood mixed with the water as our boots splashed.

The Busai lost her footing, only for a moment.

I came down on her sword-arm. Her hand and forearm dangled as she turned about, screaming in retreat.

The Erskan archer was down, slightly injured. Visada dragged her toward the great wall.

I almost slashed at Monu until I recognized her. She was covered in blood and blades of grass.

A Busai lunged at Monu; I stepped in the attacker's path, deflected the blade, and then reamed my sword into the Busai warrior's lower abdomen.

I whirled around and saw the charging Busai force. They were less than five-hundred feet distant.

Monu was fighting to my right with another Busai.

I had the left.

I tried to turn to the Great Wall but had to engage another attacker.

This Busai was weak. We only cross swords once and I was able to rip my blade across her face. Her skull was nearly cut into two parts.

Monu was knocked down to the water by one of Kale's original four escorts.

I got between Monu and countered the Busai blow as it headed to Monu's exposed thigh.

The Busai warrior backed away, a stunned look on her face.

I pressed in and struck downward.

Sparks flashed in the rain as our swords collided.

She continued blocking, reeling on her boots.

I hit down again and swept my steel blade high right to bottom left.

She stepped back.

Crossing my strike, I flashed metal again, high left to bottom right.

Rainwater arced several feet into the air off my blade.

It rang after each spark of steel.

I pressed on.

I pounded her sword down.

Alternated my attacks.

Rolled my wrist with each downward blow.

Finally she could not recover from the powerful strikes.

In a straight downward motion I stabbed into her chest.

Her bones cracked and blood gushed from her heart.

Her sword dropped.

Mouth open, the Busai collapsed to her knees, while blood spurted onto my thighs.

I pressed the heel of my left boot into her right breast and pried my blade from her body.

"Stay down!" I told Monu.

The ground rumbled as the Busai cavalry charged toward us.

My view was consumed by hundreds of threatening, mounted warriors that converged on our location.

I slammed my sword into the mud and drew the StacGun. I fired as fast as my finger would allow.

Two hundred feet.

The ground shook so hard my teeth chattered.

One hundred feet.

I fired the gun.

I gasped for air as Erskan warriors blew past me, right and left.

Waves of splashing water obscured my vision and drenched Monu and I.

A horse skidded to a stop beside me. I grabbed my sword, holstered it and the StacGun, and took the hand that pulled me up.

The Erskan horse flew a colorful standard which signaled the others to avoid running into us.

Monu was pulled up to another rider's horse.

The sound of rapid gunfire filled the air.

Then the charging forces collided in a tremendous crash that jarred our horse and made my jaw clench.

Screams.

The clash of hundreds of swords.

Horses squealed.

We pushed toward the great wall, against the flow.

The Busai attempted to surge toward my position.

Treaslok warriors flowed in to support my own warriors. They countered the attempted Busai advance.

The war wagon was drawn toward us and the battle.

As we retreated, I saw the Erskan warrior on the top of the armored turret aim over the heads of the Erskan and Treaslok warriors.

Though we were outnumbered, the odds would quickly be in our favor.

"Are you injured, Torino?" the Erskan mounted warrior shouted to me, riding hard to the gate.

I knew her. "Riko?"

"It is my turn to help you," she said.

"I am not hurt," I said.

We plowed past the gate, followed closely by the rider carrying Monu.

"Thank you," I said. I jumped from the horse.

I ran upstairs to view the field. Riko turned about and joined the battle again.

The war wagon fired the Crest-Leeland heavy machine gun at the enemy.

Tracer fire lit up the ground. Bullets arced into the mass of Busai warriors.

The Erskans, trained and prepared, split to form a fire zone between the war wagon and the enemy. Thankfully, they pulled the unknowing Treaslok out of the line of deadly fire.

In only thirty seconds, suffering heavy losses, the Busai sounded a retreat horn.

Our forces disengaged and allowed the Busai to flee.

Trained teams grabbed fallen Erskan and Treaslok warriors from the field and returned to the security of the great wall.

I estimated two- or three-hundred fallen Busai; our casualties were a fifth as bad.

Within minutes we had evacuated the battlefield.

The war wagon and its escort rolled in and the gate was shut and barred.

The last of the Busai rode beyond range of the seeing eye glasses.

I turned away from the wall.

"Visada, are you well?" I asked.

She slowly reached the top of the stairs. A trickle of blood ran from her left shoulder. Her face was bruised. "I will be."

"We are done for now. Go tend to the wounded, and yourself. That is an order."

"Understood," she replied. She turned about and made her way down the steps.

"That was close," Cinzia said. She placed her hands on my shoulders. "Are *you* well?"

My coat was half-torn. I extended my hands and inspected my body. I had a few small nicks on my arms. "I believe so."

"You are a mess," Cinzia said. "It's hard to know by looking at you."

Monu bolted up the stairs, her sword sheathed at the hip. "You saved my life. I am forever in your debt."

"You are well?" I asked.

Cinzia looked at Monu with genuine concern.

In the same familiar post-battle inspection, Monu glanced at her arms and then torso. "Thankfully, yes."

Then she held up her left hand, "I did not need that part of my finger." She clenched her hand into a ball and then spread her fingers. The top quarter-inch of her smallest left-hand finger was cleanly cut away.

"Go," Cinzia said. "Get that cleaned and bandaged."

Monu gave me an Erskan salute and then excused herself.

Peto, arms crossed, stood slightly behind Cinzia. She shook her head. "It is no wonder that the Erskans are such warriors."

I looked at her with a question on my face.

"You killed at least seven Busai, and you injured their leader." She walked beside Cinzia and gave me an Erskan salute, "The Erskans could leave the Treaslok to certain death. Yet you fight. You have earned my respect."

I nodded and smiled in appreciation.

"You were good," Cinzia said. "I have never seen you move so fast."

"Alexi and Mermak," I said. My strength on the battlefield had come from --

"We know they are alive," Cinzia consoled. "And we can assume they are in the mountain fortress."

We had hope for our frey.

"This is not over," I told her. "If I have to go to the mountains on foot... I will get our frey."

But for the Busai – I had made a new enemy.

We heard a rumbling noise behind us, inside the great wall. The stone ledge shook under my boots.

I stood between Cinzia and Peto. The three of us moved over so we could look down from the wall to where our warriors had dismounted to recover from combat.

Four-thousand warriors, Erskan and Treaslok, looked up at us.

On the base of the stairs Monu and Visada stood next to one another, waving their arms at the warriors.

The rumbling noise became clear.

The warriors were cheering.

"Tural!"

"Tural!"

"Tural!"

Their voices washed over us in waves.

Peto lifted my blood-stained right hand into the air for all to see.

"Tural!"

"Tural!"

"Tural!"

"I will help you find your frey," Peto shouted to Cinzia and I over the din of cheers. "All of us will help you."

The Treaslok warriors, once banished to the far-flung border and mistreated by Corrigan, respected Erskan leadership and commitment to honor.

"Tural!"

"Tural!"

"Tural!"

I looked over my shoulder, toward the north, and unsuccessfully attempted to see the mountain range.

Somewhere, high in a formidable palace, Alexi and Mermak were held prisoner.

I squeezed Peto's hand and faced the cheering warriors below.

"Thank you!" I shouted over the din.

Now, there was more than hope alone.

# *About the Author*

K. McVey has been a rubber fetishist and BDSM enthusiast since the 1980s.

His novels blend life-long passions for science fiction and adventure with pulse pounding erotic dominance & submission.

When not traveling to kink events throughout the world, he collects original fetish art to complement a growing latex and leatherwear wardrobe. K. lives in the USA with pet racing motorcycles.

www.ingramcontent.com/pod-product-compliance
Lightning Source LLC
Chambersburg PA
CBHW051648260626
47170CB00004B/1399